WHISPERS OF FORBIDDEN LOVE

By
Ivelin Baychev

Grosvenor House
Publishing Limited

This book is published by
Grosvenor House Publishing Ltd
Link House
140 The Broadway, Tolworth, Surrey, KT6 7HT.
www.grosvenorhousepublishing.co.uk

This book is a work of fiction. Any resemblance to
people or events, past or present, is purely coincidental.

A CIP record for this book
is available from the British Library

ISBN 978-1-80381-777-4
eBook ISBN 978-1-80381-780-4

Acknowledgements

To know that there are people out there who believe in a person who often doubted himself means more to a boy like me than all the money in the world. Thank you to all those people in a special way for the part you've had in making this dream a beautiful reality.

To my loving fiancé, A.A., my eternal source of love and inspiration, I owe you a debt that words cannot easily express. Your unyielding care and understanding are the cornerstones of my ambitions. Every word that appears on these pages is a testament to your abiding love and support.

To my family and friends, you have been the guiding stars in my darkest of nights. Your unflagging belief in my abilities and your constant encouragement have been the gas in my tank.

To my editor and the remarkable team at Grosvenor House Publishing, whose keen insights and unwavering commitment to excellence have transformed an idea into what I could only hope to find on the bestseller lists. Without your guidance and dedication, this book would never have been completed.

It is to the best in them, the readers—whose own rage and love and dappled hunger provoked this story and made me brave to tell it—to whom I owe the greatest thanks.

I owe you everything.

Chapter One

"No! If I tell him, he'll kill her." Jamie vigorously ran his hands through his tousled hair. He knew his brother had a short temper, and, God save their sister, the minute he opened his mouth, but he had no other choice. He couldn't let people in their slum neighborhood besmirch her name.

After hours of nerve-wracking pacing, running through a thousand scenarios in his head, Jamie made his way to the garage. His eyes locked on Mike, skillfully changing the oil in one of the cars left by some people he didn't know, and sighed with frustration. Since there was no easy way to break the news, he went straight to the point.

"Seems like our little sister, Chloe, has a secret lover," Jamie blurted out. Mike looked at his brother askance before returning to his business. "Won't you say something?" Jamie grunted. He'd expected his brother to jump at him sooner, yet the air in the garage electrified like a hush before the storm. "I suspected she might be having an affair for some time now, but I am planning to end it right this moment," he added in great determination.

"Instead of making things up, why don't you think about how to get rich lazily and easily?" Mike said. "That's what you're good at."

Jamie rolled his eyes in exasperation. "Make things up? I'm telling you; people have seen Chloe with some man who looked like a sugar daddy," Jamie added, pausing to examine Mike's expression. The idea of this being true made his stomach churn.

Mike pressed his lips into a thin line and glared at him. "Don't believe everything you hear. People like to gossip," he said rather blithely and hid behind the Jeep.

Jamie approached his brother, crossed his arms over his chest, and waited for some sort of reaction that would show even a small drop of concern. "Mike, won't you stop for a moment and listen to what I'm saying?" Jamie pulled on his black, oily forearm.

"Stop slandering our sister!" he uttered with a hint of threat.

"No! This is unbelievable! All you care about are your precious cars. You spend day and night in this damn garage."

"This damn garage, as you put it, is what feeds you!" Mike retorted.

Jamie paused for a moment, inwardly giving credit to his brother's point, yet it didn't mean he should care any less for their sister. "Anyway, I will find the truth on my own. I won't allow my sister to turn into a slut."

Mike lost his last bit of patience, threw the oil filter to the ground, and grabbed Jamie by the jaw, leaving black fingerprints on his gold-beige face. His anger was a wild animal, untamed and unpredictable. "Watch your mouth, will you? You're not talking about any other woman! This is our sister!"

Jamie barely managed to free himself from the strong grip and wiped his face. "Do you think I don't know that?" He stepped back. "I know what I'm saying, and I have proof."

"Oh yeah? And where is your proof?" Mike raised a skeptical brow.

"Doña Prudencia and her husband overheard Chloe talking to a man on the phone at the market the other day. Also, the butcher has seen her getting into an expensive car with some stranger."

Mike's face changed. He knew Doña Prudencia had a big mouth, but she always gossiped about things that were true, not exaggerated. "Wait, what? So, it's not just you who speaks badly about her?" Mike turned to Jamie, wiping his hands. His olive eyes were lightning bolts of fury and thunderclaps of rage. "I'll find out everything in a second," he mumbled and carelessly hurled the black-stained towel at the wall. He put on his serious expression and stormed out. Jamie rushed after him, sensing the storm was about to strike.

Once back home, the two brothers eagerly awaited Chloe in the living room. And when she came home, glowing, her smile faded away the moment she met them. The young girl recognized those faces all too well, and hurriedly whisked past them, naively thinking she would avoid the inevitable. Chloe closed the door softly and walked over to the wooden cabinet and carefully studied her face in the mirror. She took the artificial flowers out of the vase, and she hurriedly tried to put the few hundred dollars inside before Mike burst into her room and she clenched her fists in despair.

"What are you doing?" His firm voice sent a couple of chills down her spine and his piercing eyes, buried in her back, further paralyzed her body.

"Nothing!" She hastily put the vase back, still not ready to face him.

"What are you hiding?" Mike grabbed her elbow, making her turn to him, and forcefully opened her palm, smoothing the crumpled banknotes. He gazed at her as an invisible cloak blurred his eyes, before coming to his senses at Chloe's scream from the slap.

"Mike, please don't!" Jamie rushed to her rescue and stood between them. This time, it would have been hard even for him to tame his brother's wildness.

"Look at this!" Mike pointed to the money. Jamie gazed at the bills and at Chloe, words stuck in his throat, hardly believing his eyes. Chloe desperately fought to explain, but her words came out as nothing but mere whining. "Can you imagine? I can't believe it!" Mike's breathing accelerated as he raced around the room. "Now, you're going to tell me the truth – who gave you this money and in exchange for what?"

Chloe trembled, tears streamed down her pink cheeks as she tried to look into his brother's eyes.

"Speak, girl!" Mike demanded.

"Mike, let her explain!"

"I have nothing to explain."

"Chloe, people in the neighborhood are already gossiping. It's best to admit everything, otherwise it will get worse," Jamie urged her.

"I have no idea what you're talking about."

"About the man you're secretly seeing. Is it true? Do you have a secret lover?" Mike cocked his head to one side. The sheer image of his sister selling her body for money made the room spin a couple of times before him and his predatory grunting made Jamie's task of keeping him away even harder.

"Chloe, we're family, and we're your brothers. There shouldn't be any secrets between us," Jamie uttered.

"All right then! Yes, it's true! I am secretly seeing a man! So what?" she snapped, not knowing whether she had acted rightly or wrongly. But the little courage she had gathered evaporated the moment Mike lost his temper completely.

"I can't believe it! I'll kill her!" Mike reached for his belt, pulling it out of his jeans. "I'll kill her!" he wailed in rage, but Jamie blocked his way, barely pushing his colossal body back so that the belt couldn't reach her as Chloe's wobbly feet attempted to move and failed. Barely managing to regain his balance, Mike's labored breaths echoed in the room, reverberating off the walls. He clenched his fists, his knuckles turning white as he fought to contain the tempest within. In a moment of desperate self-control, he spun on his heel and stormed out of the room, the echo of his fury dissipating as the door slammed shut behind him.

The rest of the day gave enough time for the storm to pass. It was early evening when the three of them gathered in the living room. "Dinner is served," Jamie called from the kitchen. Chloe was the last to arrive, having to gather her strength so as not to shudder under his stern gaze. Mike's anger returned as soon as she sat across him.

He put down his utensils and buried his eyes into hers. "Tell me, Chloe, who is this secret lover?" His voice was calm and even, giving him a sense of hope she'd be more willing to speak.

She smiled fondly as her mind went back to the times when she was with Santiago, away from prying eyes. "I'm telling you, he's a very important person, famous, with a high status in society. I met him by accident, I swear. I didn't think I was doing anything wrong."

"Why haven't you mentioned him before?" Jamie asked.

"Probably because we fell in love. I knew you wouldn't approve of it…"

"Have you slept with him?" Mike cut in. Chloe bent her head down to her fidgeting fingers, shaking it in denial. Mike stood up from his chair, gazing at her like a ticking time bomb, waiting to explode. "Respond with words, not gestures, and look me in the eyes!" His eyes darkened and the calm, prepossessing voice was now a distant memory.

"Yes!" She stood up and met his gaze. Chloe staggered a step back from yet another heavy slap. She slowly returned her gaze to him, touching softly the corner of her mouth.

"Stop beating her like an animal, Mike. You need to respect us!" Jamie stood at her side.

"What about her? Does she respect us?" Mike kicked his chair to one side. "We care for her so much and look how she repays us!"

"Mike, I swear he's a good man." Her tears impeded the words in her mouth.

"Tell me who he is, or I'll lose the last bit of patience I have."

"What for? To find him and kill him because he likes me?" she snapped at her brother. The bitterness and pain pooled in her teary eyes. "No! I'll never tell you! You'll never find out his name!" She roared once more and ran to her room, leaving her brothers lost in thoughts and guesses.

§

Santiago Alvarez, one of the well-respected farmers in the area, parked his car at the far front side of his estate.

He came late from work, desperately hoping to avoid the celebration of his 30th wedding anniversary. Rolling his eyes with utmost irritation, he got out of the car. The sound of the guitars made him smile thinly as he slowly walked ahead, basking in the generous warmth of the sun, bracing himself for another ordeal.

"Welcome home, Don Santiago!" Magnolia greeted the owner of the mansion with a big, polite smile, taking his briefcase.

"I see the circus is in full swing!" he said blithely as Magnolia burst into choked laughter.

"That's right! Doña Gabriella has invited all of your family friends to this special occasion. You know how much she cares about image and reputation."

"Yes, I do. My dear wife has always been like this," he murmured with a slight drawl. "And my children? Are they here?"

"Yes, of course!"

"So there's no getting out!" He sighed heavily.

"There you are." Gabriella approached him with a broad, genuine smile. She welcomed him with a cheek kiss, took him by his cringed elbow, and the two of them made their way to the guests. "Ladies and gentlemen, the head of the family is finally here – my dear husband, Santiago Alvarez!" Gabriella addressed everyone present, holding a glass of champagne. "I would like to raise a toast and thank you all for responding to our invitation on this special occasion!" She raised her glass and beamed at her husband.

Santiago managed a thin smile at the guests and quickly stepped down from the small stage, carefully placed in the center. *"What was the need for all this ostentation?"* he pondered and retreated behind the table designated for them. He looked up at the ivory linen sheet tied up onto the four lamp posts, mercifully saving him from the heat. Gulping down his glass in a hurry, he ordered the servants to bring him something stronger than champagne and patiently waited for this absurd parade to end.

Gabriella followed him and sat down on the bench beside him. Her smile was gone and for a moment, the gloomy, stiff, and disaffected Gabriella had returned. She smiled from time to time at anyone passing by their table. "Santiago, can you at least pretend to be enjoying yourself and wipe the boredom off your face?" Gabriella hissed in a low voice, cautious not to be interrupted or seen by any of the guests.

"What's the point of all this show?"

"Show? It's our 30th wedding anniversary, for God's sake," she hissed in his face.

"Your drink, Don Santiago!" Magnolia left the shiny silver tray on the table.

"Thank you, Magnolia. You're free to go!" Gabriella dismissed her and she sped off to hide among the guests.

Lucia and her husband approached their table, and Santiago greeted them with a smile. Gabriella, on the other hand, pulled away from her husband as he stood up to kiss their daughter and gave a short, amicable glance at her son-in-law.

Santiago's happiness resurfaced on his face once he turned his attention to his daughter. God had blessed him with a daughter after his firstborn son, Diego, and the second boy, Juan Pablo, and this gave him a sense of fulfillment in his life.

Antonio complimented Gabriella on her appearance, and politely addressed Santiago in the same joyful manner, hoping his compliment sounded genuine.

"How nice of you to say this! Of course, it would have been nicer if you really meant it, but nonetheless!" Santiago replied acidly, completely ignoring his wife's sullen expression. "How are you, sweetheart?" He turned to Lucia.

Gabriella quickly apologized for her husband's sour mood, attributing it to a bad day at work and exhaustion.

"That's quite normal for a person in his position." Antonio pretended he hadn't paid enough attention to his father-in-law's vicious attack. "Managing such wealth is not an easy task."

Santiago gazed at him, his lips curling into a thin smile. He excused himself and went to greet his sons and some of his friends who had come to the party. And when he thought he'd finished pretending to like all this, his wife approached him in the company of Father Thomas, who had been invited more out of social obligation than genuine friendship.

"Ah, Santiago, please say hello to Father Thomas." Gabriella caught him by the arm.

"How are you, Father?" He tried to sound genuinely interested.

"Very well, thank you! Can I say how life has been kind to you, Mr. Alvarez? You have an amazing wife, wonderful and charming children, a reputable home, and untold wealth."

"Which you also happen to enjoy, Father." He smiled thinly. "I know Gabriella is making quite generous donations to you." His vicious utterance made his wife avert her eyes with frustration.

"She's being nothing but a model Christian, Don Santiago." Father Thomas smiled awkwardly.

"Excuse my husband, Father! He was just kidding."

"No, I am not!" Santiago turned to her. The embarrassment pooled in her eyes. "Don't you think you are giving a little too much?" he added.

"There is no such thing as giving too much when it comes to the lives of the poor and disenfranchised."

"Are you sure this money will be properly distributed?" Santiago raised an eyebrow and Father Thomas found himself compelled to swallow nervously.

"Of course, Santiago! How can you doubt his words?" Gabriella frowned at him, her eyes shooting fire as Santiago lost interest in having this conversation.

"Forgive me, Father. I feel indisposed, and the migraine is causing me to leave you with my wife," he said and headed for the entrance of the house.

Gabriella quickly murmured an excuse and rushed after him. "Santiago, where are you going?" She caught him on the stairs at last.

"I'm sorry, Gabriella, but I can no longer endure these two-faced people who are friends with us because we are convenient for them. This includes Father Thomas, too."

"Santiago, please! He's not any man! He's a servant of God!"

"He is just another groveller in the crowd, and I cannot stand him," Santiago hissed and went upstairs.

Gabriella rushed after him, but he slammed the door shut in her face as soon as she reached their bedroom. "Santiago, open the door!" she shouted, pounding on it in vain. "Please, we need to talk! Where were you all day? I called your work, but you weren't there again. Santiago, open the door!" Gabriella screamed, fighting back her tears. The oppressive silence made her finally give up. She smoothed her scarlet velvet suit, a shade lighter than her hair, and went back down to the guests, praying the guests would restore her gloomy mood.

Santiago let out a heavy sigh and sat on the edge of the bed, rubbing his hands over his face. His mind was a tired engine, sputtering and struggling to keep up. Their marriage had been on the rocks for years – the constant shouting, the quarrels, the lies he had to make up every time he crossed the threshold of his home. His real joy now was Chloe. His eyes brightened and a genuine smile appeared on his lips as he took out a small photo from the inner pocket of his suit. "Oh, Chloe! Sweet, little Chloe! I love you! You're the only one who brings joy to my gray days," he whispered, kissing the photo before putting it in the pocket of his pants. He lay down and stared at the ceiling, dreaming of seeing her again.

Chapter Two

Santiago had woken up at dawn, before anyone else in the house. He bathed and chose one of his best suits, hurrying to better skip family breakfast and the morning small talk with his wife, which could easily turn into a fight over something trivial. He surreptitiously exited the house and went straight to his car. Thankfully, Magnolia was the only one to see him leave the hacienda at this early hour. His rush was suspicious and opened the gate to bitter memories, but she tried not to overwhelm herself with it, at least not now. She crossed her arms on her chest and shook her head in disapproval. After all these years, he hadn't changed. Magnolia kept her gaze on the car as it drove away and returned to her modest room on the ground floor.

Santiago pulled over to the side of the road where Chloe was waiting for him. She shivered from the cool wind brushing against her skin through her thin cardigan. Chloe got into the car, and they drove to their secret hideout – a small, abandoned barn, which she still wondered if was on Santiago's land.

"What's wrong, my love?" Santiago piqued at her unusual, anxious behaviour.

"Nothing," she muttered, and they remained silent for the rest of the journey.

Once they arrived, they got out of the car, but she hesitated to go inside. She eyed the barn's entrance, and chills ran down her spine. "Santiago, I want to go back!"

"What's going on?"

"Nothing! I just don't want to go inside. Please, let's go!" Her voice shaking, she opened the car door from her side. She once again glanced toward the barn's entrance as Santiago caught her look and headed straight for it. "Santiago, don't! Don't go inside!" she shouted after him. Her heart bounced in turmoil as she knew her brothers were inside, and this was dangerous.

"Chloe, are these your brothers?" Santiago stopped several steps before the two men, surprised to find them there.

"Yes! They found out about us and wanted to talk to you." She fought to hide the panic that threatened to engulf her like a tidal wave.

"So, this is our man!" Mike crossed his arms on his chest and tilted his head to one side. He scrutinized the man, taking in every detail – his greying hair, the wrinkles etched around his striking blue eyes, and his bushy eyebrows.

"What a shame, Chloe!" Jamie sneered. "He's not even young! This old man could be your father. How disgraceful!"

She placed her palm on Santiago's shoulder in a blatant attempt to hide the trembling. Her breath came fast, and the fear crawled on her face and hid in her big, wet eyes. Knowing her brother's temper, she sensed the seemingly peaceful meeting was going to end badly and she had to avoid it.

Santiago took off his hat and gripped it tightly. "I may be old, but I am an honourable man! Otherwise, your sister wouldn't have fallen in love with me." His voice was unwavering, sincerity evident in his eyes. His posture and appearance exuded nothing but nobility.

Mike grabbed the lapels of the man's suit jacket as Chloe's expression drowned in horror completely. "What a sly man you are!" Mike hissed in the man's face. "Not only a cheater, but also a trickster."

"Mike, please! You promised you wouldn't hurt him!" Chloe implored, tears streaming down her cheeks.

"Mike, let him go!" Jamie grabbed him by the wrists, trying to pull him away.

The old man staggered for a moment from the light push but luckily managed to keep his balance. When he regained control of his body, he gazed at Mike, studying him intently. "I too wanted to meet you. I would have asked Chloe to introduce me," Santiago said. "It's a pity that circumstances are not so pleasant."

"Maybe for you! Because you're doing everything secretly, and you're using naïve young girls like my sister," Mike growled.

"No! I don't hide or take advantage of her naivety. I love her quite sincerely, and I am ready to answer for my actions."

"And how do you intend on taking responsibility?" Jamie asked.

"I'm ready to get together with her, but not under pressure!" Santiago replied firmly. He glanced at Chloe and smiled gently at her wet yet beautiful face.

"Would you marry her?" Jamie asked, causing every muscle in Mike's body to cringe.

"My life, my future, everything I possess will be hers. I am ready to take responsibility for my actions,"

Santiago continued as his eyes bobbed between Chloe and her brothers.

Mike grabbed him again, his blood rushing to his head. "Yes, you most certainly will. Your bones in your body will be in hundreds of pieces when I finish," he threatened. He punched the old man in the ribs as he squirmed onto a bale of straw.

Chloe kneeled, caressing his face. She threw a quick, freezing glance of disdain at her brother while Jamie desperately fought to keep him from lashing out at Santiago again. "Mike, please, leave him alone!"

"He lies. I won't be fooled by the words of a hypocrite!"

Santiago winced in pain. Chloe glared at her brother again, his posture like a storm brewing on the horizon, urging them to leave. The regret gnawed at her tormented mind. It was a mistake to have led them here, to introduce them to Santiago. It was late evening and the wind of emotions threatened to become a tornado unleashed from its chains.

"Chloe, how can you like him? Are you sure you love him? He's much older than you are," Jamie queried quietly. "It must be for the money. Otherwise, I don't see why else you'd have anything to do with him." Mike's threatening gaze made him shut his mouth instantly.

"I don't care about his age. I love him and I need him. He gave me his word, and I am sure he will keep it. I trust him."

"I don't give a damn about his word. You two will separate and we are going to move!" Mike asserted.

"What? Mike, we can't! After all we'd been through to settle down here!" Jamie gazed at him.

"The problems have never stopped since the day we came to this damn place!" Mike slammed his hand on the table. "I will not allow her to do the foolish thing of marrying this old man. It's absurd!"

"That's not a solution," Jamie said and sat beside his sister. "Come on! Admit it! The sole reason you want to be with him is the money."

"You must think I'm unscrupulous and only interested in his money like you. Well, that's not true! Even if it were, you, of all people here, should be interested in marrying him because he has a lot of money," Chloe snivelled.

"How much money are we talking about exactly?" Jamie's curiosity got the best of him.

"I don't know," Chloe replied. "He has mentioned several companies, many acres of land, and a wealthy mansion outside of town, which he shares with his sister and nieces. But nothing more."

"He must be one of those rich people who exploit workers like those who drove us from our lands," Mike pondered out loud. Memories of their home and parents flooded his mind and the price they'd paid when they'd moved away. "No, you will not marry him," he added and stormed out of the room.

The morning had brought the much-awaited peace that everyone in the house had lacked for the past few days. As the soft sunlight filtered through the curtains, Mike and Jamie sat at the kitchen table, their voices mingling with the comforting aroma of freshly brewed coffee.

"Listen to me! It would be unforgivably stupid to stand against Chloe's marriage to Mr Alvarez,"

Jamie said. "Think about what we can ask for in return. He has everything! This man is loaded, highly respected, and, to top it off, he's head over heels for our sister." Mike peered at him from behind the mug of coffee, lost in thoughts, and the suspense got the best of Jamie while he waited for some sort of reaction. "Mike, say something!" he whined at last.

"I don't like to go back on my word. I already said we were moving, and that's that."

"Why do you have to be so stubborn?" Jamie sighed heavily. "This is absolute madness. All these years of hardship and work…" Jamie paused for a moment, unsure if he had to continue. "We can expand your business with the money he has. He can even help us move out from this slum. Don't be selfish!" His voice succumbed to the frustration.

Mike lost his temper for a moment, slammed the table hard as the mug bounced a few inches from the surface. "You're the greediest person I have ever known. All you ever think about is money!"

Mike stood up, kicking his chair to one side, and turned to leave before Jamie blocked his way with lighting speed. "I'm not greedy, I'm practical. Mr Alvarez may not be young, and he may not be the fairy tale prince we were dreaming of for our sister, but they love each other," Jamie countered. "It would be worse if she had fallen in love with some poor guy who didn't have a cent," he added, unable to decipher his brother's facial expressions.

Mike was painfully coming to terms with the sad reality, and no matter how difficult it was to admit it, Jamie was right. Yet he was a man of his word and principles. Solid as a rock, they had guided his life and shaped him into the man he was. He wouldn't exchange the family's pride and dignity for any amount of money in the world.

The several bell rings made them look towards the door in unison. Santiago Alvarez stood at the old but cosy home that was perfectly in line with the rest of the houses along the steep road. He nervously played with his hat in his hand, summoning his strength to face Chloe's brothers.

"What brings you here?" Mike raised an eyebrow, stunned from the unexpected visit.

"I came to see Chloe."

Mike motioned his had to come in, and as he did so he quickly called for Chloe to join them in the living room. Mike arranged a pair of chairs in the centre of the room and stood before them with his arms crossed like a cop in an interrogation room. "I won't be the one to talk," Mike said emphatically. "We're listening to you, Chloe!"

Chloe's eyes stung with tears, her heart tearing apart. She gazed at him; his soothing glance was a tranquil harbour amidst the raging storm of her thoughts. She pushed herself not to cry as tears pricked her eyes. "Look, Santiago," she started hesitantly, "my brothers have recently had many troubles because of our relationship. I can't be selfish. We must move, far from here."

"Move?" Santiago exclaimed. His gaze bobbed between her and Mike's dark, smoking eyes. "They could go, but you will not go anywhere," he said tersely. "You will stay here with me!"

"Our sister comes with us," Mike cut in, powerful and relentless.

"I made a vow to take responsibility for Chloe and marry her. I truly love her. She's everything to me. I won't lose her."

"Please, Santiago," Chloe pleaded, "I don't want to be the cause of any more trouble for my family."

Santiago sighed deeply at the thought of losing her. "I understand," he said softly. "I don't want to cause any more problems either."

Mike's expression softened a little at Santiago's change of tone, yet the anger lurked inside him like a coiled serpent, ready to strike at any moment. "Then what do you propose we do?" he asked.

"I think it would be best if I left for a while." Santiago aimed his gaze at Mike. "Give you all some space to work things out. But I am not going to give up on her."

Mike narrowed his eyes but didn't comment. His gaze fixed on the old man until the sound of the front door closing made him aware he was gone.

Chapter Three

Santiago reached the main road then slammed on the brakes – the screech of the tires adding to the chaos in his mind. An overwhelming sense of impasse squeezed the air out of his lungs. He declined another phone call from work as nothing seemed to matter after the morning he just had. And when he arrived home that night, he took an ample amount of time before meeting his wife and her usual grumpy mood. He parked his Jeep in front of the house and barely paid any attention to Lucia and Antonio arriving home too.

"What's wrong with your father? He's become quite rude. He doesn't even say good evening anymore," Antonio remarked after watching him walk away.

"I don't know."

"I hope he's in a better mood when I ask him to lend me more money. We lost quite a large sum in the casino," Antonio said.

Lucia stopped and arched her brow appraisingly. "You lost a large sum of money. I don't like gambling," she said tersely. "I'm only accompanying you because of the pressure you put on me!" She frowned at him and entered the house.

Santiago Alvarez went straight to the little study room where Magnolia met him at the door. "Don Santiago, will you be having something for dinner? Her tone warm and polite.

"No, thank you," he said and went behind the desk. "Did you prepare my room?" He placed his wide-brimmed hat on top of the desk and gazed at the woman, who crossed her hands behind her back, hiding her fidgeting fingers.

"Please excuse me, but your wife forbade me when she found out what I was doing," she said, stepping a little closer to the desk. "Please do not put me between a rock and a hard place. I cannot argue with anyone, and I don't know which orders to follow."

Gabriella cleared her throat, and Magnolia turned around. Gabriella dismissed her with a stern gaze. She narrowed her eyes, her lips pressed together, sensing her husband had been running around outside. Santiago only peered at her under his brows. Even at home, she was dressed in her usual sophisticated style – dark coal pants, a white blouse, and an ivory poncho. Her hair was neatly gathered in a French twist as usual, and she stared at her husband, offended by his attitude. "After so many years of marriage, I have to see you giving cause for comment to the servants about our family affairs," she said bitingly. "Isn't it a shame? I ask you to show respect to our children and not to discredit me in front of the staff," she added.

Santiago rolled his eyes at the tedious monologue of his wife, but he let her have her say.

"Your behavior is scandalous and they don't deserve it, Santiago!" she hissed, making him gaze into her icy blue eyes, exuding coldness, and repulsion. "You will sleep in our bedroom as you always have, as is customary for married couples. Are we clear?"

There was no response. Not a single comment.

The woman exited and left her husband in the study, whose expression was tired – tired of engaging in endless quarrels and dealing with every grumpy look on his wife's face.

As luck would have it, both his and his daughter's marriage looked alike – utterly unhappy. The single real difference was that his daughter never loved Antonio. Lucia had been forced into marrying him merely out of convenience for both parties. His family was broke, and Antonio was left without a cent to his name, while Gabriella wanted to hide the shame from the cruel world – which would gossip and judge her – for Lucia had once been raped by some drunkards.

Antonio was sitting in the upholstered indigo armchair contemplating his wife who had long since fallen asleep. He gently placed the book on the polished round wooden table and with a cautious shuffle, he approached the bed, its quilted surface rumpled from the night's unrest. His trembling hand, a nervous intruder, traced a tender path up Lucia's leg, the warmth of her skin igniting a trail of sensations that spread like wildfire through his fingertips. But before his fingers reached the delicate terrain of her knee, her sudden awakening shattered the fragile tranquility. Startled, she recoiled from his touch, her gaze a mix of terror and defiance.

"I am sorry. I didn't wish to wake you," he murmured, his voice barely a whisper, carrying the weight of both regret and longing.

"Please, don't touch me!" Lucia's voice quivered, her eyes fixed on him, a mixture of fear and anguish.

"When will I be able to?" His frustration seeped through, tainting the air with a bitter edge. "It's been a year, and you never allow me to touch you – as if you think I am going to hurt you."

"I am sorry, Antonio, but this is exactly how I feel." Lucia's voice was laden with the weight of her past torment.

"I am sorry for what has happened to you. But I was not among those who raped you," he insisted, his tone a blend of remorse and exasperation.

"Please, don't remind me!" she pleaded with a hint of hostility, a desperate attempt to ward off the haunting memories clawing at the edges of her consciousness.

"You're the one reminding me every time I am trying to make love to you," he snapped, his patience crumbling like the fragile facade of their fractured intimacy. He rose abruptly from the bed, the duvet slipping to the ground with a soft thud. Lucia clutched the other cover's end to her chest in a blatant attempt to find solace and safety in the thin shield. "I married you to help you overcome this, but you must help yourself too." His voice surged with a mix of irritation and desolation. "Lucia, one day, I will get fed up and will find another woman to give me what I don't get from you."

"You're doing it anyway. I know you've been seeing other women." Lucia's accusation hung heavy in the air, puncturing the fragile bubble of their strained confrontation.

"I don't want to." Antonio's words carried a hint of remorse, his defenses crumbling under the weight of their tangled emotions. "I'm sick and tired of seeking outside what I have in my own bed." He reached for her, his touch both tender and insistent, a desperate attempt to bridge the chasm between them.

But as his lips grazed hers and trailed down to her cheek and neck, the nightmare engulfed her, the memories of her violation flooding her mind with a suffocating force. The scene of her ordeal replayed in vivid detail – the shadowy figures, the dank stable, the haunting echoes of horses' frenzied neighing. She couldn't bear it. With a sudden surge of strength, she pushed him back and fled from the bed, her sobs echoing through the room.

"Lucia, wait!" Antonio's plea followed her, but she was already out the door, her father's comforting embrace offering the only refuge in the turmoil of her shattered sanctuary.

"What's wrong, sweetheart?" He caressed her hair, gazing upon her eyes as they welled with tears.

"Nothing! Your daughter is a little tense," Antonio said wearily.

"Come on, little angel. Let's get you back to bed," Santiago prompted and called Antonio outside. When the two men were left alone in the small hall on the second floor, Santiago glared at him with ultimate disdain. "It's not the first night I've been awake from my daughter's cries." Santiago's words were like daggers, piercing his son-in-law's skin.

"That's because it's not the first time your daughter hasn't fulfilled her marital duties."

"Don't ever make her do anything against her will!" Santiago pointed his finger at him.

"Our intimate relationship is not your business, my dear Father." Antonio reprimanded him with sarcasm. "Don't stick your nose in my family."

When Antonio decided the ordeal had finally ended, Santiago brought him back with one abrupt pull. "Listen to me! One more night of suffering for my daughter, and your marriage is over."

"And you think it's that easy?" Antonio emitted a choked laugh.

"Well, it's certainly not impossible. You're nothing but parasite who managed to hide his existence in my house."

"My only responsibility is to hide the shameful rape of your daughter." Antonio raised his voice, tired of putting up with Santiago's vile comments. "And please, my dear Father, don't you threaten me because I can easily go to your wife and tell her about the affair you're having."

Santiago's face went as white as a sheet. The little corridor spun several times before his eyes. His lungs deflating, and the oxygen in the hall had gone. The one image in his head was how he could kill Antonio without any sense of remorse whatsoever.

"Yeah, I know about the luxury residence you've bought for your mistress and how you're planning to run off with her, marry her, and live there." Antonio smiled wickedly, revealing Santiago's carefully guarded secret, which he had confided only to Magnolia. "I know everything, dear Father, and be grateful and I haven't told your wife about it."

"What are you waiting for?" Santiago snapped, pointing to the bedroom where his wife was with his eyes.

"Are you fighting?" Gabriella appeared at the door, half asleep.

"No, we were arguing over silly things, weren't we Don Santiago?" Antonio said with vague semblance of a smile. "We're just talking about some financial issues."

Santiago's blazing glare threatened to set the whole mansion on fire. "Son of a bitch!" he murmured under his breath. "I rather rot in hell than letting myself be extorted by a bastard like you."

Chapter Four

Chloe had been smiling for the first time in a week. She let happiness take full possession of her. Santiago had promised to show her and her brothers something, and he skillfully navigated through the traffic until they arrived at a place none of the Williams had ever been before. He parked his car in front of an elegant peach-colored house. The simple yet luxurious facade could enchant even the most critical taste.

"Santiago, where are we?" Chloe asked with a smile.

"This is going to be our new home," he replied, smiling tenderly at her, and giving her a light kiss.

Jamie couldn't take his eyes off the large floor-to-ceiling windows on the front facade, while Mike was reminded of what he had agreed to. Frankly, he found it a little humbling, confronting his own ego, prejudices, and morals. Chloe tucked a tendril of hair behind her ear as Santiago opened the car door and helped her out.

"This is the place. Do you approve?" Santiago asked, as excited as Chloe as they took a short walk around the house.

"Of course! The house is magnificent." Her smile wouldn't leave her face.

"This is our new home. I just purchased it."

"Don Santiago, I must say you have a discerning taste. The house is more than impressive," Jamie complimented and returned his full attention to him. "And what about us? You're not going to leave us to live in the slum, are you?" His grin faded as he posed the question. Mike pushed him with his shoulder, obviously trying to get him to stop talking.

"There is enough space for you both as well," Santiago said simply. "Of course, if you wish to share it with us," he added, glancing at Mike's stone-cold face. Chloe rested her head on his shoulder, still comprehending the too-good-to-be-true moment. She had never thought that one day she would live in such an exquisite palace.

"No, it's not right, señor," Mike said tersely, crossing his arms on his chest. "A newlywed couple should live alone. We should not intrude with our presence."

"Mike!" Jamie scolded him. "We accept, of course, Don Alvarez." He patted him amicably on the back, happy as a bird soaring high in the sky. "We've never separated from our sister. We won't do it now either. We'll be glad to live together in this house."

"Of course! I want everyone to be happy." Santiago smiled thinly, taking Chloe's hand to show her around the house. For a long time now, his heart had been jumping with elation to spend some alone time with her.

"Mike, come on! Let's explore our new home," Jamie said, but Mike shook him violently, as if to come to his senses. Jamie had to take several steps back, careful not to trip on the marvelous tiles.

"This isn't ours! And it never will be!"

"You know what? You're the best at ruining everyone's mood!" Jamie hissed with annoyance and headed to the upper floor.

Time marched on tirelessly, calling Santiago to finish the tour of the splendid house. He hurriedly excused himself, stating he had urgent tasks at work and left Chloe and her brothers at the house. The frustration was evident in his sigh as he parked his car at the far end in front of his home and went straight to the stables and asked for his horse to be saddled.

The wind lashed against his face as he rode. As he kept on, the thrill of speed and solitude intertwined, forming a temporary escape from the labyrinth of worries and responsibilities. The corners of his mouth curled upward in a rare display of joy, a smile etching its way across his weathered features. It was as if the weight of the world was lifting, and the freedom from life's constraints painted a vivid sense of liberation. He was enjoying the peace and quiet, which threatened to be ruined at the sight of Antonio riding ahead on his horse. Santiago stared at his son-in-law, riding masterfully towards him. He took off his hat, put it on a small, round rock next to where he was sitting and pondered if Antonio had followed him.

"Don Alvarez, we are waiting for you." He swiftly dismounted. "Are you coming?" Antonio tied up the horse's bridle as Santiago disregarded his presence. "Very well, we can talk about the topic we hadn't had the chance to finish."

"You are terribly mistaken, Antonio, if you think you can scare me." Santiago's eyes grew darker. "You will not get anything from me." His anger woke up immediately as if putting gas into a fire.

"I don't think so." Antonio twisted his lips into a wicked smile. "Not only will you buy us a house of our choice, but you will also transfer a considerable amount of money into my account, so Lucia and I do not suffer any deprivation in the future. You won't give everything to your mistress, will you?"

Santiago jumped out of his seat and punched him. The young man fell on his back and it took him a while to come to his senses from the hard hit. When he finally did, he barely stood on his feet as the pain in his back grew bigger by the minute. "So, you will refuse me, Don Alvarez! Then, you will suffer the consequences."

Santiago glared at him from under his bushy brows and hardly restrained himself from punching him again. He grabbed him by the jacket's lapels, shaking him vigorously. "Don't you ever dare threaten me! I demand you show respect!" He finally pushed him back, pointing at him with a finger for added effect. "You won't see neither money, nor house. With every single day I am more convinced my daughter is not out of danger with you." Santiago's contempt was reaching new heights. "You dare to mistreat her under my roof, I cannot imagine what it will be like if you live separately."

"Is that your final word?" In that case, I feel inclined to tell the whole family about your mistress, my dear Father."

Santiago Alvarez gazed at the man for a moment. His lips quivered into a small grin, leaving Antonio completely baffled by his inexplicable reaction. "I'll save you the trouble. I will personally inform them right this instant." He grabbed his hat that he'd thrown on the rock, hopped on his beautiful horse and, in a moment, he was galloping towards his home. Antonio followed him with his eyes before jumping on his horse and following in a desperate attempt to reach him.

Santiago Alvarez spurred his horse, masterfully holding onto the bridle with one hand and his hat with the other. The wind made him squint. The net of tears made it difficult to see the road ahead. The racing anger and thoughts blocked his hearing as Antonio approached quickly, shouting for him to stop. But his only goal now was to rid himself of this burden as soon as possible, regardless of the consequences.

As he pivoted to face the path ahead, a flash of metal and the screech of tires tore through the serenity, the scent of burning rubber mingling with the pungent musk of the startled horse. Santiago's gaze locked onto the looming vehicle that was barreling towards him like an unstoppable force. The horse let out a shrill, primal neigh, its hooves striking the ground with a thunderous rhythm. Santiago's senses heightened, the thud of his own heart echoing in his ears, the acrid taste of fear on his tongue. With a swift, desperate movement, he relinquished his hold on the bridle, the leather slipping through his fingers like a fleeting dream. In an instant, he was airborne, the ground rushing up to meet him with a primal ferocity. The world spun, a blur of earth and sky, the wind howling past his ears, whipping his hair into a frenzied dance.

"Don Alvarez? Don Alvarez!" Antonio screamed in alarm, witnessing the horror that played out before his eyes. When he finally reached him, he kneeled next to him, gazing down at his face. The man emitted a few ruckles before peacefully rested his head on the cold, hard ground.

Antonio darted off to the mansion. He jumped off his horse and approached the family.

"Antonio, what happened? Where's Santiago?" Gabriella uttered in annoyance.

"He had an accident!" Antonio said, trying to catch his breath.

"An accident?" Gabriella hardly absorbed the shock. "What accident?"

"Hurry! We don't have much time! One of you, call an ambulance!" Antonio said and took Lucia and her mother in the car, while Juan Pablo and Diego went inside to call a doctor.

"Papa? Papa? Dios!" Lucia cried as she ran towards him, pushing the men aside and carefully examined the man lying before her eyes. His hat laid aside; his face peaceful. His eyes closed. "For God's sake, what happened?" she demanded, needing an explanation for this tragedy.

Gabriella froze in place. Her husband laying on the ground, still and lifeless. She turned to Fernando, sparks of anger shooting towards him. Thousands of regrets for having drank that much gnawed at his mind. And now, his recklessness had taken the life of Gabriella's beloved husband. "You will pay for this, Fernando! I blame you for this murder!" Gabriella vigorously punched him in the chest before Antonio grabbed her hands and tried to calm her down.

"I swear to God, Doña Gabriella, it isn't my fault!" Fernando fought for words to explain. "The horse came out of nowhere, and it was too late to swerve, and…"

"You silly son of a bitch! You killed him!" Gabriella grabbed Fernando, shaking him violently.

"Papa! Papa! Please, open your eyes!" Lucia cried, caressing her father's forehead, still warm. Lucia considered him asleep.

"Gabriella, please, he's still alive! It's no one's fault. He fell alone." Antonio caught her shoulders in desperate attempt to subdue her rage.

"Oh, God!" Gabriella murmured and let the sorrow grip her whole being.

Chapter Five

The outing the Williams family had organized on that beautiful spring day turned out to be an excellent idea. Chloe and her brothers had a chance to spend more time together, especially now that they had prepared for Chloe's move to her new home. As Chloe poured orange juice, she caught a glimpse of Mike's sullen expression. "What's wrong?"

"Most probably this will be the last time we'll be together like this." His voice resembled the pain in his chest.

Chloe gazed at him, and her lips curled into a vague, meaningless smile. "Why are you saying this? I am going to marry, not die." She rubbed her palm against his arm to comfort.

"To some extent, there is something that will die. You will move, and will take care of your new home, as it should be," he continued. "I didn't think it would be this soon." A few tears pricked his eyes, but he didn't let them spill out.

"No matter where I go, you'll always be my brother, and I'll always love you," Chloe said, hugging him fondly. Mike lowered his head and put his hand to his forehead. "Are you crying?" Chloe teased.

"No, of course not!" he replied, shifting his gaze back to her. "I was thinking... You're my little sister, and now you're a woman about to get married. You know how difficult it was for me…" Mike paused, unsure if he wanted to revisit old, bitter memories. "I approve of this marriage, and I wish you all the happiness in the world," he managed instead.

The melancholy floated in the air through the whole outing until late afternoon. The three of them reminisced about distant memories from their childhood, which made them laugh, breaking the scattered clouds of sadness. They were children again; playing hide and seek and arguing when Jamie cheated by peeking through his fingers while counting. When the trip came to an end, they hurriedly packed what was left and returned home.

"Chloe, here's some money. Could you go buy a bar of soap? A cheap one will do. Oh, and shampoo too. We're all out," Mike said. She smiled at him and nodded in agreement. "Did Don Alvarez call today?" he continued, rather intrigued.

"No! He hasn't." Chloe thought for a moment. It was unusual of him not to call for an entire day. "He must have a lot on his plate at work," she murmured with a thin smile and left.

"I hope he doesn't play around and fool her, because if he does, I will kill him and not bat an eye!" Mike's voice carried a sense of threat, his eyes staring for a while at the door after Chloe.

"Mike!" Jamie exclaimed. "They are getting married in two weeks. It's time to start putting more trust in him."

The short silence filled the room before Mike spoke again. "I can't! There's something… fishy about this man. He may be rich and respected and all that, but I still can't trust him."

Chloe went down the street before turning around at Doña Prudencia's cry. "Where are you going?"

"I have to buy some things."

"Wait! Come with me!" The woman stopped her. "I will give you what you need," she added and both headed to the indoor market. "How are you, my dear?" The woman's voice seemed concerned.

"I am good. Very good, actually," Chloe said. The sincere grin on her face served as evidence as they passed a few stalls of assorted fruits and vegetables.

"I can hardly imagine you're good, after such a tragedy. Tell me, what happened?"

"What tragedy?" Chloe stopped, baffled by her words that had erased her smile in the blink of an eye.

"Oh, no! Don't tell me you haven't heard!" The woman gaped at her. "Miguel!" she screamed at her son. "Give me the newspaper! The one from today! Hurry up!"

The woman flipped through several pages until she came to the small article. Chloe's head spun several times as she read through the title. 'Don Santiago Alvarez's family is saddened by his sudden death'. The air became heavy with the mingling scents of freshly brewed coffee, exotic spices, and the sweet fragrance of ripe fruits; a cacophony of aromas that usually enticed the senses but now felt like an overwhelming assault on her frayed nerves. Chloe stood frozen; her eyes fixed on the words that seemed to blur into a meaningless jumble. Santiago's untimely death reverberated through every fiber of her being. Her hand instinctively reached for the edge of the desk counter, fingers clutching at the smooth surface for support as if the ground beneath her had turned to quicksand.

"Isn't that your fiancé?" Miguel asked. "The article says he had a wife and children. They were a big family. He died in an accident with a horse," the man summarized succinctly as her eyes instinctively went back to the small black and white picture of the noble man.

Her breaths came in short, shallow bursts, each inhalation a struggle against the invisible weight pressing down on her chest. A wave of dizziness washed over her, as if the air had turned thicker, suffocating her with its oppressive weight. Her vision blurred, and the once-familiar market seemed alien and distant, its edges melting into a haze. She refused to believe what she'd just read.

"It's him, isn't it?" Doña Prudencia turned to Chloe. "I recognized him as soon as I saw the photo… Chloe, wait!" the woman screamed after her, but the girl didn't stop. Her look was hollow; the tears immediately rolled down her face. She grabbed a few fruits from one of the stalls and threw them in a desperate attempt to soothe her anguish.

"Why!" she screamed. Her heart was a heavy stone that broke under the lighting. She didn't know what to do, nor where to go. It seemed the sky had fallen on her as it was more and more difficult to breathe.

Finally, Doña Prudencia managed to get her back to the little shop. "Calm down, my dear! He won't return even if you cry out your eyes," she said and soothingly caressed her hair.

"Maybe you'd want to go and pay tribute to his family?" Miguel said.

"I don't even know where he lives," Chloe sniveled.

"There is an address in the article, if you wish…" Doña Prudencia reached out for the newspaper.

"Please, don't! Don't show me this Godawful news again!" she begged.

"Maybe it's best to call your brothers, so they'll take you home," Miguel suggested, but Chloe refused. She only had the faintest idea of what had happened and couldn't even think of how, or what to tell her brothers.

A family! He had a family. Chloe tried to absorb the news that had hit her like a ton of bricks. Bitterness, like a venomous vine, coiled around her heart, its tendrils seeping into the once-burgeoning garden of love she had nurtured for Santiago. The news of his carefully concealed past was nothing but a calculated blow, casting shadows over the tender memories they had shared. The tempestuous storm raged within her, tugging her in opposing directions, torn between the need to mourn the loss of the future she had envisioned and the searing desire to confront Santiago, to demand answers that might never soothe her ache.

"It's better this way. At least he won't fool you anymore," Miguel stated.

"How's it better? She has certain rights. She must demand what's hers!" his mother insisted. Her mind dreamt up ways of helping the poor girl – maybe Chloe would give her some of the money she would demand from the widow? "Wait here, girl!" She turned to Chloe. "As soon as we close, we'll drive you!" She skimmed through the article again. "Here! It says his wife is merciful to the poor."

Chapter Six

Mike sat on what appeared to be a bench covered in a moth-eaten, tattered blanket. He desperately needed to stop his leg from bouncing. It was past ten, and Chloe had been missing for hours. His rage was turning into worry, and back into rage again. Jamie appeared from the kitchen into the cozy living room, which was separated from the kitchen by an arched wall. He held a seemingly expensive, already-opened bottle of champagne with three glasses in his hands. After pouring himself a glass and leaving the bottle on the table, he poured one for Mike while sporting a goofy grin on his face.

"Two weeks, my brother, two weeks! After all this time, we'll finally live as we deserve." Jamie sighed contentedly after taking a sip of champagne and handing a glass to his brother.

Mike stood up from his seat, emptied the glass in Jamie's face and shattered it against the green wall. "What's wrong with you?" he roared. "Don't you see the time? How long does it take to buy soap and shampoo?"

It took a moment for Jamie to regain his normal breathing after wiping his face clean. "Damn it, Mike! What's wrong with you?" he hissed. "She must be with Don Alvarez, enjoying some alone time together," Jamie added but his words only made Mike's irritation grow bigger.

"Get dressed! We are going to the police!" Mike said, and without leaving him time to reply, he slammed the front door and got into his car. And when Jamie joined him, he pressed the pedal to the metal, and the car roared into the night.

"Don't you think it's too early to get the police involved?"

"I don't care!" Mike pressed on the accelerator. "She's never been out this late. She wouldn't do it."

"They are so many things we thought she wouldn't do, but she did," Jamie said, earning a vicious glare from his brother. "Anyway, it's the right thing to do."

"We'll look for her and, in the meantime, we'll inform the police. They may help," Mike said, speeding downtown to the police station.

৯৯

The devastated family had gathered in the dining room. The long, dark, wooden table was full of all sorts of dishes, which no one had touched.

"I don't want Fernando and his friends in this mansion, anymore!" Gabriella roared, fuming over the death of her husband. She had let her anguish turn into rage and could barely control herself. "They killed him, and they deserve to end up in prison!"

"Mom, that's enough!" Diego said. "Antonio had already explained to you that it was an accident."

"You may think so, but I will not be fooled with this story."

Magnolia rushed from the dining room, spotting the man at the door. "Fernando, what are you doing here?

Doña Gabriella is still livid. She shouldn't see you in here." She hurried to send him away.

"She has visitors," he murmured.

"At this time?"

They both scurried outside. Her eyes widened at the sight of the three strangers standing by the parked car. She approached carefully as the image of the girl grew familiar. It was her. The girl from the picture she had seen in Santiago's pants, but the other two people she met for the first time. She carefully looked at the girl, who cried and trembled, dressed in a short summer dress and her thin pink cardigan, which barely protected her from the bitter wind.

"How may I help you?" Magnolia asked politely.

"Is this Santiago Alvarez's home?" Doña Prudencia asked.

"Yes, it is. I am sorry but Don Alvarez passed away."

"We are aware of his death. This is why we are here," the woman said, seemingly angry.

"I am sorry but who are you?"

"Can you inform his wife that Chloe Williams insists on seeing her," Miguel demanded.

Magnolia froze. The girl's presence hit her like a tidal wave, completely overwhelming her. "Please, go! You shouldn't be here!" Magnolia's heartbeat accelerated.

"Not without talking to his wife," Doña Prudencia insisted.

"Magnolia, who is it?" Gabriella called in the distance.

"Some strangers are looking for Don Santiago," Magnolia said in horror.

Gabriella approached the people, finding them odd and impudent, paying little attention to the crying girl.

Chloe wanted to go home; she had never wanted to come here. What was the point? The man she loved had lied to her and, more importantly, he was dead.

"What do you want?" The woman's words came like a slap in the face, leaving Chloe reeling and stunned.

"Look, Mrs Alvarez, we need to talk to you about a touchy subject," the woman said. "This is Miss Chloe Williams, the girl your husband deceived after having had a roll in the hay with her."

"How dare you?" Gabriella growled.

"We dare because it's true." Miguel hurried to defend his mother.

Gabriella stood in front of them, dismayed by the whole story the strangers were telling. The slanders they poured came like shockwaves, rippling through her body. The anger deep inside her resurfaced instantly. "Get out of my house immediately!"

"What? Ah, no! How is that possible?" Doña Prudencia jumped to Chloe's defense as the young, poor girl didn't even know why these people had brought her to this house. "We are here to help this little girl to demand her rights, and we won't go anywhere before we settle the matter at hand."

"Who are you?" Gabriella asked.

"We are friends of the little girl and came to help her," Miguel said.

"To help her? You're slandering my respected husband," Gabriella snapped. "If you had any respect, you wouldn't be here. Get out!"

"Very well," Miguel said. "Don't cry when her brothers come. They're much more ill-tempered, and then you'll have to take responsibility for Chloe and… her baby."

The lie slipped off his tongue, but it was too late to go back on his word. Chloe gazed at him, bewildered by his words but said nothing. She wished she'd been braver and faced the elegant woman, but she didn't dare to lift her eyes off the ground. Gabriella dragged the girl into the house. Chloe's heartbeat accelerated, matching the speed of blinking.

"Magnolia, gather the whole family," she ordered from the salon.

Chloe's face turned crimson. Embarrassed, she wished she could escape, but her feet were too weak to run or even move for that matter.

When the whole family gathered, Chloe's body winced. The many eyes on her were like daggers through her, and she didn't even dare to face them.

"Mother, who is this girl?" Diego asked. Chloe's heart skipped a beat at the welcoming voice, yet she stood in the marvelous salon like a bird with a broken wing.

"Speak, girl. Isn't that why you're here?" Gabriella screamed at her face as she shivered violently.

"Mother!" Juan Pablo exclaimed.

After what appeared an eternity of silence, Chloe murmured, "Please I don't want to be here! Let me go!"

"Well, since you are here, let me introduce you to my family. These are my children!" She showed each one of them separately. "As you can see yourself, even they are older than you." She stood by Antonio. "This is my son-in law, coming from a respected noble family. Me – you already know who I am – the faithful wife devoted to her family and home."

"What's with the formal introduction?" Antonio said impatiently. "I don't understand."

"You will! In a moment!" Gabriella returned to the girl. "This girl states her name is Chloe and claims to have been romantically involved with my late husband!" Gabriella said at last, utterly disgusted as she repeated the words again.

"What base slander!" Lucia jumped over the girl but luckily didn't hit her as Diego caught her in time.

"There is more to it. The two peasants outside, who brought her, state she's pregnant – with my husband's child," Gabriella added in an indignant tone. "Shameless but intimidated! What? Did your strength fly away?" she snapped at Chloe's face.

"This is a heavy accusation, miss." Diego stood up from the leather armchair. "You need to be careful."

Chloe stole a short peek over his muscled body and the lower part of his jaw, but she lowered her head immediately.

"That can't be true." Juan Pablo stood up as well. "Our father was a respected man with an excellent reputation!"

"I think so too," Gabriella added.

"Then why did you let her in, Mother?" Diego narrowed his azure eyes at his mother.

"Because I believe in my husband's devotion, and I wanted to show her how difficult it would be to besmirch the memory of him." Gabriella raised an irritated eyebrow at being questioned disrespectfully in front of a stranger by her own son.

Diego approached her and Chloe's knee shivered. There was something about him, something she couldn't quite figure out, but his presence accelerated her heartbeat to the maximum. His perfume, his voice, his posture, his whole attitude made her head spin, ready to faint in his arms.

"Please, tell us, who did you come with?" Diego said in a low voice.

"With two other peasants of quite dubious appearance. It must be them who made her tell such lies," Gabriella interjected.

"Come on, tell us everything!" Diego raised his voice in impatience.

"I don't want to say anything! I want to go home! Please let me go!" Chloe had finally found a way to speak. She gasped at his penetrating gaze, making him look appealing and repulsive at the same time.

"You can't go before we clarify things," Diego said.

"All I am going to say is that I loved Santiago! And yes, he made promises to me." Chloe's tears rolled down her cheeks. "But I never knew he had a wife and children. I swear!" she lamented.

"It's better for her to go! She said everything she had to say," Antonio said.

"No, we must let her talk," Diego interrupted.

"Why?" Antonio grumbled. "She is nothing but an ordinary intriguer who wants to make some money from the situation."

Chloe gazed at him. For some reason, she wanted to slap him – hard.

"That's true!" Gabriella grabbed her by the elbow and dragged her to the front door. The rest of the family remained in the salon, hardly believing the meeting they had just had. "Magnolia, make sure this piece of filth goes away and never comes back."

Magnolia did as she was told and followed her outside. "Chloe, wait! I believe you!" Magnolia ran to reach her. "I knew about you two. Don Santiago told me the whole story. I want you to know he really loved you," she added once the heartbroken girl turned to her. Her eyes winced in sadness, and Magnolia wished she could do something for her, but there was nothing more to be done other than saying goodbye.

"If he loved me, why did he lie to me?" Chloe screamed in tears.

"Magnolia, what are you still doing there?" Gabriella called from the entrance door.

Magnolia panicked, and Chloe turned to go. "I was making sure she's leaving." She cleared her throat and went slowly inside.

Doña Prudencia and her son were impatiently waiting in their car. When the girl appeared, she was bombarded with questions, but Chloe was too utterly upset to answer. Right that moment, she didn't even want to be around them. They had brought her here and she could hardly forgive them for the ordeal she had been subjected to.

"What are you talking about, girl? You can't walk," Miguel said, "we're too far away from home."

"Leave me alone." Chloe plucked herself from his hands and ran off into the darkness. She walked aimlessly ahead, unsure if she was heading in the right direction. Her hands were crossed over her chest, protecting herself from the cold wind which was making her face numb from the tears streaming down her cheeks. She refused to believe this was all true; it was a nightmare, the worst in her life, and she desperately hoped she would wake up and everything would go back to normal.

As she walked across a bridge, she stopped in the middle and gazed down at the bottomless precipice. "If we cannot be together here, we'll be together there," she mumbled before climbing to the outer side of the railing. Her eyes shot to the dark sky, stars sprinkling all over it. She was reciting a prayer and didn't even notice the car, pulled over in the middle of the road.

"Miss! Don't do it!" the man shouted, and Chloe instinctively turned back.

Chapter Seven

Chloe slowly opened her eyes, taking in the scent of the sheets and relishing the heavenly sensation. As she lifted the duvet, her gaze fell on her underwear, and her tumultuous thoughts caused her to gasp and cover her mouth with her hand. "What the...?" A burst of urgency formed in her chest as she threw the duvet aside and feverishly examined the room. When her eyes landed on her clothes, she quickly slipped into her dress and cardigan, pressing her fists to her chest as fear began to crawl over her body. "Where am I?" she whispered. She strode down the narrow corridor, glancing at the doors of the other bedrooms lining both sides. She hurried past them and walked downstairs.

"Ah, you're already up?" Mr Brighton rose from his armchair and approached her.

"Where am I?" Chloe looked at the man, unease poking her mind. She took a step back, causing him to stop in his tracks.

"This is my home!" He cast an inquisitive glance at her. "You were going to jump off a bridge last night."

Chloe bent her head, ashamed of her actions. "Why am I here?" She mustered the courage to meet his gaze. The middle-aged man briefly grinned before his expression turned serious again.

"Well, you fainted before I could ask where you lived." He cleared his throat. "Bonnie? Bonnie, did you set the table for lunch?"

Lunch? What time is it? Chloe's thoughts raced in her head as she remembered she hadn't returned home since yesterday afternoon. Her brothers must be worried sick. She had never stayed out all night before.

"Yes, Mr Brighton! The table is set!" the chubby housekeeper replied, adjusting her glasses. Her cold gaze lingered on Chloe for a moment before she turned back to her master, smiling.

"Thank you, Bonnie," he said, and the woman disappeared unnoticed. "Shall we?" He gestured towards the lunchroom.

"Um… it's very kind of you to offer, Mr Brighton, but I must go home! My brothers must be worried."

"Please, call me Edward!" He smiled, pleased to hear her speak more than a word at a time. "Here's what we're going to do: we'll have lunch, and then I'll drive you home."

Chloe's hesitation crept onto her face, but she nodded in agreement at his suggestion.

They made their way to the exquisite lunchroom. The table was laden with all sorts of foods and drinks, resembling a tasting menu in a fancy restaurant. Chloe took her seat, her eyes darting across the mouth-watering dishes. She quickly dug into her salad as famine prevailed. She paused mid-bite when she noticed Edward's gaze fixed on her, and she instinctively stopped with puffy cheeks.

"Oh no, no!" Edward exclaimed. "Don't stop! I'm glad to see you have such a good appetite. I don't want you to go home hungry."

Chloe finished chewing and swallowed the last bits of her meal. "You have an exquisite home, Mr Brighton… uh, Edward."

Chloe forced a thin smile and took a quick look around the room. From the chandelier to the silver cutlery she was eating with, everything was shining and spotless. Edward was the wealthiest of all farmers in the nearby vicinity. Of course, he heavily relied on the other business deeds he was involved in.

"Thank you, Miss…?" Edward prompted, realizing he didn't know her last name.

"Chloe! Chloe Williams." She smiled awkwardly. "Do you live here alone?"

"I rarely come here at all," Edward said before sipping his Chardonnay. "But, yes, I am here alone. I mean, Bonnie and Malcolm take care of it while I am away."

"So, where do you live?" Chloe asked, munching on her salad.

It took a while for Edward to respond, his eyes lingering between Chloe's lips and her breasts. She was indeed a gem he had found, and he wouldn't think of losing her. "Um, Boston," he blurted out, trying to take his stern gaze off her lips. "But I travel a lot."

Chloe smiled, winning the battle over her anxiety. She was getting to know him better and by the time lunch was over, she had confessed everything that had happened before they met.

Edward dropped her off later in the afternoon, expressing his interest in seeing her again. Chloe nodded eagerly and smiled, but the wave of grief hit her as soon as she turned to enter the house. She locked herself in her room and sat in front of the mirror, picking up the vase that once held money given to her by Santiago Alvarez. Her lips curled into a bittersweet smile as she reminisced about their time together. Her expression saddened but this time she didn't cry. Instead, she let go of the emptiness inside her in the form of a small, inaudible sigh.

The banging on the door snapped her out of her thoughts and back to the harsh reality. She walked over the door, unlocked it and returned to her seat without saying a word, nor opening the door.

"Mike, please promise me you won't act recklessly," Jamie pleaded as they entered the room.

"I can't promise this," he replied curtly.

"Then, let me speak to her first."

"I appreciate your concern, but as the oldest brother, I am the head of this family, and she is my sister." Mike halted in the middle of the room, his gaze fixated on her unkempt cardigan.

"Where have you been? We've been worried sick about you. We thought you were with Don Alvarez for hours," Jamie prodded, urging her to speak.

"Did he do something to you?" Mike's voice grew louder, his patience wearing thin. "That old son of a bitch!" Mike bellowed. "I'll find him and make him pay!"

"He's dead, Mike! Don Santiago Alvarez is dead!" Chloe gathered her strength and buried her gaze straight into his eyes.

"Oh my God!" Jamie gasped at the bombshell.

As soon as she spoke those ugly, awful words, she burst into tears. After an eternity of begging, Chloe finally found herself compelled to tell her brothers the whole story. She recounted how she found out about Don Alvarez's death, her harrowing experience in that Godawful place, and the ultimate embarrassment she had been subjected to. Her fingers fidgeted on the topic of her suicidal thoughts. She buried her stare towards her feet, sparing them the story about Edward Brighton. She was hesitant as to whether she was ready to deal with the inevitable barrage of questions about who he was.

When she finished, Mike wiped a couple of tears from his cheeks and left the room. He ran his hands over his face, and in the next second, his anger turned into pure insanity. He grabbed the table and flipped it upside down, sending everything crashing to the floor. He snatched the blanket and threw it to one side in a fit of fury. But it still wasn't enough. He picked up the bench and hurled it to the other side of the room. He grabbed the nearest chair and smashed it against the wall, leaving the back of it in his hands while the rest shuddered in pieces on the ground.

"Mike, stop! What the hell are you doing?" Jamie rushed into the kitchen, startled by the loud thuds coming from the other room. "Do you want to bring the whole house down on our heads?"

Mike glared at him, his eyes burning with a fierce intensity. His chest heaved as he tried to calm himself down. "Were you in there? Did you hear what Chloe just told us?" His voice was raspy with anger.

"Yes, but it wasn't her fault. And you don't have to take it out on the furniture," Jamie replied, trying to reason with him.

Mike arched an eyebrow at him, his expression still dark with fury. "This old maniac played with our little sister for months. His entire family made her feel like a cheap wench going after their money. Don't you understand? What if she had jumped off the bridge?" Mike's intense gaze made Jamie's facial muscles twitch involuntarily. "The blame for this is on you!" Mike roared, before Jamie could even defend himself. And without warning, he punched him, sending him falling onto his back.

"Mike, please stop!" Jamie screamed as Mike straddled his legs around Jamie's hips, pinning him down and raining punches down on his face.

Chloe rushed into the kitchen, finding her brothers rolling on the floor and destroying everything in their path. She screamed at them to stop, but they didn't even notice her presence as they were engulfed in an inferno of fury.

When Mike finally put his anger to bed, the room looked like a tornado had torn through it, with broken furniture and shattered glass scattered everywhere. Chloe was helpless, overwhelmed as she watched her brother's fight. Jamie was lying on the floor. It took a while for him to come to his senses, a small trail of blood appearing in the corner of his mouth as he struggled to catch his breath. His wavy messy hair was even more tousled than it normally was. And when he straightened his body, Chloe had to clean off the few pieces of glass stuck to the back of his shirt.

"When that old bastard was talking miracles in the expensive house, this brat made his accounts." Mike clenched his fists and teeth, fuming. "I knew it! I just did! And I let myself be fooled and gave the go-ahead to this madness," he roared as if mad at himself.

"Mike, please, everything is over," Chloe said in low voice.

"Oh no! Everything is far from over," he mumbled. "Everyone will pay dearly for what they have done to you! When I finish with them, then it will be over!" His chest bobbed from the heavy breathing.

"For God's sake, what are you planning to do?" Chloe whined.

"Chloe, give me the address of Alvarez's family." He gazed at her intently. His nostrils moved fast from his erratic breathing.

"Mike, no!" She shook her head in refusal. She'd discovered his intentions, and so had Jamie.

"Chloe!" Mike growled. "It will be either you, or I'll go to that ignorant, greedy woman, Doña Prudencia and smashed her head before she could say a word."

Chloe could only blink. Her fear suffocating her, she reluctantly gave him the address. Mike sank the tip of his teeth into his lip, saved the address in his phone and stormed out to the backyard in a desperate attempt to calm his nerves.

Chapter Eight

The woman standing near the front door appeared to be in her late 60s, calmly looking around as if waiting someone other than the servants to notice her arrival. Her platinum blonde hair was gathered in a French twist, adding a sense of superiority and refined nobility to her appearance. She handed her black coat, adorned with beads and crystals along the sleeves, to one of the servant girls and dropped her carry-on sized suitcase at the entrance.

"There is more luggage in the car," she ordered politely, addressing the servant girl. "Please see to it that it is taken great care of."

"Yes, ma'am," the girl replied in an intimidated voice, fixing her gaze on the lady's wrinkled eye corners. "Let me inform them of your arrival."

"No need!" Isabella retorted with scolding eyes. "I know the way!" She straightened her back and marched confidently into the dining room. "How lovely it is to see the whole family gathered for supper," Isabella declared in a firm and emphatic voice, demanding her arrival to be acknowledged immediately.

"Mother! What are you doing here?" Gabriella rose from her seat to greet her, caught in great surprise of her unannounced arrival.

The two women barely made a hug, plastering wry smiles on their faces, but Isabella did smile quite fondly at her grandchildren. She took the free seat at the other end of the table, without waiting to be invited. She rested her elbows on the table and nodded to Magnolia to bring her cutlery and glasses. "I heard about the tragedy of your husband and came for a visit," Isabella stated matter-of-factly, without a trace of pity in her voice. After settling comfortably into her chair, she turned to her grandchildren. Diego and Lucia found her attitude to be quite inappropriate, but Juan Pablo found her to be charming and bold. "That's life, kids! Everyone ends up there one day! Now it was your shameless father's turn," Isabella quipped in a sarcastic tone.

"Mother, please show some respect," Gabriella scolded her from her seat directly opposite her. Isabella raised an eyebrow but let the remark pass.

"Antonio are you still here?" She raised a quizzical brow, glancing at him as Magnolia arranged the utensils in front of her.

"Of course, Doña Isabella. This is my home," he replied.

The old woman pursed her lips in bewilderment and relaxed in her chair. "Oh well. If it doesn't feel humiliating for a man your age to not have a roof over his head and hide his presence at my daughter's house…" she said bitingly and signaled to Magnolia to pour her a glass of wine with a glance.

Diego shrugged in his seat, and Juan Pablo emitted a choked laugh at the biting tone of his grandmother. Gabriella immediately scolded him with an icy cold stare, and he sipped from his glass while avoiding eye contact.

"Mother, how long are you planning on staying with us?"

"One would think you want me gone as soon as possible," Doña Isabella remarked.

"Of course not! I'm glad you came to see us." Gabriella forced a courtesy smile.

The rest of the dinner proceeded in much the same fashion. Isabella regaled them with stories of her life in New York and her constant travels around the world, enchanting her grandchildren but boring Antonio and Gabriella. "So, how's life here, kids?" she asked, changing the subject. "Are there any pretty girls conquering your hearts?" Her tone sounded genuine.

"Not yet, Grandma!" Diego smiled at her.

"Well, I suggest you hurry," she said, her tone biting. "You don't want to end up in Lucia's predicament, I suppose."

Antonio nearly choked on his sip of wine, while Lucia shrugged in her seat, her skin growing hotter. Luckily, her chocolate complexion didn't betray her embarrassment. Diego sat still, uncomfortable in his seat, while Juan Pablo rolled his eyes and emitted a chocked laughter at his grandmother's blunt language. Gabriella was about to lose her patience. Her mother's behavior was unforgivable, and her words were offensive and stinging.

"Oh, don't take it personally, honey! It's not your fault," she said, trying to soothe her granddaughter's wounded pride. She smiled warmly at her. "After all, you were, what, 20 when you got married, and we all know your mother likes to take care of things." She peered at Gabriella, and her face muscles twitched as she pursed her lips, trying to control them. Gabriella rolled her eyes at her mother, threw her napkin on the table, and stormed out of the dining room. Antonio thought it best to join her, leaving Isabella and her grandchildren to finish dinner on their own.

"Oh, Grandma, I'm so happy you'll be around," Juan Pablo cheered. "We've been needing someone to lift up our spirits."

Antonio only glared at him on his way out. "Don't pay attention to Isabella's words, Gabriella," he said, sounding melancholic.

"My mother is a pain in the ass!" she growled. "She always has been and always will be."

"Gabriella, language!" he exclaimed. "She might hear you!"

"I don't care!" she murmured. "How rude of her to show up on my doorstep without any prior call." She rubbed her forehead, trying to soothe her light headache.

"I was thinking," Antonio said in a rather joyous voice, "why don't you take a trip to your mansion in Atlanta? It will help you relax and distract from all the problems here."

"What a good idea!" She turned to him and curled her lips into a contented smile. "And you and Lucia can accompany me. You know I don't like taking trips on my own."

And with the morning's arrival, Gabriella gathered the family to announce the trip.

"That's great!" Juan Pablo cheered upon hearing the news.

"We haven't taken a trip in decades. I think Juan Pablo is right," Diego agreed.

"No! You'll stay and take care of the mansion and your grandmother! She's old and needs someone around!" Gabriella's words echoed in the airy salon. "Lucia and

Antonio will accompany me!" Gabriella added brusquely, leaving Juan Pablo and Diego disappointed. Lucia furrowed her brows in slight reluctance too. "I hope you don't mind, Lucia?" She raised a questioning brow at her daughter.

Lucia put her cup of coffee on the small square table, making a sound as the china plate hit the glass surface. "As you wish, Mama."

"I must reckon it's an elegant way for you to avoid my presence." Isabella gazed at her daughter profoundly. "But it's too obvious, my dear."

"No, Mother! I'm not trying to avoid you. I just thought it would be nice to take a short break after my husband's death."

"Why not take Diego at least? You may need a man while you're there!" Isabella sipped her tea.

"Mother!" Gabriella growled at Isabella's sardonic, most offensive innuendo.

"Your luggage is in the car, Doña Gabriella!" one of the servant men informed her and made his way out.

"Ah, at last! Let's go!" Gabriella stood up from her seat and smoothed her black trousers before catching Antonio's elbow as both headed for the car. Lucia said goodbye with the rest and followed, rolling her eyes in exasperation.

The old car pulled up a few yards away, making a creaking noise as it came to a halt. Gabriella and the rest of the family cast a glance at each other in perplexity. The men exuded strength and steadfastness as they approached the house, which made Lucia's curiosity even bigger.

"Magnolia, see what these men want!" Gabriella got into the car with Antonio. "Lucia, come on! What are you waiting for?" her mother called from the car, snapping her out of her gaze.

"How may I help you?" Magnolia turned to the strangers.

"Is that the Alvarez family's home?" Mike said in a hoarse voice, sending chills down her spine.

"Yes, it is!" She creased her lips into a polite smile. "What do you need?"

"We're here to talk to Mrs Gabriella Alvarez and the rest of the family!" Mike stated firmly just as the car moved behind the turn and out of sight.

"I'm afraid you just missed her. Mrs Alvarez went on a trip and will be back in a week. May I ask who's looking for her?"

"Mike and Jamie Williams – Chloe Williams's brothers," Jamie said tersely. Magnolia clenched her jaw tightly, grateful that Diego and Juan Pablo were standing not far behind.

"Who are these men?" Diego turned to his brother, as he shrugged, and both approached. "Magnolia, what's going on?" Diego queried with an appraising look. His voice was pleasant and calm.

"Uh, nothing!" the woman stuttered. "These gentlemen are looking for Mrs Alvarez, but I already told them she's not present."

"Are you here for the interviews?" Diego asked politely as he met Mike's stern gaze.

"What interviews?"

"The interviews for the mansion administrator position," Diego clarified.

"We have nothing to do with those interviews."

"We're here to discuss a more important and delicate topic." Jamie gazed at Juan Pablo.

"In that case, you will need to wait for my mother's return," Juan Pablo replied in a lightly catching voice.

"Magnolia, please kindly see to it that the gentlemen are well refreshed on their way back. The weather is too hot!" Diego whispered in her ear and yanked his brother's arm, who was glued in place and grinning goofily at the strangers.

After the brothers left, Magnolia returned her attention to Mike and Jamie and carried out the offer Diego had made.

"We cannot wait for Mrs Alvarez's return. The matter at hand is urgent," Mike insisted, but Magnolia shrugged apologetically. "We won't leave until we speak with someone! Call the two gentlemen. They will surely be interested in hearing us," Mike said. "Jamie, go and find the boys!"

"No, no! Wait!" Magnolia stood in his way. "Don't worry them. I will speak with you. Follow me!" She gestured towards the easternmost part of the mansion, where she hoped they could talk in private.

In the distance, Jamie noticed the two gentlemen getting into their luxurious BMW and leaving the hacienda. Diego trusted his mother's judgment and Magnolia would be capable of handling the situation at hand and conducting interviews for new grooms and an administrator position after Gabriella had let Fernando go.

Chapter Nine

The black BMW zoomed through the village streets as the Alvarez brothers raced to meet Father Thomas to organize a charity fundraiser. Gabriella had tasked her sons with the job; Diego had accepted it eagerly, but Juan Pablo found it to be a real annoyance.

"Are you going to explain to me why you're looking around like someone's chasing us?" Diego peeked at his brother.

"We should have stayed to find out about the two men who came."

"I'm sure Magnolia will take great care of them. Why should we care who they are?" Diego peered at the speedometer.

"It's our duty to know everything that happens at home."

"Why should we care who our new grooms will be? Since Dad is gone, it's Mom who cares about hiring and firing the employees."

Juan Pablo grinned at the memory of their appearance. "Did you see them? Have you ever seen such men before?"

Diego threw a quick glance at him, sighed, and shook his head. "Stop acting like a horny donkey. When act like this, everything shows up, and one day your little secret will come out," he warned his brother with a hint of irritation.

"I never thought I would meet such handsome men. What faces! What bodies! They look like real cowboys!" Juan Pablo exclaimed, his excitement evident in his voice.

"Stay out of trouble. I know you."

Juan Pablo leaned back against the leather seat, lost in thought, picturing the handsome men right in front of him.

⚬⚬

Magnolia quickly briefed them on the night Chloe had been there, speaking in hushed tones. "Please, you must go. I am risking my job here, as it is," she begged. "I advise you not to do anything irrational. Mr Alvarez is dead, and he can no longer take care of her," Magnolia continued. "If you're here to settle your accounts with Mrs Alvarez, there will be a huge scandal, not fruitful for anyone."

"Don't think you can send us away so easily." Mike clenched his teeth. "We're not going anywhere, even if it causes a big scandal."

"Please, don't!" Magnolia shivered. "I'm really touched by your sister's story, but I'm a servant here and I'll be in huge trouble for letting strangers into the house."

"Magnolia? What are you doing here? And who are these people?" Isabella startled her from behind. "Are these the new workers my daughter mentioned?"

Magnolia's face paled and the words got stuck in her throat.

"Yes, ma'am," Jamie said emphatically. Magnolia glanced at him, as puzzled as Mike.

Isabella invited them in and briefly scolded the poor, shaking-with-fear housekeeper for not having done so already. It was improper to discuss such topics in the remote parts of the mansion, as if hiding a life-threatening secret. "Please, be seated!" Isabella pointed to the L-shaped leather sofa and returned her attention to the brothers with a gallant smile. She sat across the small table on the chair she usually took and ordered Magnolia to prepare some coffee.

"Um... Doña Isabella, we've already discussed everything. The boys are probably busy and would likely want to go. We shouldn't keep them!" Magnolia said in a shaky voice, sensing some sort of threat in Mike's voice. His determination was evident in his eyes, and the idea of them working here shocked her to the very core.

Isabella gave her a short, scolding look, making Magnolia's blinking match her heartbeat. As if regretting what she'd said, she left to fetch the coffee.

"Forgive my housekeeper! She's an excellent employee, but sometimes she doesn't know when to keep her mouth shut." Isabella smiled fondly at the men. Jamie responded to her tender gesture, but Mike remained impassive. "What are your names?"

"I'm Jamie Williams and this is Mike."

"Are you brothers?"

"Yes, ma'am," Mike replied simply, while Jamie carefully took in the sight of the salon. His eyes darted in all directions, as if assessing the family's wealth in detail. He found the idea of working for the Alvarez rather appealing, though part of him reminded himself they were supposed to be their enemies; the ones who stole the innocence of their sister. The house was magnificent, the horses more than beautiful and, frankly, the lady who invited them in had an amicable attitude. For a moment, Jamie lost himself as to why they had come before he returned his attention to her.

"Ah, yes. You look very much alike," Isabella said, gazing at their faces and their dark eyes for a full minute. "Have you served in the military?"

Jamie shook his head.

"Well, you may as well have," Isabella said. "Now, that's what I call real men!" She stared in awe at their bodies. They exuded nothing less than masculinity and power, and Isabella found herself drawn to their humble, yet imposing postures. "Not like some slackers who managed to sneak into my daughter's house."

Magnolia placed the small wooden tray, holding a pot of freshly brewed coffee and three china cups, down on the table. "Shall I pour?" She glanced at Isabella, who nodded her approval without taking her eyes off the two gentlemen. Despite their cheap clothes, there was something in them that Isabella found rather intriguing.

Magnolia's eyes wandered upon Isabella for a moment, her hand trembled involuntarily, and the hot coffee spilled over Mike's pants. He bit his lower lip to stifle a wail as the heat sank into his thigh. "Oh my God! You silly old—" Isabella grunted from her seat as Magnolia hurriedly gave him a napkin. "Are you okay, Mr. Williams?"

"Please come with me! Let's remove the stain before it sets," Magnolia signaled for him to follow, and he did. She skillfully navigated him to the restroom and turned on the cold water. "Please go! You saw for yourselves; there is no one you could talk to at this moment."

Her brows furrowed with concern, and she completely forgot the stain on Mike's pants.

"Very well, Magnolia," Mike said rather calmly. "I believe my brother already gave an answer to the job proposal." He stopped the water. "Expect us tomorrow!" he added with an emphatic tone and quickly returned to the salon. "Jamie, come on, let's go!"

"Wait! Are you going? You haven't even finished your coffee, and we haven't even discussed the terms of employment," Isabella stuttered.

"We will," Mike said flatly. "Tomorrow," he added and whisked out, leaving Jamie behind. He smiled politely at the lady, curtly bowed as a goodbye, and rushed to catch up with his brother.

Magnolia hurried inside Gabriella's room and leaned against the locked door as soon as the brothers left. The memory of her insult flooded her mind and momentarily turned the panic to hatred and anger. She approached the nightstand, and threw a long, fervent glare at Gabriella's picture. Now that the brothers had left, she had time to think calmly over the matter. Her stern gaze fell again on her mistress's framed photo on the nightstand. "Now you can say I have betrayed you, Mrs Alvarez," she murmured in a low voice. "I will help these boys and there is nothing you could do to stop me." Determination flared in her eyes.

When Mike parked in front of their home, his eyes instinctively dwelled on the window of Chloe's room. Chloe waved at him lightly and curled her lips into a small smile. Inwardly, she was burning with anticipation to find out what they had discussed with Gabriella Alvarez. Chloe greeted them rather reluctantly when she saw their grumpy faces, both looking engrossed in their thoughts. Mike opened a bottle of cheap tequila and sat at the table, drinking up the first glass. His body stern, he sighed and grimaced from the bitter aftertaste.

"Did you speak to the family?" Chloe finally asked.

"No, we couldn't," Jamie said, glancing at his brother, who wasn't in the mood for interrogation. "Mrs Alvarez was not there." Chloe inwardly sighed and, without noticing, the relief showed on her face in the form of a small smile. "But don't worry, we'll talk to them," Jamie added.

"How so? Are you really thinking of going back to that mansion?"

"Yes. Tomorrow," Jamie said with a sigh. "Tomorrow and many days after."

"I don't understand." Chloe widened her eyes to Jamie, then to Mike, completely baffled.

"We're starting a job at the mansion," Mike turned to her.

"What?" Chloe shrieked. "This is absurd!"

"Keep your nose out of this! We've already made up our minds." Mike peered at Jamie as if looking for his support on this.

"Yes," Jamie confirmed in a flat voice. "We've already made up our minds, and there's nothing you can do," he repeated and went to his room.

Chapter Ten

Juan Pablo turned up the radio and danced in his robe with a glass of exquisite wine in his hand. Now that his mother was not here, he planned to take full advantage of her absence and have the best time, which was number one on his to-do list. As the music pulsed through the room, memories of his younger days flooded his mind. The neon lights casting a kaleidoscope of colors across the dance floor, the infectious energy of the crowd, and the pulsating music that seemed to seep into every pore. With a wistful smile, he swirled his wine before Diego rushed into the study room. He furrowed his brows, covered his ears from the blasting radio, and quickly ended the little party.

"What is this noise, Pablo?" His tone was high. He often shortened his name to show his brother he wasn't in a mood.

"What? Can't I have some fun?" Juan Pablo protested, slumping on the couch, "You are worse than Mama." His gaze went to the ornate bookshelves, their rich mahogany exuding a timeless elegance, basking in the warm glow of a crystal chandelier.

"You are not alone! You're disturbing Grandma."

"She doesn't care! If she did, she would have come to complain by now." Juan Pablo gulped the rest of his wine. "Here! Take one glass and join me!" His eyes flickered with enthusiasm.

"Instead of wasting your time, you'd better help me with the charity fundraiser with Father Thomas." Diego went behind the desk and opened the folder on top of a thousand other things.

"What a tut!" Juan Pablo grunted and poured himself another glass, while Diego skimmed through the tasks and activities Father Thomas had given them, with the deadline being the following week.

"Stop being lazy and come help your brother." Diego glanced at him from under his brows and returned to the list of activities. "Would you tell Magnolia to bring me coffee?"

"I haven't seen her all day. I think she's not home."

"How so?" Diego looked up at him, but his brother only shrugged.

"She is taking advantage of Mom's absence too. It's only you who can possibly think of work," he giggled, tipsy from the wine.

Diego shot a lasting, irritated gaze at him that made Juan Pablo's laughter even louder. For a fleeting moment, Diego went back to those times when they were ten. He gazed at his brother with a ghost of a smile on his face. He'd always be the mischievous little kid he used to be and perhaps that would never change.

"Ah, here!" He took out a piece of paper and skimmed through it quickly. "The children's protection is an extremely important project, but we'll need more than the council's help." Diego peeked at his brother, grateful to see his face serious. "Organizing only spectacles, however, won't be enough to raise the necessary funds."

"Well, it depends on the spectacles." Juan Pablo raised his glass in a toast. Diego arched his brow and tilted his head to one side, ready to hear his brother's ideas. "A rodeo could work," Juan Pablo added.

"I didn't know you liked rodeos."

"I love them! Mostly because there are cowboys! Strong and brave!" He had put his goofy, dreamy look on his face again. Diego shook his head as a way of dismissing his suggestion. "Like the men who came today," Juan Pablo added, sitting at the edge of the desk.

"Again, this nonsense!" He peered at him from under his eyebrows. "Don't get distracted," he added in flat voice, and kept skimming the other documents.

"I am dying to see them one more time. I wonder if they will come back again," Juan Pablo said and went back to the couch, murmuring some ideas as his brother asked for his opinion.

The night rolled into the early hours of the morning, and the two brothers could barely hold their heads straight. A couple of hours later, the first rays of the sun generously bathed the lands around the hacienda in yellow warmth. The phone's loud, insistent ring echoed through the walls of the salon, reaching the rooms upstairs. Magnolia sprinted to pick it up, before the shrill noise woke up everyone in the house.

"Honestly, I am worried about the mansion," Gabriella said. "And my mother? Does she behave?"

"Yes, yes! Absolutely," Magnolia assured her. "Diego and Juan Pablo are also doing well. They are performing their duties conscientiously and thoroughly."

"How nice to hear," Gabriella exclaimed in satisfaction. "And what about the new workers? Have you had any luck finding suitable candidates?"

Magnolia paused for a short moment, pondering the thought of Gabriella finding she had let the brothers of her late husband's mistress into her house. She shivered but managed to regain her voice. "Yes, Doña Gabriella. We did find two men."

"Only two?" Gabriella sounded disappointed. They were wealthy, noble people and she'd expected at least a dozen candidates to have shown interest by now.

"Yes, but don't you worry, Doña Gabriella! They are the most suitable people for the job," she said in slow, emphatic voice as she held the handset to her mouth.

Isabella cleared her throat, taking aback Magnolia from the landing of the stairwell. Her eyes were upon Magnolia who rushed to finish the conversation, gazing at the old lady. She had chosen a classic, elegant black skirt, falling below the knee, and a white lace blouse with the same color suit jacket on top. Her hair was in the usual French twist, revealing her diamond earrings, a gift from her late husband.

"Was it my daughter?"

"Yes, it was." Magnolia released the blow of air she had held for a moment.

"I hope she said she'd never return." Isabella walked down the stairs carefully, holding the wooden, state-of-the-art rail too strong. Magnolia hardly managed to restrain her laugh and informed her the three of them would be back by the end of the week.

Isabella and her daughter had been on bad terms for almost 20 years. And their relationship had got even worse since Gabriella's father died. To her, her mother had become more frivolous, indulging herself in the company of various men, spending her beloved father's money on vacations and whims.

"Are my grandchildren here?" Isabella asked.

"Yes, they're still sleeping! They must have stayed up late last night."

"What a pity! I wanted to take a stroll around the hacienda with them," Isabella grumbled in discontent. "Anyway, would you like to keep me company?" Magnolia stared back at her, bewildered to be asked but nodded her agreement.

Isabella joined her grandchildren for lunch in the formal dining room. Another young servant girl tended to the table as Magnolia was impatiently waiting for Chloe's brothers to return. When they finally showed up, she scurried to meet them.

"Look at these horses, Mike!" Jamie's eyes widened at the sight of the beautiful stallions. "Each one must cost a fortune," he continued. Mike's facial muscles tensed but didn't comment on his brother's awe. "Of course, these people are bathing in money," Jamie added.

"Good afternoon, Magnolia," Mike greeted. His voice was cold, leaving Magnolia under the impression that this was his usual mood.

"I was expecting you. May we have a word in private before you start?"

Mike signaled with open palm for the woman to lead the way.

"Look who's back!" Isabella grinned, accompanied by Diego and Juan Pablo.

"We were waiting for you! Are you starting a job in the hacienda?" Juan Pablo put his goofy grin on his face, holding his breath for a full minute.

"That's what we have come for," Jamie replied, crooking his lips into an awkward smile.

"Magnolia said that you were sent by an agency," Isabella said promptly. "There must be other workers coming too?" Her eyes curiously walked over them.

"No, ma'am! It's only us," Jamie murmured. Both brothers looked at each other for a moment and went on with Magnolia's lie.

"We don't need more people to do our job in the best possible way! Be sure of that!" Mike reassured them, a shade of malice in his tone.

Magnolia rolled her eyes in desperation. Her thoughts raced in her head, wondering if she had made a mistake by letting them start here. She gazed at Mike, wondering if his voice showed bitterness, or even hatred, or if it was her imagination. Jamie caught the rim of his hat and nodded, as Magnolia pointed the way to the stables. She quickly showed them around the mansion, asking Marcello to introduce them to the others.

For the first couple of days, they were doing some auxiliary work around the hacienda, and by the end of the week, they were diligently doing their jobs without having to be supervised. And during this short time, Mike and Jamie were the hottest topic of conversation and the center of attention to every servant girl.

Isabella was strolling down the long corridor, screaming in dire need of someone to attend to her needs. "Magnolia! Magnolia!" she screamed again until the woman appeared from one of the boys' rooms. "Where is everybody?" she roared. "I have been seeking someone to fetch me a jug of water, but the other maids are nowhere to be found, and neither are my grandsons."

Magnolia only shrugged. The other two servant girls were on the small wooden balcony, facing the west side of the hacienda. Positioned at the corner, it revealed a stunning vista towards the garden, bathed in all sorts of flowers and a small part of the stables. The two girls giggled audibly, ogling Jamie and Mike. "Careful, girl! You'll start drooling any minute," Dominga teased.

"I believe Grandma is looking for you," Diego snapped, disrupting their secret awe.

The girls gasped in surprise and hurried inside, trying to make their way through the brothers in embarrassment. Juan Pablo threw a quick, menacing look after them and rested his elbows on the railing. Diego quickly caught up with his staring and emitted a deep, irritated sigh. "Oh no! This again! If Martians landed in the front yard, they wouldn't have garnered such attention."

"Aren't they just gorgeous?" Juan Pablo missed his brother's bitter comment.

"Juan Pablo, stop! You're acting like a fool." He nudged him in the ribs.

"I can't even say who is the more handsome one..." His eyes jumped between Mike's broad shoulders and clipped, short raven-black hair, and Jamie, who had a slimmer, yet well-built body. His messy, wavy hair frivolously spilling a little above his penetrative gaze, maybe a shade lighter than his brother's.

Jamie lifted his gaze involuntarily. Juan Pablo's eyes momentarily dwelled on his cherry lips encircled by the well-trimmed beard. He smiled awkwardly at the two brothers as Diego pulled his brother away, ashamed of being caught observing the workers.

Once inside, Juan Pablo headed for his room, but Diego stopped him, giving him another lecture on proper manners in front of the servants.

"Don Diego…" Dominga's voice became hesitant after seeing their heated conversation.

"What is it, Dominga? Don't you see we are busy?"

"The taxi just pulled up. Your mother is home," the girl announced.

The two brothers looked at each other in bewilderment and hurried downstairs.

Chapter Eleven

Magnolia raced through the stables, her heart pounding in her chest. She frantically searched for Mike and Jamie, finally spotting them cleaning the stables and hurriedly informing them of Mrs Alvarez's arrival. They were finally going to meet her. Mike strode purposefully toward the house, nearly knocking Jamie down in his eagerness to get there.

"What are you thinking, Mike?" Jamie hissed, aware of the other grooms and servants staring at them. Mike glared at him; his temper flared up like wildfire. Now Mrs Alvarez was here, and he couldn't wait any longer. A sense of dread crawled over Magnolia's body as she trembling at the imminent threat. She had hoped Gabriella's absence would give him time to heal but, alas, this wasn't the case.

"Don't worry, Magnolia. We'll do our best to be discreet," Jamie assured her as she hurried off to the house. "Mike! Come to your senses!" Jamie snapped at him.

"Why? Have you forgotten why we're here?" Mike glared at Jamie.

"Of course not, but what do you plan to do? You're going to walk in there, and what? Kill her?"

Mike stood there for a moment, trying to regain his composure and let his anger subside. He inhaled from the wind that breezed across his face, trying to steady his nerves but every time he thought about what this woman had done to his sister, his vision blurred, and blood rushed to his head. He looked at Jamie. "Honestly, I could kill her, and I don't care if I end up in jail." His eyes narrowed.

"How nice!" Jamie emitted a sarcastic laugh. "Go inside and slaughter her like a Christmas turkey. Then I will let Chloe know the prison's visiting hours, as I don't have money for public transport to there," Jamie said and left his brother alone.

They had an opposing stance on how to get revenge on Gabriella Alvarez. They often argued about this at home, both carefully planning the moment they would meet her. And now, she was several yards away as Jamie's body stiffened at the realization it was going to be harder than he'd imagined.

A few workers carried all the luggage inside the house and up to the masters' rooms as Diego and Juan Pablo gave way to them on the staircase.

"Why do you look so serious?" Gabriella caught their attention.

"No reason, Mama!" Diego swallowed nervously before rushing down to give her a welcome kiss. "We weren't expecting you so soon."

"To be honest, I could have stayed a few more days in Atlanta." Lucia smiled.

"But then we wouldn't have been able to spend so many romantic nights in our bedroom," Antonio said, barely able to lay his lips on her cheek as Lucia moved her head to one side. He curled his lips into a small smile before caressing her cheek with the back of his finger. During their time in Atlanta, they had slept in separate rooms, and Antonio had missed her presence next to him in bed. Lucia bit her lower lip in mild horror but managed to keep her composure.

"Excuse me, but our flight had a huge delay, and I have a terrible migraine," Lucia said and rushed upstairs, leaving the rest to catch up with small talk in the salon before Gabriella and Antonio followed her.

It wasn't even a day before everyone fell into their routines in the mansion. Gabriella turned her attention to the tasks at hand in the mansion. Antonio went out with friends as soon as he caught up on everything that had been going on in the hacienda and Diego, Juan Pablo, and Lucia chatted about the vacation, and Isabella locked herself in her room.

"Magnolia! Magnolia!" Gabriella called from the salon. When the woman appeared from the kitchen, she stood next to Gabriella and hid her grumpy face behind a polite smile. "I saw a pickup parked outside. Does it belong to the new workers?"

"Yes, ma'am."

"Call them in! I want to meet them!"

Magnolia forced herself to remain composed. Her face paled. "Come on, move! Call them in!" Gabriella's voice startled her, and she only nodded.

"Remember what we talked about?" Jamie asked with a hint of concern on his face, but Mike didn't respond. He simply strode ahead through the grass, wearing clothes too dirty to match the grandeur of the mansion.

"Doña Gabriella?" Magnolia's voice broke the silence in the salon. "The boys are here."

She turned around to face them. A surge of unease immediately washed over her, and she swallowed nervously. Their appearance was imposing, even from the considerable distance between them, but she managed to greet them, nonetheless.

"Would you bother telling me your names?"

"I am Jamie Williams, and this is Mike Williams." Jamie took off his cowboy hat. "Ma'am!" He cleared his throat.

"Are you brothers?"

"Yes, we are!" Jamie smiled awkwardly.

Gabriella's knees trembled lightly as Mike took a small step towards her. His expression was unyielding, like a rock in a turbulent sea. Luckily, her trousers were loose-fitting, perfectly hiding the discomfort she found herself in. "I thought there would be more people. The work in the hacienda had doubled since I had to fire some of our ex-employees for causing the death of my husband," Gabriella said.

A vivid image of her husband made Mike's jaw clenched. He sank his nails into his palm, bringing himself back to reality. "Don't worry, ma'am! We are not afraid of work!" Mike said in a low, thick voice, sending further chills to the woman's back.

Gabriella stood there, gathering all the confidence and nobility she possessed. She lifted her head slightly, her blue eyes gazing at the two men in superiority. "Well, you look like responsible people!" She smiled thinly. "And that's exactly what we need! People who will conscientiously fulfil their duties," she added.

"Don't worry, ma'am! We always do our duty! That's why we came here, and we won't leave until we finish our job. Properly!"

Mike's categorical voice left a sense of threat in Gabriella. She gazed at him; his face was straight, and it was impossible to decipher his thoughts or emotions. When she had nothing more to add, she sent them back to work, leaving Mike even angrier and Jamie with more chaotic thoughts than before.

Dusk had fallen over the village when Mike and Jamie made their way home. Chloe was waiting for them at the window, as she usually did. Once in the living room, she quickly laid the table, calling them from their room. "Come on, boys!" she shouted, inviting them to the table, but neither of them sat down. "What's wrong?" Chloe asked, her eyes too big for her small face. "Did something happen at work?"

"Nothing! We finally met Doña Gabriella Alvarez." Jamie murmured.

Chloe's stare shifted. Memories of her bitter past flooded her mind momentarily. She gasped.

"This woman..." Mike paused. "She's exactly how you described her to us. A despotic monster who likes to control people and humiliates everyone who stands below her." The pure hatred was evident his voice.

"Boys! Don't you think that's enough?" Chloe said, worried their revenge was turning into obsession. "You already met her. You saw for yourselves what she's like. What else are you planning to do?"

Mike peered at his sister before his eyes dwelled on Jamie as he rubbed his chin.

"Judging by the way he spoke to her, I believe he'll accept my proposal," Jamie said, examining his brother's moves.

"What proposal?" Chloe asked as the uncertainty crept into her stomach.

"We'll act as I told you." Jamie ignored his sister's question and turned to his brother.

"I don't promise anything," Mike said in a dismissive voice.

Jamie turned to him, watching as he stood by the window. "Don't be so stubborn, Mike," Jamie hissed in exasperation. "Tell us, then, what are you planning to do?"

"If you don't want to get involved, then don't!" Mike shouted, making Chloe shiver.

Tears pricked her eyes. "Mike, please, let it go!" Her lower lip trembled.

"I'm sorry, Chloe, but I can't," he said. "My hand won't flinch when I smash her. I can kill her in cold blood," he mused, staring blankly into the room.

Chloe gasped in horror. Her brain struggled to decide if he meant it, or it was just the heat of the moment.

"Did you hear him?" Jamie jumped in. "I can just picture it – boom, boom, boom... blood everywhere... a raging man breaks into the house of a noblewoman and kills her and her whole family... heads everywhere..." Jamie snuffed out the candle. "Then, the scandal breaks and, in the end, we're rotting in jail. Well done, Mike, well done!" He clapped ironically at Mike's recklessness.

"Then do it your way!" Mike roared. "Seduce the daughter! I am not this kind of man!" Mike glared at his brother. "I am rude, brutal, and I will take full responsibility for my actions." His anger burned like a hot iron.

"You are monsters!" Chloe screamed, running to her room.

It was well past midnight. Chloe was turning from side to side in bed. It was unusually hot for a spring night. Sweat broke out on her forehead. Her bare feet barely touched the ground, trying to catch up with her brother who was heading steadfastly towards the giant mansion. Mike opened the door and turned right to the salon where Gabriella Alvarez and her children were calmly sipping tea. He glared at them, and the gun went off. The horrific sound echoed in her ears. The golden bullets fell one after another, as did the people standing in the marvelous salon. The red stains on their white ethereal gowns grew wider.

She jumped up to a sitting position in her bed. Her mouth wide open gulping the crispy air from the open window. She threw her blanket aside and rushed to her brothers' room. When she adjusted her eyes to the ambient light of the streetlights, she cast a glance at her brothers sleeping calmly in their beds.

Chapter Twelve

Mike and Jamie diligently combed the horses' manes. Jamie had an open admiration for thoroughbred horses. Each one of the horses in the hacienda cost a fortune and required special treatment and supervision, which even he had been deprived of. His face fell as the sad reality of how unfair life could be sank into his brain. Antonio approached them as Jamie whistled to his brother, signaling this must be the husband of Mrs Alvarez's daughter.

"Hey! You two!" Antonio shouted nearby, his face as gloomy as Jamie's. "Are you fully aware of your duties?" he asked in a stern, superior voice before stopping a few feet away from Jamie. His light brown eyes flickered wickedly, and the expensive suit he had chosen to wear made him look older than he was. Antonio, however, found it appropriate as it underlined his pomposity.

"We are professionals," Jamie said, glancing back at his brother. "We know our work well."

"I must warn you I am exacting and demanding," Antonio said with a note of disparagement. "The stables must be thoroughly cleaned, and the horses must be well taken care of, along with all other duties your job entails."

"We know what we're doing, Mr..." Mike paused, pondering how to address the gentleman.

"Call me Don Antonio or Mr Garcia," the man said firmly. "And if I have any doubts about your work, I will consult with the agency that sent you. I hope I have made myself clear!" he added.

Jamie lowered the front rim of his cowboy hat in response to the man's words. Mike stared at the man walking away, as if pulling a thorn out of his flesh.

Antonio went back into the house and climbed the stairs straight to his bedroom. He had to change his shirt for a new one, as he always did when he was in close contact with the grooms or near the stables. "Are you ready?" He turned to Lucia.

"Almost," she said, carefully applying the last stroke of mascara.

"I spoke to the new workers," he said, adjusting the collar of his shirt and gazing back in the mirror as he reached the upper buttons. "I don't like them. Especially that Mike Williams."

"Why? Did he insult you?" She paused for a moment as her eyes widened at his reflection in the mirror.

"No, he didn't," Antonio said tersely. "I don't like the tone they were holding. They seem quite cocky, and there is something in their attitude…" Antonio stared at his suit jacket as if trying to identify what was so utterly repulsive about them.

"Well, what matters is they do their job properly, don't you think?" Lucia said blithely, hurrying up to finish her preparation.

Once ready, Lucia got in the car, frantically trying to hide her wrath and boredom as they had to attend a high-profile engagement reception at the club. Frankly, she didn't like Patricia Gonzales, nor her fiancé, but she was one of Antonio's dear friends, and Lucia was rather compelled to attend.

The guests at the engagement party were scattered around the tall tables. The ballroom buzzed with voices, clinking glasses, and Lucia immediately regretted not insisting on staying home. The waiter kindly smiled at the newly arrived couple, offering them a glass of champagne from a tray too overloaded with glasses that he was barely keeping hold of in his left hand. Lucia forced herself to offer a kind smile back to him and an even more sincere one when the engaged couple approached them.

"Thank you very much for being here," Patricia said, giving a welcome kiss to Antonio and his wife. Lucia greeted the woman, who was dressed in a short, tight red dress with a V-neck too deep for the occasion.

This dress is suitable for a bachelor party, not an engagement one, Lucia mused silently and returned her attention to the hosts.

"It's a real pleasure to have you here, especially you, Lucia," Sebastian, said in a polite, amicable voice. "We rarely see you."

Antonio glanced at him. Jealousy pooled in his eyes, but he forced himself to smile. "Yes, of course! It's a momentous occasion, and we couldn't have missed it. Isn't that right, sweetheart?" Antonio smiled at his wife, as she forced herself to smile back. She took a small sip from her glass, hoping her feelings towards this small talk and utter tedium would not be noticed behind the rim of the flute.

"Excuse me, but I'm going to take Antonio away from you," Patricia said, grabbing his arm. "We have a lot to talk about."

Lucia watched them go with a semi-curious look as they joined a group of women dressed almost as scandalously as the hostess herself. "Your fiancé is very beautiful," she said, turning her attention back to Sebastian.

"I'm sure we'll be blissfully happy," he replied joyfully. "Like you and your husband are." His eyes lingering on the sparkly necklace she wore. "Is something bothering you?"

"Not at all." Lucia tried to smile but her lips only quivered. "I'm not accustomed to these types of parties and places, even less so after my father's death."

"I had the honor of knowing him," Sebastian murmured with a note of sadness in his voice, which lasted a moment. "He was a delightful, sophisticated man." He sipped from his glass and moved his eyes onto her lips. "I hope your mom and sister are doing, okay?"

"My sister?" Lucia fixed her perplexed gaze on his dark chestnut eyes.

"Don't you have a sister?" he asked reluctantly. "I've seen him in the company of another girl. They were coming to the club quite often."

"No, I don't have any idea who are you referring to," she said as her body stiffened.

"She looked like in her early 20s," Sebastian continued. "I saw them myself couple of times together and thought she was your sister."

Lucia managed a thin smile, utterly uncomfortable and, as if on cue, Antonio interrupted them. "Your fiancé is calling you," Antonio said. Sebastian quickly made an excuse and walked away. "What were you talking about?" Antonio turned to Lucia, with a trace of curiosity.

"He was telling me something about Dad," she said simply, gathering her thoughts.

"Don't lie! He was flirting with you, wasn't he?" Antonio leaned in, hissing in her face. Lucia frowned at him, trying to understand his abrupt change of attitude. "He's getting married soon, but I know him like the back of my hand. He doesn't miss a chance to lure any woman he meets. You won't be alone with him." He reached out to catch her, but she quickly slipped from his grip.

"You know what? If you're going behave jealously, I don't need to be at this notorious party," she said briskly and turned to leave.

"Where are you going?" he said through clenched teeth, throwing a quick glance around them.

"I'm going home! And if you don't want me to make a scene, you'd better leave me alone," she said and stormed out of the hall.

⁂

Gabriella Alvarez was on the verge of a nervous breakdown. Her mother had asked some of the workers to help her move pots of flowers and the entire house was now covered in mud tracks on the carpets from the living room all the way to her mother's bedroom. When they finished, Isabella caught Jamie's elbow and they made their way downstairs, leaving Gabriella to deal with the mess.

"What are you doing?" Gabriella yelled at the men, fixing her gaze on her mother and scolded her for treating the workers as if they were her best friends.

"We're helping your mother get downstairs," Jamie said.

95

"Who allowed you to enter the house?"

"I asked them to come," Isabella replied in a bored tone. "Can't I use the workers in the mansion?"

"They have other duties here! And look at the mess you made with your dirty boots. Next time, be good and clean your dirty feet!" The vein in her neck pulsated almost as fast as she was spilling her bile.

"Don't insult them!" Isabella jumped to their defense. "You need to learn to respect humble people." She turned to the workers, smiling amicably. "Don't pay much attention. I'm sincerely grateful for your help."

"This won't happen ever again!" Gabriella growled, ignoring Mike and Jamie's presence.

"They will help me anytime I need them, since you forbid the other workers." Isabella turned to her daughter. "You're trying to keep me upstairs in my room like a rubber plant, so I won't be a burden to you."

"Don't speak to me like that, especially in front of strangers!" Gabriella roared, tears welling up in her eyes from her frayed nerves.

"Don't scream at me! I'm your mother, and you need to respect me! You can't order me around!" Isabella lost her patience, and headed shakily toward the kitchen as Gabriella ran upstairs in frustration.

Mike tried to follow her, but Jamie managed to grab his hand before he could touch the second step. "Mike, don't! I beg you, for the sake of our parents," he said in a trembling voice, and they left.

Gabriella paced around her room, unable to quell her anger. She stepped outside and headed to the small terrace, hoping the fresh air would invigorate her. "Juan Pablo!" she exclaimed at her son leaning over the railing, observing the workers in the garden. "What are you doing here?" Her astounded look bobbed up and down the length of the satin robe he had put on.

"Uh... nothing!" he stuttered as his mother caught him off-guard. He hurried to cover his chest and tightened the sash of his robe. "I was making sure the new workers were doing their job properly." He cleared his throat.

"Who hired you as a supervisor? And you can't walk around in your bedtime robe," Gabriella hissed, pulling him inside. "Get dressed! Father Thomas wants to meet with you. Your brother is probably downstairs, waiting," she commanded, finding it hard to swallow the bitterness. "This is more than unacceptable," Gabriella told herself as she sped downstairs, flew past her son, and rushed to the stables. "You two, approach, hurry up!" she ordered. When the two men did, she found herself uncomfortable with their half-naked appearance. "First, none of you are permitted to enter the house without my consent, even if my mother tells you to. Secondly, could you be so kind as to put your clothes on? This is an honorable house, not a nudist beach. We do not want to watch your bodies. If you do not obey, I will ask the agency to send over other workers." She glared angrily at Mike, who was standing right before her. As Jamie was putting on his vest, Mike remained immobile. She threw one last menacing glare at him and turned to leave, utterly raging from his insubordination. His vision blackened with fury, he grabbed the leaf rake and lifted it effortlessly, ready to strike.

"Mama?" Lucia called from a distance. "Can we talk?" she tried to keep her balance on her high heels in the muddy garden.

"Inside! Not here!" Gabriella snapped.

Lucia's gaze dwelled on Mike for a moment, who stared back, losing his sense of gravity. His heartbeat accelerated to the maximum in no time. With each thud, it threatened to rip open his chest and he didn't even notice dropping the rake to the ground. The rage evaporated as quickly as her enchanting ocean-blue eyes sank into him. An overwhelming sense of connection made him furrow his brow. The urge to touch her rippled through his body. He swallowed, and his eyes fell on her lips before their eyes met, like two magnets drawn inexorably toward each other. A surge of warmth spread through his body, as fast as the jolt shot through hers. Her presence made him shiver to the core of his bones. Lucia bit her lower lip as the thought of touching his chest crossed her mind.

"Come on, girl. What are you waiting for?" Gabriella's voice distracted her for a moment. Her brain was in tumult; her legs walked ahead, but her eyes stared back at Mike.

The whole moment passed much faster than Mike wanted it to, but its liveliness haunted him even now as they were driving home. "I can't drive!" Mike slammed on the brakes under Jamie's frightened gaze, and exhaled the air he had held in for too long. The impression Lucia had left on him had paralyzed his whole being. The image of her was still vivid in his mind, and it took him about a second to find out it would haunt him forever.

Chapter Thirteen

Over the next week, Mike was not himself. He was unusually quiet, avoiding being around others at home for no apparent reason. The restless nights kept him awake and he often wandered through the dead streets of the neighborhood in the middle of the night. Chloe had tried to speak to Jamie about him without any results.

"Jamie?" Mike said in a quiet voice, drying his face with a towel over the sink in the kitchen. "Let's go out and have a drink or something." He kept staring at himself in the square mirror hung on the tiles.

"Ask him what's happening with him," Chloe whispered in Jamie's ear while Mike was putting on his denim jacket and cowboy hat, waiting for his brother outside.

Mike headed for the pub few blocks away as Jamie meekly followed him in silence. Once there, they sat in the back garden of the pub, choosing a table at the far end away from the loud voices and crowd. "Well, will you tell me why we're here?" Jamie asked impatiently, looking at Mike.

"Can't I ask my brother for a little time together?" Mike retorted, arching a brow at Jamie. But they both knew each other well; they almost never went out for a drink together unless they had a special occasion to celebrate or needed to discuss something Chloe shouldn't know about. "I agree with your plan," Mike blurted out.

Jamie's eyes shone with pleasure and surprise and he couldn't hide his contented grin. "I don't want to hurt or kill these people anymore," he added in a low voice.

"Very well." Jamie smiled as the waiter came to serve their table. Once he retired among the crowd, Mike turned to his brother.

"What is the plan?" he asked, taking a long sip and sighing as the tequila immediately stung his tongue.

"I'd say you can focus on Lucia," Jamie started. "I noticed how she looks at you, and she seems more interested in you than in me." Jamie threw a quick glance at Mike, whose stare changed at the mention of her name. "Once she falls in love with you, we're going to expose her to the world as they did to Chloe." He shifted to make himself more comfortable in his chair. "But we need to be careful. She's married, and if her husband finds out, we're done," Jamie said. There was a long pause and quick exchanging of glances before the brothers could speak again, each drinking from his glass.

"What about you?" Mike finally asked, half-curious to find out the rest of the plan.

"I'll see what I can do," Jamie replied, leaving his glass on the wooden table. "I have something in mind, and if it turns out the way I think it will, we'll gain more than just revenge," he added with a wicked smirk.

Mike looked at him intently and warned him to be careful about his actions, or else he'd break every bone in his body. Jamie stood still, a couple of chills running down his spine at the thought that his brother might carry out his threat. Mike stared at him for a moment, trying to discern his brother's intentions through his penetrating eyes. It was about money, Mike thought.

Jamie Williams would do anything as long as he could benefit.

It was well past midnight when the two brothers returned home. Mike went to Chloe's room and stood at the door. She was peacefully sleeping in her bed and his lips curled into a small smile. It was nice to have her home and know he could protect her. He changed into his pajama pants and as soon as he laid his head on the soft pillow, his eyes closed in a deep sleep.

The next morning, they left the house later than usual, hoping to avoid any trouble with their masters. Jamie's tension grew higher when they arrived. His eyes moved in all directions around the hacienda, as if seeking someone.

"Boys, I've brought several sacks of fertilizer. Can you help me unload the car?" One of the workers shouted as Mike and Jamie volunteered to give him a hand. As they lifted the sacks, Jamie caught a glimpse of Juan Pablo making his way out from the house.

"That's it!" Jamie murmured to himself, summoning all his strength to lift the sack onto his shoulder. But as he tried to hoist it up, the sack slipped from his fingers, and fell to the ground with an inaudible thud. Jamie quickly bent over, clutching his waist, and groaning in pain.

"Dios! Are you okay?" Juan Pablo rushed to Jamie's aid. "Shall I call your brother or Magnolia?"

"No, no! I'll be fine," Jamie murmured through his pain. "Can you help me reach the servant's changing room?"

Juan Pablo wrapped Jamie's arm around his neck, and they slowly made their way to the room. "Thank you very much, Don Alvarez," Jamie murmured in pain, curling his lips into a half-smile and hissing once again in pain in front of the door.

"Call me Juan Pablo," he said politely. "I'll come with you."

Jamie nodded in agreement, and Juan Pablo took a quick look around before joining him inside, barely suppressing his joy amidst Jamie's ordeal. The thought of spending some alone time with the him made his blood boil for less than a second. His eyes shone, his beaming smile glorious on his lips. Jamie thanked him once again, nervously swallowing under the piercing gaze of Juan Pablo's grey-blue eyes.

"You don't look quite well. Shall I call a doctor?" Juan Pablo regained his composure, his eyes fixed on Jamie's dark, pained gaze with concern.

"No, it won't be necessary," Jamie replied, slightly shivering from the proximity of the man. "A light massage with sanitizer and ointment should alleviate the pain," he said, pointing toward the bathroom. As soon as Juan Pablo disappeared from his sight, Jamie quickly took off his vest and waited near the table.

"Is it necessary to take off your vest?" Juan Pablo stood at the bathroom door. His thoughts baffled, he managed to swallow in intervals.

"I thought it might be more comfortable for you to apply the ointment, Mr Alva— Juan Pablo," Jamie said as he put his hand on his waist again. "Now, shall I turn around?"

Jamie stared down at his boots, his breathing labored as Juan Pablo approached. His mind was in tumult. *What am I doing?* He cursed himself inwardly as two cool fingers touched his scorching waist. This whole scene looked a lot better when he rehearsed it in his head. Now, he found it simply ridiculous, but it was late to go back.

Juan Pablo carefully applied a second layer of the ointment and started moving his fingers in circles on the injured area. The contact with the cold substance made Jamie shiver violently.

"Does it hurt?" Juan Pablo asked, sounding worried from behind.

"No, just a bit ticklish," Jamie replied with an awkward smile, trying to ease Juan Pablo's concern.

As Juan Pablo leaned in closer, his hot breath brushed against Jamie's lower back. His muscles clenched, and he swallowed convulsively, a sense of guilt and awkwardness rising in his throat.

"Does it still hurt?" Juan Pablo asked, and Jamie shook his head. His brain numbed, he couldn't feel any pain, just the man's gentle finger running in circles. The proximity paralyzed him, giving Juan Pablo a chance to examine him much better. His back and shoulders were definitely not as broad as his brother's, but he found him perfectly to his liking. His skin was perfectly toned, soft and smooth under his fingers. He slowly started moving his hands in a wider circle. He wanted to get to know every inch of Jamie's body, and he finally had the chance after weeks of watching him from afar. Jamie swallowed, turning his head to one side. His eyes trailing Juan Pablo's hand sliding from his shoulders down his arms.

"You are probably training in a gym. You have quite sturdy biceps." Juan Pablo threw a quick, lusty look at them and closed the tube as Jamie instinctively turned to face him. "Your girlfriend is a lucky girl," he said casually, breaking the awkward stare they gave each other.

"I don't have a girlfriend," Jamie said a little above a whisper. His eyes hidden behind mysterious curls of his hair, a trace of tension was coming and going in waves, making his muscle clenched harder. He was standing there, half-naked allowing another man to gaze at his chest and his eyes. He had to run as fast as he could and as far as possible, but his feet were nailed. He gazed down nervously, and when he gathered his strength to lift his eyes up, he sank into Juan Pablo's fathomless eyes. "You have beautiful eyes," he murmured under his breath, trying to remember why he had staged all this insanity as Juan Pablo broke a light unengaged grin. Jamie parted his lips. He was gripping the vest in his hands too tight, rubbing his palms in it, trying to wipe off the cold sweat. Juan Pablo was dangerously close to him. He wanted to take a step back but the table behind him blocked his move. "I think—" Jamie said, but Juan Pablo placed his finger on Jamie's lips.

The lust threatened to explode in every possible way. He could no longer bear the flames inside him. He closed his eyes for a second and let the urge of passion prevail as he sucked on Jamie's lower lip. The sweet taste of his mouth spread through his veins like a shockwave, leaving his body in a state of weightlessness, as if Jamie was the first man he had ever kissed.

"Pablo!" Diego swung the door open, mouth gaping in disbelief at the humiliation. Juan Pablo looked in his direction. His brain went numb. The room became a theater of mirrors, reflecting his embarrassment in a thousand angles. Jamie feverishly put on his vest, praying the earth would open and engulf him.

"Diego! Wait!" Juan Pablo rushed after his brother, leaving Jamie to regret what he had started. "Let me explain!" Juan Pablo said as Diego waited outside, desperately trying to erase the image from his mind.

"Not here! In my room! Immediately!" he said, and marched back to the mansion.

"Please don't tell anyone what you saw!" Juan Pablo begged him once they reached his room, leaving the door open, vigorously trying to find his words. Diego slammed it shut, and before his brother could say another word, Diego punched him in the face. Juan Pablo staggered several steps back but managed to remain on his feet. Once facing his brother again, he gazed at him with a mixture of anger and sorrow. "So, is this your way of supporting me?"

"This is not a game, Juan Pablo! This is something of great concern!" Diego said angrily.

"Don't turn it into a drama. It was just a kiss. What's so serious about a kiss?"

Diego arched an eyebrow at him. "It's not about the damn kiss," he growled. "It's about who you're kissing."

"You sound like Mother again," Juan Pablo blurted out wearily.

"I sound like a brother who is worried about you," Diego snapped at his brother recklessness. "You are an honorable man, Juan Pablo. You come from a prominent, respected family. You cannot just kiss the first worker who crosses your path, let alone under everyone's nose," Diego paced around the room, trying to collect his thoughts. When he finally softened, he gave his brother an apologetic gaze for punching him. "And the kiss?" he returned to the matter. "Was it consensual?" Juan Pablo stood there silently, staring at his feet. "I can't believe it! How can you be so irresponsible?" Diego continued. His blood rushed back into his head, and he had to try hard to restrain himself from hitting him again.

"Will you tell Mother what you saw?" Juan Pablo dared to ask.

"No! I won't tell her anything!" Diego swung the door open and stepped out, his mind racing with thoughts of the potential scandal, which could rock the reputation of their prominent, respected family. "Not because you deserve it, but because I want to spare the family the scandal that would follow." He shot Juan Pablo a fiery glance and slammed the door shut. He rushed down the stairs, straight to the garden, where Jamie was watering the newly planted flowerbed, berating himself for being this foolish. Though, if Jamie was honest with himself, everything had gone as planned – he had kissed Juan Pablo and now had a witness to the scene. He instinctively smiled at the blend of flowering perennials. "You! Mr Williams!" Diego called out in a firm, demanding voice. "Can you come here for a moment?" Jamie followed him to the side of the main entrance, out of earshot of the other servants.

"Shall we not go to the servants' room?" Jamie suggested.

"I can't set foot in that room now, thanks to you and my brother," Diego snapped, looking him straight in the eye. Jamie didn't know if he should speak or not. "What my brother did is unforgivable, but your behavior is worse," Diego said bitingly.

"I must assure you…" Jamie tried to explain himself.

"He is irresponsible and doesn't realize what he's doing. You shouldn't take advantage of him, and I will make sure you won't!"

"I assume you'll be speaking to your mother about this?" Jamie asked.

"No, I will not!" Diego said firmly. "I don't want to create any trouble or cause any scandal for our family, and I know you need this job."

"Thank you very much, Mr Alvarez!" Jamie smiled simply. The unexpected nobility eased his troubled mind. "And just so you know, I may be a worker and poor, but I am not an unscrupulous person."

"Diego!" Gabriella interrupted, walking towards them, watching them move apart. "What were you discussing with Mr Williams?"

"Nothing, Mama! I informed him to be careful with the newly planted bushes at the further end of the garden," Diego blurted out, disgusted with himself for lying to his mother. He emitted a long, deep sigh and followed her inside, hoping the situation wouldn't spiral out of control.

Chapter Fourteen

Jamie and Mike were arguing about something that had made Mike's blood boil fast. He noticed Lucia, or Mrs Garcia as she had formerly introduced herself to Mike, approaching them. "Isn't she the most beautiful woman in the world?" Jamie murmured admiringly, as his brother looked at him out of the corner of his eye.

"Jamie? My mother wishes to talk to you," Lucia said with a melodious voice, accelerating Mike's heartbeat in no time.

"What for?" Mike said abruptly, causing Lucia to turn her attention to him. Her face was serious as she carefully hid her admiration towards Mike behind an iron mask.

"I have no idea. She'll tell him. Could you follow me, please?" she replied, turning her attention back to Jamie, feverishly fighting her instinct to gaze at Mike. Jamie put his hat on and followed.

"I am coming too." Mike took a couple of steps forward and stopped when she turned to him.

"No! Not you!" Lucia rebuffed him.

"Why not?"

"She wishes to talk to Jamie." Lucia gazed at him as the violet shades in his eyes made her shudder.

"What's wrong with you?" Jamie hissed through clenched teeth. "Doña Gabriella is calling for me and we don't need to annoy her! We are obedient servants who can obey orders, are we not?" Jamie winked at him, and they walked away.

Lucia led Jamie to the small study room and announced him before going about her business, leaving him in the company of Gabriella and her mother, who was meekly sitting in her chair and sipping her tea from an exquisite china cup. He took off his hat and greeted them with a broad, heartfelt smile.

"You were calling for me, ma'am," he said timidly, slowly taking a few more steps with hesitation. The unwelcome thought of Diego Alvarez having confessed the awkward scene in the servants' room troubled his mind. This inevitably meant it was the end of his undercover story, and the entire plan for revenge would go down the drain. And if that happened, he did not want to be anywhere near Mike. *No need to panic, Jamie, Diego Alvarez said he wouldn't tell.* He tried to calm himself inwardly and gazed at the elegant woman behind the wooden desk.

"Yes, Jamie! I wanted to notify you we are ceasing your work in the hacienda," Gabriella announced.

Jamie's face went pale, and he thought to himself, as his blood froze in his veins, *shit!*

"Only until the end of the week!" she added after a pause, nearly giving him a heart attack. "There will be an important event this Saturday, and it's best if there aren't too many people around," Gabriella added with a thin smile, casually throwing glances at her mother from time to time.

"Oh!" Jamie exclaimed with great relief. "I thought we were getting fired."

"Now, why would you say something like that?" Isabella arched a brow.

"Mother, would you let me talk to him?" Gabriella cut in. "He's my employee, not yours!"

Isabella said nothing, nor did she protest. She leaned back in her chair, lazily sipping her tea, so Jamie found it best not to dwell on the question.

"May I ask what this event is?" Jamie's voice seeped with hesitation, yet his curiosity prevailed.

"It's a charity event, a rodeo I believe, organized by Father Thomas and my sons," Gabriella explained. "You won't mind, I hope?"

"Of course not! A little break never hurts," Jamie mumbled. "I haven't asked my brother, but I would be delighted to attend this feast. It will probably be fun and interesting.

"The invitations are sent to people who can make donations," Gabriella reprimanded, crushing Jamie's high hopes.

"Of course! What was I thinking?" The utterly foolish thought made his face grim, but he managed to nod his understanding.

"Of course you may come!" Isabella said.

Gabriella turned to her mother, offended by her insubordination, and for contradicting her decisions in front of the workers.

"Oh, Gabriella, don't give me that look!" she remarked. "The rest of the servants will be extremely busy, and additional help will not be superfluous."

Gabriella pondered her mother's suggestion and had to admit she had a point. "Very well, Jamie! You and your brother may come!" she said, smiling slightly. "You know,

I find you exceedingly kind and amicable. You have good manners, but your brother…" She paused for a moment. "He's quite rude and arrogant, even aggressive."

"No, Doña Gabriella, I assure you! He's impetuous, yes, but he has a good heart!"

Gabriella gazed at him with a shade of distrust but didn't argue further. She sent him back to his work, and Jamie excused himself, put back on his cowboy hat, and left the room, grinning from ear to ear.

Back home, Jamie and Mike were arguing again. The damn mansion was tearing the family apart. Chloe tried to stop them, but they weren't listening. She didn't know how much longer she could endure these tense quarrels.

"That's ultimate stupidity. Why did you demean yourself and beg her?" Mike said angrily.

"Come on, it will be fun!" Jamie said. "Beautiful ladies, music, and horses," he added, smiling.

It sounded like a real feast, and Chloe wished she could be there too. Of course, this was out of the question, and she remained silent as her brothers kept on arguing.

"Yes, it will be fun – for all those wealthy brats, who will come with their families and show off their great generosity," Mike said as he sat on the bed. "What's more, it's for charity! We have no place there at all."

"That's a great opportunity to keep an eye on—" Jamie stopped and peered at Chloe. "To follow our plan." He cleared his throat.

"What's with these secrets?" Chloe whined, returning her attention to them.

"Jamie's plan of revenge is for me to seduce Lucia Alvarez, break her marriage and make her fall in love with me, so we can humiliate her in public," Mike blurted out.

Chloe stood up from where she was lying with a cushion in her embrace and went to Mike. She sat beside him and begged him to cease their retaliation immediately.

"Why did you tell her?" Jamie snorted. He wasn't in the mood to listen to his sister's moralistic prejudice.

"She's our sister, and she deserves to know our intentions," Mike said.

"Boys, please, you're playing with fire."

"It's too late to stop now!" Mike said firmly. "We'll go to the notorious rodeo. Let's see what good that will bring." He gazed at them and went to his room.

Mike Williams didn't care much about the party or the money. If it were up to him, he'd rather stay home. He agreed because Lucia would be there. This woman – she had lit up his interest from the second he had laid his eyes on her. The most beautiful woman in the world; her eyes, her face, her everything. Mike undressed himself and put on his pajama pants. He laid down and stared up at the ceiling as the pictures of her resurfaced before his eyes. She stood on the balcony, gazing at him, and again while talking. Her sweet voice chiming in his ears, her eyes made him yearn for her like no other woman before. At times, he found her to be a bit snobbish, which he couldn't tolerate. Yet something in her had rocked his world and he hated himself for that.

Hours slipped through his grasp like fine grains of sand as he found himself ensnared in a silent rapture, a prisoner in her crystal image. A minute later, in the quiet turmoil of his mind, he grappled with the idea of seducing her. Their worlds akin to distant galaxies and yet, this wasn't his main concern. She was married and didn't appear unhappy in her marriage. With a heavy sigh that felt like the weight of a thousand collapsing stars, he turned his gaze to one side, feeling the weight of the moment pressing against his closed eyelids, a universe of longing and restraint warring within him.

The week sprinted along before Saturday arrived imperceptibly. The mansion bustled with guests and musicians who played their guitars at the hacienda's entrance, further lifting everyone's spirits.

"What? You're going to keep me in my room while there's a party in the mansion?" Isabella whined at her daughter, peering through the window at the arriving cars.

"What will you do at this gathering, Mother? All the guests are young and... You'll feel out of place!" Gabriella huffed with displeasure.

"Young? I saw the Mendoza family is on the guest list, and they're practically mummies. I wonder how they're still alive, reeking of a cemetery," Isabella snorted.

"This is precisely why I don't want you there! You'll start arguing with them and ruin everything."

"If you don't allow me to get out of here, I will start right now." Isabella reached to open the window before Gabriella rolled her eyes in exasperation and found herself forced to agree.

In the next room, Lucia was putting her earrings on, as Antonio was uncomfortably standing behind her, staring at her reflection. He put his hands on her shoulders, admiring her beauty. "There may be many beautiful women in the world, but you are incomparable to them." His fondness was evident in his voice and it made her smile. For a moment, a strong urge of passion set him on fire, and he reached to kiss her cheek. Lucia instinctively turned her head to the other side, as his glare sank into her reflection in the mirror. "At least I will have the pleasure of pretending to be happily married in front of others," Antonio said in bitter disappointment. He squeezed her shoulders hard at her rebuff. "Be careful and act like a kind, loving wife," he snapped at her before leaving the room.

He quickly joined Gabriella in the salon as the Alvarez brothers appeared from upstairs, dressed in black suits for the occasion, which immediately met their mother's disapproval. "Today, we have special guests. I want you to be nothing less than glamorous. Get changed! It's not a funeral. And be punctual," Gabriella reprimanded them. Juan Pablo and Diego only looked at each other for a moment and returned to their rooms.

Antonio stood up from the leather sofa and went to Gabriella's side. "What's on your mind, Gabriella? What's all this fussiness about?" He had nosed out her hidden agenda and the curiosity got the best of him.

"The niece of Rafaela Mendoza will come too. And, between us, she might be a good party for one of the boy." She smiled.

"Are you looking for wives for your sons?" Antonio arched a quizzical brow.

"No," she said rather blithely. "I am considering my options. I don't want them to end up with some peasant women," she added and walked to the formal dining room, where the girls had almost finished laying the table for lunch.

Chapter Fifteen

The last time Gabriella had organized such party was at her 30th wedding anniversary with her late husband. Although the party had been exquisite, the memory of it was grim. She pushed the unwelcome thought to the back of her mind and made her way through the gaps between the parked cars towards her mother, who was in the company of Mike and Jamie, screaming joyfully at the musicians and expressing her love for parties.

"Jamie!" Gabriella pulled him to the side. "Since you're here, please take care of my mother. She becomes quite frivolous at such gatherings." She glanced at her mother, who was trying to dance with one of the musicians.

"Of course, ma'am! We'll look after her!" Jamie nodded. Gabriella thanked him with a smile, and he returned to his brother and the amicable lady.

"What did she tell you?" Isabella asked. "Not to take your eyes off me because I'm mad and crazy, am I right?"

"You know your daughter quite well." Jamie smiled, relieved for not having to tattle on Gabriella.

"Well, she is my daughter, for better or for worse!" Isabella said, gazing at the green vintage car slowly coming to a stop in one of the empty parking slots.

The elderly lady struggled to climb from the back seat, helping herself with a cane. She was taking small, careful steps on the gravel path and gave Gabriella a heartfelt hug once she managed to reach her. A young lady appeared from the back seat and went to the other side to help the man, too thin and fragile to raise from his seat.

"Who are those people, Doña Isabella?" Jamie asked.

"Two mummies who have gotten out of their sarcophagus. Rafaela Mendoza and her husband, Adolfo Mendoza," she said, quickly introducing them. "And the scarecrow with them is their niece, Penelope."

Mike and Jamie giggled, but they had to agree. The couple looked quite old, maybe in their late 70s at first glance, and their niece seemed rather odd. "Your daughter has many friends," Mike said.

"I doubt she invited them without any reason," Isabella said, scrutinizing them from afar. "My daughter doesn't do anything without a hidden agenda. She must be looking for a fiancé for my grandsons," she said.

"Is that how your granddaughter got married?" Mike asked hesitantly, earning an inquisitive look from Jamie.

"Of course!" Isabella snorted. "How else would Lucia ever marry a rascal like Antonio Garcia?" the woman said and headed for the arena where the rodeo would take place as Jamie and Mike followed.

Gabriella Alvarez and Rafaela Mendoza were dear friends for many years. They shared similar views on customs, values, reputation, and traditions.

"Your home is delightful, Gabriella," Penelope exclaimed at the entrance. "I hope I can have one like yours someday." She glanced towards the stairs where Lucia and her husband were coming down, accompanied by Diego and Juan Pablo. The whole family had gathered, and they headed to the dining room.

Gabriella and her family took their usual seats and let the guests choose theirs. Soon, Magnolia and Dominga started bringing out all sorts of food and drinks until the table's surface was almost obscured.

"You look radiantly happy with your wife, Antonio," Rafaela said. Her eyes were almost invisible behind the sharp features of her face. Her hair was gray, tied up in a low roll updo.

"Yes, I am, Doña Rafaela. Lucia and I are thrilled to be together." He tried to sound sincere. "Every day is like an everlasting honeymoon," he added and peeked at her, and Lucia forced herself to return a sincere smile.

"That's sweet of you to say! And so it should be!" Rafaela placed her salad in front of her husband, whose head had bent down for a short nap at the table. She pushed him a bit to resume his posture, tucking his napkin in the slightly unbuttoned suit, and returned her attention to Antonio. "You're quite lucky, Antonio. A beautiful and prominent woman like Lucia is rare to find."

Gabriella smiled fondly at the compliments addressed to her daughter. "Those who marry my sons will also be blessed with luck." She turned to Diego and Juan Pablo, who adjusted in their seats, uncomfortable and surprised at the sudden point. "I know I am their mother, but they are also remarkably handsome." Gabriella put her hand on Diego's, who rolled his eyes at her for putting him in the spotlight. His skin burned, and he forced himself to take a sip of his wine.

"You must be around a lot of women who intend to marry you," Penelope said, smiling at them and revealing her slightly crooked front tooth. Diego pierced her with his icy blue eyes and she found it hard to maintain long eye contact.

"No, not yet! We are most certainly not in a hurry to marry!" Juan Pablo gave his brother a little nudge, and Penelope returned her gaze to her rocket salad.

"Don't linger for too long, boys!" Rafaela threw a quick glance at them. "Youth is short, and time flies. Before you realize it, you'll remain bachelors. It's not good to remain alone,"

"It's never too late for a man to marry, Doña Rafaela. You married at 51, did you not?" Diego threw a sarcastic yet polite stare at the woman, who adjusted in her seat uncomfortably.

"What about you?" Antonio turned to Penelope, attempting to break the uncomfortable silence.

"I am definitely ready to take this step!" Penelope exclaimed, using her hand to remove a bit of green salad lodged between her teeth. "I have always wanted to see myself in a white dress," she continued, her face taking on a dreamy expression as if she was imagining the ceremony. She stared at the two Alvarez brothers, as if assessing who'd be the better husband, with Juan Pablo currently in the lead.

"You might want to hold off on that for now," Juan Pablo blurted, a little too loudly, drawing everyone's attention to him. "I mean, it's hard to find the right person." He leaned forward as his eyes caught Penelope's, who stared back at him with her large, wet, brown eyes, and giggled in response.

"That's true," she agreed before returning to her meal.

After the sumptuous lunch, everyone moved to the backyard where the audience had already started choosing their spots to watch the brave men take on the wild stallions. Rafaela opted to stay indoors, due to the fact she was too old for such a show and wanted to take care of her snoring husband. Gabriella and her family took their assigned seats, while Jamie and Mike followed Isabella as she made her way to the second floor of the hayloft, where they could get an excellent view of the wooden-walled arena, reminiscent of a Roman theater.

"Isn't this view amazing, Mike?" Jamie beamed with excitement.

"Yes! Yes, it is!" he muttered under his breath as if he couldn't be bothered. This place was filled with people entirely unfamiliar to his world, but the notion of watching wild horses, he found rather enjoyable.

Excitement filled the air as everyone gathered. Antonio was seated with Gabriella and Lucia on either side of him, while her brothers stood behind them, with Penelope joining them. The musicians were positioned in a line on the ground floor, entertaining the guests. Father Thomas welcomed everyone who had joined them today and announced the start of the rodeo. The first cowboy appeared, standing on the back of a horse, waving a lasso in his hand. Then, the second rider skillfully swung from side to side on the back of the maddened animal, giving the spectators an excellent show.

"This rider is awesome, isn't he?" Juan Pablo exclaimed, gaping at the rider who was holding onto the horse's side while the stallion galloped in circles.

"More or less," Penelope replied, standing next to him. "I prefer other types of shows, like ballet, for example." He turned to her and arched an eyebrow with boredom and returned his attention to the next cowboy in the arena.

Lucia lifted her head, surprised to see the brothers and her grandma directly opposite to where she was standing. Her eyes dwelled on Mike as his penetrating gaze engulfed her, and she found it difficult to endure the fire in his eyes. She refocused her attention on the arena, stealing occasional glances at Mike, her lips twitching into ghostly smiles each time she encountered his enigmatic gaze.

"Stop staring!" Jamie hissed, catching his brother's stare. "Her husband is right next to her."

"I can't help it," he said dryly, briefly looking down at the horses. The gate opened, and the next rider flew into the arena, falling three seconds later.

"What a jerk!" Isabella muttered, holding a drink in her hand. Jamie and Mike were having a lot of fun with Isabella at the party. She wasn't quite the 'royal' her daughter tried to portray herself and her family to be, and they clicked quickly. Isabella danced with the musicians, drank whisky from a hip flask with the workers, and did many other things she tried to hide from her daughter.

"Ladies and gentlemen!" Father Thomas said into the microphone. "Don Gabriel Garrido is offering $5000 to the rider who manages to stay on the back of a stallion for 15 seconds."

"$5000?" Jamie's eyes lit up. "I would have tried without even thinking."

"No point! The money is for the orphanage," Mike said.

"No, dear! The rider also gets something! That's the arrangement," Isabella pointed out.

The next cowboy quickly jumped on the stallion's back. He skillfully gripped the bridle of the stallion, trying to balance on the horse's back, but ended up sprawled face down on the earth just as fast. Gabriella put her hand on her chest in horror as her heart threatened to jump out. She instinctively averted her eyes to Antonio, who was quite disappointed at the sight, as if he had bet on it.

"I am too nervous. I think I will go back in," Gabriella said in a mildly horrified tone.

"There are too many people. It will be difficult to pass unnoticed. Wait a little longer!" Antonio leaned closer to her.

"I am used to horses but not to this type of spectacle. I am horrified. What if something bad happens? I can't stop thinking about what happened to my husband."

Antonio caught her hand, and she smiled, trying to pull herself together and not allow her imagination to run any wilder than it already did. Lucia took another surreptitious peek at Mike. He leaned on the wooden railing in his full power and masculinity, and Lucia found it hundreds of times harder to ignore him.

"Attention, ladies and gentlemen," Father Thomas distracted her, "Don Gabriel increases his reward to $20000 for the person who manages to stay on the stallion's back for 15 seconds!" The crowd gasped and cheered, but no one seemed to dare to ride the wildest of the stallions on the ranch.

"What happens now? Where are the real men?" Isabella screamed at the crowd in the arena. "Will anyone take the bet?"

"$20000?" Jamie's ears perked up. "This is a whole fortune! If only I could ride the stallion…"

"You, maybe not, but I can." Mike's determination was evident in his voice.

"What? You're going to put on a little show, eh?"

"You might have forgotten that we grew up on a ranch, but I haven't. Here, let me refresh your memory," Mike added and disappeared into the crowd.

With the sum offered and what Juan Pablo and Diego had collected so far, they could already start the project. Juan Pablo furrowed his brows with anticipation before his brother brought him down to earth. "Stop dreaming, Juan Pablo!" Diego murmured. "Apparently, nobody wants to do it!"

"That's why Don Gabriel is offering this kind of money. He knows well nobody would dare to take the risk." Gabriella turned to her sons.

Lucia gazed down at the next cowboy, who was getting ready to fly into the arena, and this time she wasn't timidly grinning; she was glowing. Mike straightened his cowboy hat, made sure he had positioned his body well on the horse's back, and gripped the short mane as tightly as he could. His eyes pointed at Lucia as if dedicating this last round of rodeo to her before the door opened and the wild horse flew into the arena. Lucia gasped. Her breathing quickened, matching the speed of her heartbeat. The crowd broke into cheers and whistles as the horse galloped madly in circles. Mike had to adjust himself several times on the stallion's back as it made abrupt halts at the wooden fence.

Juan Pablo nervously stared back and forth at him and his watch, counting the seconds. But for Jamie, time had stopped. "He'll hurt himself," he said to Isabella, fear resurfacing on his face, his eyes locked on his brother.

"He won't! Look how firmly he's gripping the horse's hair!" Isabella cheered, patting vigorously on the wooden rail. "How many seconds have passed?"

"I don't know! I didn't watch!" Jamie replied and grabbed the hip flask from her hands, throwing his head back.

The horse made another brusque stop at the wooden fence, making Lucia hold her breath. She stared at him, nervously swallowing in intervals, her gaze exuding panic and admiration. She blushed at her baffled thoughts and looked again at Mike, who finally landed on his feet.

"He made it! More than 20 seconds!" Juan Pablo cheered as the crowd's applause deafened.

"This is what I call a man. A man and a half!" Isabella broke into loud cheering, and Jamie hugged her in his moment of rejoice.

Mike went to the middle of the arena, fell to one knee, and took his hat off in a gesture of a small bow. His heart bounced and danced at Lucia's glorious smile. Father Thomas went to the arena, shook the man's hand, and gave him the cheque with the amount written on it, but Mike could only carelessly gaze at Lucia and hardly paid any attention to what the man was saying. He raised the cheque above his head and ran off to where the Alvarez family was gathered.

"Mr Alvarez!" Mike spoke, trying to adjust his breathing. Lucia instinctively turned to see him, smiling at his nobility. "Here!" He handed him the cheque.

"The money is yours!" Gabriella jumped from her seat to return the cheque.

"I insist on it myself, ma'am." His voice was firm. "Everything is for the orphanage. I don't want anything for myself." He swallowed, and his gaze went back to Lucia, losing himself in the depths of her eyes.

"What a jerk!" Antonio mused quietly. He furrowed his brows at the man in a mixture of puzzlement and envy. Juan Pablo hugged him and patted him on the back for too long, and Diego pulled him back. Mike threw a last short peek at Lucia, then turned and disappeared into the back without saying another word.

"What are you talking about?" Jamie walked fast behind him, trying to catch up with him. "And why are we going home? The show isn't over yet."

"Mine is. We have nothing more to do here!" Mike said firmly and put the key in the starter. The car roared, and they drove home after the glorious afternoon they had spent.

"I was scared to death," Jamie said. "But I am so proud of you." He nudged Mike joyfully. "And what if you had injured yourself?"

"I knew what I was doing!" Mike replied blithely and stared at the road ahead.

Chapter Sixteen

Lucia saddled her mare for a short ride around the hacienda. The fresh air brushed against her face, her golden curls bouncing as the horse trotted. Her mind was filled with Mike and her smile evaporated at the intrusive thought of her husband. She sighed in a desperate attempt to shut the door to the hell she'd been living for far too long.

She reached the mansion's parking area. The horse steered to the left, and her shoe caught the end of a man's denim jacket, causing him to crumple violently to the ground. Magnolia gasped in the distance as Mike sprawled on the ground. Lucia quickly dismounted her horse, threw her hat to the side, and kneeled next to him as he was trying to come to his senses.

"Dios mio!" Lucia's voice trembled with horror. "Are you okay?"

"How is he? Is he hurt?" Magnolia asked, horrified by the bloody blotch on his vest.

"Yes, he is. Call a doctor!" Lucia ordered, but Mike stopped her. He tried to stand up, but his feet were weak, and the women helped him stand.

Once in the servants' room, he took off his jacket, clenched his teeth from the pain, and removed his vest. Lucia rushed to the bathroom and fetched a first aid kit. "Is it serious?" She turned to Magnolia, examining the wound in more detail.

"No, but it is heavily bleeding," Magnolia said.

Lucia sent her to fetch gauze and bandages, and Magnolia rushed out instantly. Lucia crouched down next to the wounded side, soaking a swab with alcohol. "Does it hurt?" She immediately stopped as his muscle twitched, and he pulled back with a loud gasp. She glanced at his dark eyes, which held hers for a moment.

"A little," he said, rubbing his hands on his legs, trying to control the pain and even out his breathing.

"We can get a doctor, but I don't think it's serious," Lucia said.

Mike took a longer, inquisitive look at her as she soaked another swab in alcohol. "You're... strange." He clenched his teeth as she rubbed the swab against his skin. "You seemed remarkably annoyed when your brother came to talk to us, and today, you are alone with me without hesitation."

It took a moment before she spoke again. "I am doing it because it is my duty. As for my brother, Juan Pablo seems to seek friendship with you and Jamie." She glanced up at him.

"It is unacceptable someone like you seeks friendship with someone like us." Mike held his breath for a moment, his heartbeat pulsating in his ears.

"Of course!" Lucia said in a mild voice.

"So, we are unworthy of your attention," Mike said bitterly, as if she had wounded his pride more than his body.

"Neither are you unworthy, nor are we indifferent. And I think I am showing this to you now!"

Mike glanced at the tips of her teeth as she sank them into her lower lip. A wave of passion and lust washed over his body, and an urge to taste her mouth bogged his mind. It took him a full minute before he stirred clear of his indecent thoughts. "But, nonetheless, you are not hiding your superiority."

"Do you think I am superior to you only because I believe the line must not be crossed?" She raised a brow at him in slight offense. "Everyone should know their place, don't you think?"

"Are you sure? Are you sure that the line hasn't already been crossed?" Mike swallowed and locked his unwavering gaze with hers.

Her mind reeling, she attempted to decipher an answer within the depths of his eyes. Yet, all she discovered was her own overwhelming longing to kiss him. She let her hand glide over his broad, rugged chest, feeling his heart pounding beneath her palm, and the charged air between them surged to a voltage neither could bear. The intimacy with the man who had consumed her thoughts all morning unveiled a world previously unknown to her senses, a torrent of lava coursing through her veins. "I am afraid I don't understand what you mean," she whispered, her hand gliding over his chest.

Mike swallowed and glanced down at her hand. The cool air in the room and her hot breath mixed tantalizingly, making it easy for him to confess the story behind his arrival. "I wish I could tell you, but I feel disarmed before your eyes," he said slightly above a whisper.

The wooden door squeaked open. "Lucia!" Antonio exclaimed, glaring at their inadmissible proximity.

Mike turned away from her face, and Lucia stood up quickly, taking a few steps back. She threw a quick glance at Mike, confused by her own behavior. "As you can see, Mike... er... Mr Williams is injured," she stuttered as her husband stood there, trying to decipher the unusual kindness of his wife.

"What does this have to do with you?" Antonio replied, consumed with jealousy.

"I am the reason for the accident."

"No, it wasn't your fault. I wasn't paying attention and got in her way, and she couldn't steer the horse," Mike jumped in her defense.

Lucia looked over her shoulder, trying to catch a glance of Mike talking behind her. His deep, velvety voice, mixed with a subtle rasp, completely lured her mind as if it were whispering sweet secrets meant only for her.

"The wound needs to be cleaned well. You don't have much experience in first aid. Let someone with more knowledge deal with it!" Antonio said, barely containing his rage.

"I'm doing my best," she snapped at his bitter taunt.

"Doña Lucia, your husband is right," Mike said, more to himself as a reminder that she was married. "You're wasting your efforts," he added melancholically as if his heart and thoughts sank in a pool of remorse.

Lucia turned to face him, wanting to know if he really meant it, but Magnolia and Jamie rushed into the room. Antonio went closer to her, gently kissing her cheek, staring fondly at her sullen expression. "Magnolia, please attend to the man's wound," he commanded. "If he needs a doctor, we'll phone someone at once," he added and dragged his wife out of the room. Once outside, Lucia plucked herself from the tight grip before Antonio completely lost his composure. "You shouldn't have attended to his wounds, regardless of whose fault it was!" he flared.

"Don't blame me! I was only fulfilling my duty," she snapped in response to his unfounded attacks. "What did you think I was doing?"

"What do you want me to think when I saw you with him, half-naked?" His eyes sparked with fury as his insecurity tightened its hold.

"I couldn't clean his wound while he was dressed."

"There are plenty of people who could have done it – Magnolia, the servants, the vet."

"He's not an animal!" Lucia gaped at his lack of sympathy.

"No man would like to see his wife around another man, regardless of the circumstances."

"What's going on?" Gabriella interrupted them.

"Nothing important, Gabriella," Antonio sighed with irritation.

"But you attached major importance to it." Lucia glared at him before strolling back to the house.

The night had rolled in quickly as Lucia gazed at the dark blue horizon through the window. Her mind was preoccupied with the conversation she had with Mike. His words still echoed in her ears, as if he were standing behind her, repeating them. She turned, but the room was empty. She gazed out the window, replaying random scenes in her mind. The conversation with Sebastian about her father and the young girl flooded her mind. Lucia went to the bookshelf and took down the framed picture of her late father. She gazed at it for a long time, not wanting to question his integrity, especially after his death. But what if the stranger girl was right? What if her father wasn't the paragon she had always believed him to be? And was Mike referring to the same girl? How would he know? Lucia returned the photo to the bookshelf. The questions in her head threatened to set her brain on fire, and she didn't have answers to any of them. She quickly changed into her nightgown and got ready for bed as the knock on the door took her out of her musings.

"May I come in?" Gabriella peeked through the gap of the ajar door.

"Of course, Mother!" Lucia replied, inviting her in.

Gabriella stood in the middle of the room, examining her daughter's tranquility. "Where is your husband?" she asked with a hint of irritation in her voice.

"He went out!" Lucia said blithely. She picked up a magazine from her nightstand and started turning the pages at random, skimming the headlines just to avoid eye contact.

"Where?" Gabriella raised her voice.

"I don't know. He wanted to clear his mind," Lucia said, keeping it brief.

"Are you not even a bit concerned? Is it right for your husband to go out at night?" Gabriella's eyes flickered with anger and surprise at her daughter's negligence.

"What's wrong with that? He's a free man," Lucia said.

"He's not free. He's married. To you!" Gabriella snapped. "You can't leave him alone. You're risking ruining your marriage."

Lucia looked up at her mother. She wanted to find the connection between all the troubling memories in her mind. "Are you speaking from experience?" Lucia asked.

Gabriella's expression changed, caught off-guard by the question. She stood up from the bed and turned around so as not to face Lucia or show any signs of weakness. "You felt secure with Dad. You trusted him. You didn't suspect anything was wrong even when he was late for work. And if he weren't dead, you still would have lost him because he would have been with another woman," Lucia said firmly but respectfully, watching her mother turn back to face her.

"How dare you talk to me like this?" Gabriella roared.

"I dare because I am right. My case is different. I don't care if he sees other women." She stood up from the bed, her heart pounding, but she needed to pluck the needle from within her before it poisoned her whole being. "If I am a bad wife, he can divorce me whenever he pleases." She gathered her strength and gazed at her mother's infuriating eyes.

Gabriella shook her head in disbelief. Her daughter's marriage was on the downturn, and she couldn't allow such a thing to happen. She couldn't bear the thought of people gossiping about what a bad daughter she had, or maybe worse. With a last glance at her daughter, she said nothing and closed the door from the outside.

The morning was as gloomy as the night before, and the same intrusive thoughts were still hanging in Lucia's head as she stared down at Mike, who occasionally looked up at the small wooden balcony in her direction. He wasn't just a worker, she mused. As she'd grown up, she'd encountered hundreds of workers come and go in the mansion, and none of them were like him. None of them made her stay in the chilly morning air, staring with such curiosity at a man.

"Are you worried about him? It was a minor incident," Magnolia said, startling her.

"I am worried, yes!" she confessed in a low, quiet voice.

"The wound is not serious." Magnolia tried to wash away Lucia's concerns.

"No, it's not that. I am concerned about how he stares, how he speaks... he is acting strange," Lucia said, peering at Magnolia who bit her lower lip with fear but managed to hold her straight face on in front of the young woman.

"Can I help somehow?" she offered.

"No, thank you. I am thinking of checking up on some things, but I will do it myself. I think I know the way." She gave Magnolia a small smile and went inside.

Magnolia rubbed her forehead and sighed. If only they knew the truth... She went into the kitchen, murmured something to the maid in charge of polishing the plates and cutlery. Mike quickly thanked them for the lunch and went out leaving Jamie alone with her. She sat at the table beside him, looking for a moment at him, hoping she'd find answers to the thousand questions that threatened to split her mind "I don't trust your brother," she finally said. "He's good, with a good heart, but rancorous, and this is dangerous." Jamie lifted his eyes to her. "He's not even pretending. He's talking too much in front of Mrs Lucia," Magnolia added, as her voice trembled with concerns that pooled in her voice.

"What do you mean?" Jamie's face straightened.

"She's suspecting something." Magnolia swallowed. The guilt for letting them start working in the mansion grew bigger each day, and it was now threatening to suffocate her. "What are you planning? You're not completely honest." She nearly burst into tears as she stood there, begging him to come clean.

"It's a secret I cannot share," Jamie said in a firm voice. "But I promise you, there won't be any violence or hostility. If we fail, we'll go! And no one will ever find out about us." Jamie drank up his juice and sank his gaze into her eyes as a form of assurance and went out to seek his brother.

He found him alone in the most eastern part of the mansion. He pulled him from his work, glancing with precaution now and then so as to not to be overheard. "Magnolia is worried. She said Lucia is suspecting you," he said in low voice. "You don't believe my plan will work out, do you?"

"No, I don't," Mike said tersely. "And we're not having this conversation in here," he added. He turned to leave, but Jamie pulled his arm to stop him.

"If we're patient and level-headed, the plan will work," Jamie insisted, which made Mike's blood boil.

"Seducing and deceiving Lucia Alvarez is impossible," Mike said emphatically, irritated by Jamie's persistence to have the conversation anyway.

"Exactly! Seducing is the key word," Jamie said through clenched teeth, making sure they were still alone. "You think I don't see how you look at her? When she's around, you transform into another man! I have warned you to be more careful."

"I don't care if you warned me!" Mike kicked the wall in anger. "You think I'm pleased to be sweeping my enemy's yard and stables?" he roared loudly. "If I were alone, I would have done much more by now." His eyes fired bullets. His anger was hardly controlled. "But she is the one who stops me! Lucia Alvarez!" He kicked the wall again as if mad at himself. "Something happens to me when I see her! Her voice, her eyes are transforming me, and I cannot hate her." Mike ran his hands vigorously on his head and down to his face. "I have never felt this way with another woman," he added.

Jamie's mouth popped open, frantically wanting to have misheard his brother gushing out his feelings, without the smallest trace of shame or concern in his voice. His cheeks puffed with air before he emitted a long, deep sigh. He returned his gaze to his brother. "Everything goes to shit! I didn't expect you would fall in love! You're in love, aren't you?" He arched a quizzical brow at his brother. "We need to run! We must forget about the plan and revenge."

"I told you not to manipulate me," Mike said with an emphatic voice. "Don't play me like a pawn," he added in the same tone.

"Don't you get it? She is married. And this is too dangerous. We need to pull the plug on this whole thing."

"I don't care. I am not going to run. And I won't give up. Running means we're cowards." His stern eyes locked on his brother. "Whatever happens, it's too late to give up! We'll stay and finish what we've started at all costs," Mike said and went back to his work.

Jamie threw his hat in anger and ran his hands through his hair. Desperation seeped through his pores until it filled his whole being. He sat on a bench and stared at the tree branches swinging against the wind for hours, thinking of a possible way out, but there was none. The only option now was to let things take their natural turn and pray to God it would be for the best.

Chapter Seventeen

Doña Rafaela Mendoza and her niece came early in the morning to the mansion as Antonio had organized an outing for the two families. Gabriella, of course, quickly approved the idea and was thrilled to spend the afternoon in the company of her old friend. Thus, Diego and Juan Pablo were going to have more time to spend with Penelope.

"Where is Lucia?" Antonio asked when everyone was ready to go.

"She will not be coming! She's indisposed and prefers to stay at home," Juan Pablo said.

Antonio's face turned grim and he mumbled an apology, stating that he'd rather stay with his wife. Gabriella, however, was more persistent in him coming and quickly managed to talk him into joining them.

Lucia impatiently stared through the windows as the car was leaving the house. She went out onto the balcony, shamelessly staring at Mike and when their eyes met, Lucia turned to go back inside.

"What are you planning?" Jamie tried to stop him. "You won't go inside while she's alone."

"Try and stop me. I am putting an end to everything," Mike threatened, not taking his eyes off the balcony.

"Please, Mike, don't ruin everything." Jamie could hardly contain his anger.

"Either you leave me alone, or I am telling everyone who we really are." He threw a quick glance at his brother and went steadfastly towards the house.

Jamie furiously threw the shovel aside. "Damn you, Mike Williams! Why do you always have to be like this?"

Mike opened the door, making sure there weren't any servants around. His heart was racing in his chest at the speed of a race car. He sprinted upstairs as the coast was clear, lowering the front rim of his hat and slowly opened the door to one of the bedrooms. He scanned the narrow corridor to make sure no one was around. When he saw no one was inside, he closed the door and went down the corridor.

"Since Rafaela and her niece are back in town, the invitations never end. They want to engage my grandsons with the scarecrow." Doña Isabella was talking to someone. Mike's heart leaped in his mouth. He tiptoed to the nearby room and closed the door from inside. Scanning the room in detail, his eyes dwelled on the picture of Santiago Alvarez. He pressed his lips in a thin line, gazing at the man in the photo. Although he had deceived and made a fool of his sister when promising to marry her, the hatred was gone, or at least was deeply buried in his consciousness. He quickly put the photo back when Magnolia's voice in the corridor grabbed his attention.

"Why didn't you go out with the others?" she said, holding a few fresh towels in her hand.

"Doña Rafaela insisted on me going, but I don't want to get involved in her plots with my mother," Lucia said.

"So, it's true. They are trying to engage one of your brothers to Doña Penelope?"

"Do you still have any doubts?" Lucia said. "They don't think of anything else, but I don't want to be a part of it," she added and turned to leave. Her eyes followed the faded footprints of mud, leading to the door of her room. Her heartbeat accelerated as she opened the door, scanning quickly through the empty room. She put her hand on her stomach, trying to calm her nerves, pulled like strings of a guitar, and went to the bathroom.

Mike took a few steps, ready to follow her. He pushed the handle down, and when the door opened, he quickly retreated his hand, leaving it ajar. He furrowed his brows in hesitation. When his doubts prevailed, he turned to leave. He took a couple of small steps ahead and froze in his spot when the unexpected touch of a hand on his shoulder made him instinctively turn around.

"Are you searching for me?" Lucia gazed into his eyes. "Why are you leaving? You already sneaked in like a thief." Her eyes were like arrows piercing every inch of his body. His mind numb, he couldn't move, nor breathe.

"Maybe I am a thief." He found his voice at last.

"Yes, yes you are. You stole my peace." Lucia straightened her body. "I thought about your words – that someone of us was connected to someone of you. What were you implying?" Her lips parted, making it even harder for him to speak.

"Think what you want!" Mike replied succinctly.

She took one step closer to where he was standing. "What are you doing in here?" She stared at his dark, longing eyes.

"Maybe I wanted to find out if a lady like you would be scared of a man like me," Mike said hesitantly.

"Did you give up?" Lucia inquisitive eyes slid down onto his lips, full and tantalizing.

He said nothing. He wrapped his hand around her waist and pressed her body against his, led by his own emotions and presumptions. The warmth blossomed in his chest and sparks igniting as he leaned in close, lips brushing together, tentatively, for the first time. The smell of her perfume was dizzying. Her lips, impossibly soft against his own, made his heart dance. Lucia hardly managed to pluck herself from his grip. The offense boggled her mind, and in the heat of her turmoil, she raised her palm to his cheek in a deafening slap.

"Now, we're clear!" she said curtly. "Get out! What are you thinking? You'll insult me in my own house?" She wiped the corner of her mouth as Mike pressed his jaw tight at the unexpected rebuke.

"If only I could," he managed to say almost inaudibly, "but I can't." His eyes were like that of an innocent child. "I cannot hurt you or insult you." Mike bent his head down, gazing at the floor, unconditionally defeated in his own game.

Lucia approached him, timid and confused, and ran her fingers on his cheek.

The sudden realization that she could yearn for a man just like any other woman made her wince. Mike had lit up a spark, turned it into a fire for no more than three seconds, and now it threatened to engulf her in flames. When his eyes met hers, she slightly caught the back of his head and pressed her lips against his in another tentative, longing kiss that she never thought she could ever initiate. She closed her eyes and let the lust fill her whole being. The zing of their bodies was increasing by the second, and when their tongues met, the lava of passion spilled, burning all barriers and prejudice. When their lips finally parted, Mike slowly opened his eyes, still holding his hands on her cheeks.

"Why did you do it?" he whispered now gazing at her captivating blue eyes.

"Please, Mike! You need to go!" she said in a low, firm voice. Her breath brushed against his moistened lips; he battled the uncontrollable surge to kiss her again. But she took a couple of steps back, turning away from him.

"You didn't answer my question."

"I said, leave!" Her voice demanding, she gazed at his eyes before he put his hat and left without insisting anymore.

When he returned to the stable, Jamie bombarded him with questions, which he had no answers to. Her mixed signals confused him and yet he let himself savor the moment of his sweet defeat. He was ready to lose his heart – that was one thing he knew for sure.

"Tell me, for God's sake, what happened in there? Did you talk to her?" Jamie hissed.

"Nothing of your concern!" Mike murmured.

"Did you tell her? Did you tell who we are?"

"No, I didn't! Although she gave me this chance." Mike turned to see his brother, who stood with a bewildered expression. "I don't know what kind of people these are, but I cannot hurt her, and she knows it." He threw away his gloves to one side and went to the servants' room.

After they finished work and got home, things got even worse. A sense of betrayal and guilt gnawed at his mind. He didn't have dinner and went straight to his room without saying a word to his sister. It wasn't long after when the knock on the door took him out of his thoughts. "Go away! I don't want to talk to anyone!" he screamed from the bed, but Chloe entered the room anyway. Mike gazed at her, irritated. "Didn't I just say…?"

"I don't care what you said. I am here and we are going to talk." Chloe closed the door and meekly sat at the edge of Jamie's bed. With a deep breath, she met his gaze, unflinching, her eyes reflecting a mix of concern and unwavering determination. "She is beautiful," Chloe said after a moment of silent exchanges of looks. Mike furrowed his brow, perplexed. "Jamie told me about your feelings toward Lucia Alvarez," she added.

"Remind me to kill him when he comes," Mike murmured and averted his eyes from Chloe.

She went to his bed, took his hands into hers, and Mike gazed at her innocent eyes. "Now you know how I felt," she said. Her voice was comforting to him, but something in the back of his mind was still disturbing his inner peace.

"My situation and yours have nothing in common," he blurted out and pulled his hands off hers. He got up, snatched his denim jacket off the chair and put it on, desperate to avoid the conversation.

"To me, they do." Chloe followed him with her eyes.

"Is that so?" Mike stopped for a moment. "How is my falling in love with Lucia Alvarez even close to what that old bastard did to you?"

Chloe smiled and went to him again. She stood in front of him and gently put her hand on his heart.

"It all starts in here." She smiled fondly. "The heart wants what it wants."

"But…"

"Shh!" She put her finger on his lips. "I never wanted to be avenged. Things happen the way they were meant to." She took a step back and shrugged her shoulders. "Maybe you, too, should let things go the way they are meant to be." She smiled and quietly closed the door on her way out.

Mike stood by the open window, welcoming the cold stream of air that entered his lungs. Maybe his sister was right; maybe he should have let things take their natural course. The images of Lucia Alvarez rushed in his mind and the memory of the night Chloe was missing followed almost immediately. *No, that cannot be, no! She is my enemy*, he said to himself and went out.

Chapter Eighteen

The Alvarez family gathered for dinner with unusual excitement reeling in the house. Juan Pablo had announced he needed every member at dinner as he had important news to share.

"Doña Isabella, dinner is served." Magnolia smiled at the lady, dressed in an impeccable white suit. She rose from her seat and followed the housekeeper to the dining.

"Come on, Juan Pablo, what was it so important you wanted to share?" Diego leaned on the back of his seat, impatient to find out about the new madness his brother had plotted. He quickly greeted his sister and his brother-in-law and threw a quick, pleasant smile at his grandma.

"Well, now you are all here, there is no point in waiting any longer." He grinned and glanced at everyone with broad smile. "Well, as you all know, we had an outing this afternoon."

"Yes, with this mummy, Rafaela, and the scarecrow," Isabella said.

"Mother, please!" Gabriella hissed.

"I have decided to accept the engagement with Penelope Hernández," Juan Pablo blurted out, hardly being able to follow the mixed reactions. Isabella almost choked on her sip of wine. She grabbed the napkin placed on her serving plate, and wiped off the corners of her mouth and half of her lipstick. Gabriella and Antonio hurriedly congratulated him, and Diego turned to him with furrowed brows in great amazement, and Lucia fixed her gaze on him, speechless.

"I cannot believe my ears," Isabella said trying to find her voice. "Either your English has gotten worse, or I haven't heard correctly."

"No, Abuelita, you're hearing well, like everyone else."

Gabriella raised her glass and sipped, grinning like a kid in a candy store, as a few wrinkles appeared at the corner of her eyes.

"What are you talking about? Are you blind? How can you be engaged to this... crocodile?" Isabella hissed.

"I don't see anything wrong. Penelope is a good choice," Antonio said.

"I agree with Antonio," Gabriella cut in. "She is intelligent, smart, elegant," she added, as the smile threatened to split her mouth.

"This she may be, but to be a wife of my grandson is an utmost absurdity." Isabella glared at her daughter, fully convinced her daughter, along with Antonio and Rafaela, had forced him into this madness.

"No, Grandma! No one has forced me or advised me. The decision is entirely mine," Juan Pablo reassured her.

"Are you sure, Juan Pablo?" Lucia cleared her voice. "Aren't you hurrying with this?"

"Absolutely not!" The determination was evident in his voice. "Well, I hope there won't be any problems."

"What problems?" Gabriella said cheerfully. "I fully approve." She raised her glass for a toast.

"Well, the only one left is Diego. You should follow your brother's example," Antonio said with a seemingly genuine smile.

"Don't get your hopes up!" Diego snorted.

Isabella pushed her chair back and stood up from her seat.

"Grandma, are you not going to eat?" Juan Pablo said.

"I think I've had enough," she said as she pushed her chair in and left.

After dinner, Gabriella retired to the salon with Antonio and Lucia, while Diego dragged his brother to his room. "Now that we're alone, tell me what you have planned," Diego said, placing his hands on his waist. His eyes stern on his brother, he waited to hear a plausible explanation for his irrational behavior, if there was any.

"Wasn't I clear at dinner? I agreed to get engaged to Penelope," Juan Pablo replied nonchalantly.

"But you don't like her, you don't love her, and you're not even into women," Diego said, puzzled like a jigsaw piece that doesn't fit. "How are you going to marry her?"

Juan Pablo giggled and went to his brother. "Oh, Diego, I was talking about engagement, not marriage. A fiancé could be anyone, but a wife or husband can only be one person, and it's not going to be Penelope Hernández," he said, patting his brother on the shoulder before leaving Diego pondering if his brother's mischief could top anything he had previously done.

The news of Juan Pablo's decision quickly spread to the surrounding estates. Gabriella even called her friend the same evening to inform her of the engagement. The next day, Magnolia kept Mike and Jamie company in the kitchen for lunch, also telling them about the engagement. Mike took the news with indifference, but Jamie's sullen expression was enough evidence of his irritation. He abruptly got up from the table, walking outside without finishing his lunch.

"What's up with him?" Magnolia asked.

"I have no idea," Mike said meekly before thanking her for the lunch and returning to his work.

Jamie slammed the wooden door of the servants' room, hoping he would find some space to think. "What a treacherous hypocrite! What's taken hold in his head to get married?" he murmured to himself. He wasn't particularly concerned, but somehow this engagement bothered him. He needed to act quickly to finish his plan. It was a tricky and dangerous game, but he had no other choice and no time. His brother had already lost his guard towards Lucia Alvarez, and Jamie doubted his every move. Although he should try one more time to convince his stubborn brother they had to get out of there, if not, he had to take the reins solo.

"What's going on?" Mike startled him.

"Not much! I was refreshing myself," Jamie said, trying to ignore his inquisitive eyes. "I'll wait for you in the car," he added and darted off.

Mike changed his clothes and when he was ready to go, Lucia smiled at him. She awkwardly put her hand around her neck, as if wondering what she was doing there herself. She bit her lower lip, and Mike's gaze momentarily dwelled on them. She slowly approached, intending to give him the blissful moment again. And he started to decipher her intentions more easily with every gaze at her captivating fathomless eyes.

She parted her lips, and Mike instinctively pressed his mouth onto hers in a slow, mesmerizing kiss. They both dove into an ocean of emotions, ready to be drowned by the waves of lust and longing, passion, and love. Time had stilled. Their universes merged into one, the current sweeping them away. Lucia trembled with a slight burning sensation in her loins. Oh Lord, she wanted him, needed him with every fiber of her being. This intensity burnt in her loins making each stroke of her tongue more tentative and demanding.

Mike tightened his hands around her, pressing her body hard against himself. He craved her scent, her lips, and his head reeled in the sweetness of ecstasy. His body fully responded to her sweet attack on his mouth, and when Lucia pulled away, he caressed her silky cheeks and ran his fingers through her hair once again. Her eyes burned with desire, and Mike had no more doubts; he was madly in love with this woman. Their hands let go, and she slowly turned away, her captivating eyes disappearing behind the door.

"What game are you playing, Lucia Alvarez, what game are you playing?" He ran his finger over his lower lip, still gripped by the heavenly moment.

Once in the car, Mike skillfully navigated through the streets.

"What's up with you?" Jamie turned to him with a grumpy look.

"It's none of your concern." Mike rebuffed his curiosity, not taking his eyes off the road.

"If your silly grin has something to do with Lucia Alvarez, then I'd say it is my concern," Jamie hissed. "Mike, please listen carefully to what I am about to say and get it through your head." He sighed, allowing himself time to regain his calmest voice. "I insist we get out of the mansion, please! The plan didn't work out the way I thought it would. I'm sorry, but I was wrong."

Mike threw a quick look at him and turned his eyes onto the steering wheel. He put on his poker face and went back to where he was a while ago, his tongue exploring Lucia's mouth. A semblance of a smile appeared on his face. His inner self was dancing a small, victorious dance.

"I wasn't expecting you to fall in love, and for us to use and to deceive her brothers is too big of a risk," Jamie said, turning to his absent-minded brother. "Mike, are you even listening to me?" Jamie hissed again.

"Yes, I am listening to you," Mike replied casually. "I don't care if you made a mistake or not. I already told you; we are not leaving the house no matter what," he said with a hint of satisfaction that further irritated Jamie. He kicked the glove box angrily and leaned on the back of his seat.

Lucia was enjoying a long, soothing bath with the invigorating citrus scent of bath salts filling the air. As she inhaled deeply, she pressed her knee to her chest and rubbed her calf, running her hand up her body. She was subtly disturbed by the presence of her husband in the bathroom. "Would you please leave me?" she asked, glaring at his audacity to enter without permission.

Antonio grabbed the bathrobe that hung on the back of the door and held it out before her, admiring the sight of her velvet skin covered in foam. "Let me help," he offered, coming closer. As Lucia stood up, she made a pointless attempt to cover herself. "What's wrong with you? You're more reserved than ever," he questioned with a hint of insult.

"I'm concerned about Juan Pablo," she murmured, tightening the sash of her robe.

"He's happy because he's in love. As happy as I wish you were with me." Antonio sighed with unease. "Maybe you would have been if Gabriella hadn't forced you to marry me," he added, his voice heavy with bitterness.

Antonio brushed her hair over her shoulder, revealing her smooth, scented neck. She gasped, and instinctively followed his mouth, but then pulled back and closed her eyes. For the first time, she allowed her husband to kiss her passionately on her arm and her neck, with the most sacred love a man could have for a woman. She ran her hand through his hair and let him caress her back. When she turned around and their lips touched, she opened her eyes, startled by her own indecent thoughts of Mike.

"Antonio, please stop," she said, torn inside. "Just go. I'm sorry."

Antonio rolled his eyes in frustration, and when she demanded him to leave a few more times, he stormed out of the room in an even sourer mood. She quickly got dressed and went to the window. Her lips curled into a smile, and she flew downstairs, confident and sure of herself. She had found the answer to the countless sleepless nights she had spent thinking, and now she was ready to prove to herself it wasn't just her imagination but love in its purest form.

She looked around several times and fixed her stare at the door of the servants' room. She put her hand on her stomach before the door opened and Mike appeared before her. Catching his eye, she threw her hands around his neck and devoured his mouth, taking in every inch. Mike responded with the same passion that had spilled in her veins. His inner self dancing in the rhythm of love. His heart pounded in his chest; his brain filled with her. He didn't even care they were hiding. Lucia pulled her lips back, catching his hand. She led him behind the annex of the main building to avoid being seen. Pressing him against the wall, she kissed him again as Mike devoured every inch of her mouth.

The startling noise of a metal tray hitting the cobbled path made Lucia turn her head. Her blood froze. Her face dead serious, covered in panic, she ran away. Magnolia's eyes followed her and returned to Mike as soon as Lucia disappeared. Mike stood there, not able to think straight. He fixed his stare at the woman, who was hiding her dismay behind her hand on her mouth.

Chapter Nineteen

Magnolia paced around the room, her eyes darting around. The image of young Lucia Alvarez with Mike Williams vividly reminded her of Santiago Alvarez and the young girl. Her heart jumped in her chest. Her thoughts were a jumbled mess, with a million different scenarios racing through her mind. Magnolia tried to push them away and focus on something else, but the worry was too strong and overwhelming.

"For God's sake, Doña Lucia, how can you kiss him under the nose of your mother and husband? Have you lost your mind?"

Lucia gazed out the window of her room, unable to meet Magnolia's eyes. "Maybe I have, Magnolia."

"I have no right to judge you, but I must tell you I am disappointed."

Lucia turned to face the woman, noticing the distress etched on her pale face. She was struggling to come to terms with what had just happened – the most level-headed and prominent girl among her peers in their circles was shamelessly kissing the groom. "I can't help it, Magnolia," Lucia said, her voice heavy with emotion. "It's been like this ever since I met him."

"Please don't tell me you're mad about him because I don't believe it. You're such a responsible lady to act so recklessly without thinking of the consequences... How is it possible, Mrs Garcia?" Magnolia's words almost choked her.

Lucia wasn't sure if she had an answer to the question. All she knew was that she needed to share the jumble of emotions in her heart. "Will you tell my mother and Antonio what you saw?" Lucia asked, her voice filled with concern.

"No! Of course not!" Magnolia reassured her. "I'd rather die than open my mouth."

"Then listen to me, Magnolia." Lucia turned to the woman, determination showing in her voice. "I did it because for the first time since the day I was raped, I don't feel disgusted by a man. With Mike, everything is different. When he's close to me, I feel the need to kiss and hug him, and it's stronger than me." Lucia fought hard not to go back to that moment and battled the tears welling in her eyes.

"Please, don't give in to temptation. You don't even know him. You don't know who he is, where he comes from… nothing!" Magnolia's fear overwhelmed her, but Lucia remained adamant. She didn't care as long as her inner self insisted that he was the man. She was all flesh and blood; with all the weaknesses a woman could have for a man.

"Magnolia, Mike succeeded where my husband failed," Lucia said, holding a picture of Antonio in her hands before placing it back on his side of the bed. "We share one bed, but I don't even allow him to touch me." The painful realization she had shared too much caused Lucia to speak with a hint of regret.

"You owe him respect, Mrs Lucia," Magnolia said. "You're scaring me. I don't like any of this," she added in a low voice. "I don't know what to advise you or how to defend you."

"You don't need to do anything, Magnolia." Lucia took her gentle hands in her own and sat on the bed beside her. Magnolia's thoughtful eyes stared at her. "Just keep my secret."

"I don't know what you feel about Mike Williams, but I beg you not to give in to the temptation," Magnolia said, caressing Lucia's cheek. "You're risking too much for nothing. You're in grave danger." Her voice barely above a whisper.

Lucia stood up and stared at the woman for a while. "I am more afraid of living the way I do," she said with a trace of regret in her eyes. She gave the woman a small smile and left the room. Magnolia furrowed her brows in desperation. A strong surge of guilt gnawed at her mind, for she was the one who let the brothers in the house.

The day dragged on forever as Mike's tension got hold of him. He desperately tried not to think that Lucia might be in trouble after the recent events. When he finished changing, he left Jamie alone and went out without saying a word.

"Are you leaving?" Juan Pablo asked in a hesitant, curious voice.

Jamie turned around and swallowed. "What are you doing here?" he stuttered, hastily putting on his t-shirt.

"I came to see if you're okay," Juan Pablo said meekly. "Your back pain," he added with a mischievous grin.

"You don't need to worry about me, Juan... er, Mr Alvarez," he mumbled. "And I'm sure you have more important things to do with your time, like getting ready for your engagement," he added in a low, somewhat vicious tone.

Juan Pablo grinned. "So, you heard, huh?" Jamie nodded with a thin smile. "Well, won't you congratulate me?" He extended his hand for a shake.

Jamie lingered for a moment, thinking about what a spoiled brat Juan Pablo was, and smiled thinly. When they finished the long handshake, Juan Pablo turned to leave without saying a word. He looked over his shoulder at Jamie, a little ecstatic and content, and closed the door behind him. Jamie gazed at the bent note Juan Pablo had slipped into his hand. He opened the crumpled piece of paper that read, *I am dying to see if you dare. Wait for me at the Belmore restaurant at ten tonight.* His mouth gaped open, the thoughts baffled him, and before he managed to lift his gaze back up, Juan Pablo was gone.

Jamie remained silent during the journey home, which came as a welcome relief to Mike, who wasn't particularly in the mood for small talk either. Once at home, Jamie mumbled hello to Chloe and went straight to his room. His head was floating in the clouds. "What game is this?" he murmured to himself, reading the note again. He put it back in his pocket, sighed heavily and got ready for a steamy shower in dire hope it would help him relax.

"Chloe!" he screamed from the bathroom. "Chloe, come here!" When his sister entered, he pulled the curtain, peeked his head around it, and a cloud of steam hit her in the face. "I told you to buy a new bottle of shower gel," he hissed grumpily. "Why is no one listening to me when I am talking?"

She rolled her eyes at him and opened the steamed, mirrored cabinet, and handed him a brand new bottle.

"Here!" she said bitterly and crossed her arms over her chest.

Jamie pulled the curtain back, but she pulled it aside again. "Chloe!" he snapped. "What are you doing?" He snatched the lower edge of the shower curtain, which was glued to the outer part of his leg.

"I'm waiting for your apology," she replied, arching an accusatory brow.

"Please, go away. I have a date and…" He paused and swallowed.

Chloe widened her eyes at his stunned face as he stood under the cascading water, too embarrassed by the slip of his tongue. "A date?" She gaped. "Who is she? Mike! Mike! Did you know about this?" She rushed out of the bathroom. "Jamie has a date!"

"Chloe, no!" he shouted furiously after her. "Damn!" He pulled the curtain back, welcoming the hot torrent of water splashing over his face.

Jamie arrived at the appointed place and checked his watch for the 100th time. He sighed in frustration, muttering, "Damn you, Mike, Chloe, and everyone with their stupid inquisitions." When he was about to give up, a familiar voice startled him from behind.

"Hey there," Juan Pablo said, plastering a broad, confident smile. "I thought you wouldn't come."

Jamie parted his lips, allowing his lungs to engulf the stream of air. The flutter in his stomach paralyzed his gaze on Juan Pablo's dark purple shirt, neatly pressed against his muscled chest. "Er… no!" Jamie's voice trembled as he spoke. "I had to endure my brother and sister's inquisition," he said, trying to sound stern.

"Your sister? I didn't know you had one."

"Yes, yes I do!" he murmured hastily, as his inner self scolded him for acting like a jerk. Juan Pablo grinned at Jamie's nerve-wracking state and suggested they walk in.

The extreme discomfort hit him as soon as they entered. The place was more than sophisticated and the people at the tables were dressed in expensive suits and gowns. Jamie glanced at his denim jacket and worn-out jeans and clenched his jaw in response to his improvidence.

Juan Pablo greeted the host in a friendly manner as he walked them to their table on the second floor at the far end of the salon. When they took their seats, the impeccably groomed waitress brought the menus and left the ice bucket beside the table, containing Juan Pablo's favorite champagne.

"You're shaking. Are you still nervous?" Juan Pablo gazed at him.

"I'd be lying if I said no." Jamie smiled awkwardly and buried his gaze at the menu.

Juan Pablo caught the upper side of it and lowered it enough to meet Jamie's eyes. "Relax! I am not going to jump on you," he teased, leaving Jamie even more frustrated. "It's just a normal evening out. With a friend." His grin gave Jamie a bit of reassurance and courage.

By the time the main course was served, Jamie had gulped a couple of glasses, which had helped to ease his tension. They were talking about Jamie's adventures, the few affairs he had with the women from his neighborhood, and lots of other things he didn't even suspect he might tell Juan Pablo in normal, professional environment.

"So, would you say I am the first man you ever kissed?" Juan Pablo threw an inquisitive, curious glance at him, holding the stem of his glass. Jamie adjusted himself in his seat and cleared his throat. He gazed down at his steak and the awkward silence hung immediately over the table. "There you go! You're nervous again."

"No, I am not!" Jamie said blithely.

"Yes, you are. Every time you are tense about something, you adjust in your seat and try to avoid eye contact," he pointed out. "I was able to read body language when I was five, and yours is not very cryptic."

"You did?"

"Don't try to change the subject," Juan Pablo laughed.

"Well, if you must know – yes, you were. Happy? You got me to embarrass myself."

Juan Pablo laughed even louder, making Jamie's irritation grow. "There's nothing to be embarrassed about," Juan Pablo said. His face was serious and his eyes fell upon Jamie's cherry lips.

"And, in my defense, I didn't start it," Jamie said matter-of-factly. Juan Pablo arched a brow at him but didn't comment. "And I still don't know what we are doing here. Aren't you supposed to be with your fiancé?" Jamie gazed at him with all the confidence he could muster.

"Ah, yeah, my fiancé," Juan Pablo said blithely. "She can survive a night without me."

"I don't understand. You're getting married and asked me to come to this place."

"No one is marrying anyone," Juan Pablo giggled.

Jamie gazed at him, confused. *What the fuck is he talking about?* he mused and listened to Juan Pablo's secret plan he had arranged with Penelope Hernandez, and how it all came down to a symbiotic union with mutual benefits for both. He had opened up to her about his sexuality, but he entrusted his secret in her after

Penelope had admitted she was more interested in the money she would gain from her aunt if she married soon.

Jamie's mouth gaped open. "You didn't tell her about me, did you?" he asked, a trace of concern in his voice.

Juan Pablo reassured him with a laugh. "Of course not!"

Afterwards, they discussed a future engagement party, which Juan Pablo wasn't enthusiastic about but had to adhere to as part of the protocol. As they finished the second bottle of champagne, Juan Pablo revealed the dull and conditional life he had to lead as a member of his society. Jamie listened intently with a strong passion for the topic, glad that the awkward part of the conversation was over, and it finally felt like a bro night out.

After settling the bill, Juan Pablo and Jamie faced the invigorating air outside. The night was young, and now that they were together, Juan Pablo intended to make the most of it. "How about we hit a nightclub?" he suggested, beaming with excitement.

"What? No way! I have work tomorrow," Jamie replied, inhaling deeply as the champagne kicked in.

"Come on, don't be a buzzkill! Even Grandma is more fun than you." Juan Pablo laughed and hailed a taxi.

Once inside the club, they headed straight for the VIP booth. "Money does make the world look different," Jamie's voice blasting into his ear.

"It certainly helps," Juan Pablo replied as they clinked their glasses in an inaudible toast. After a few more drinks, they fully surrendered to the music.

It was a little before dawn when they stumbled out of the nightclub, barely able to stand on their feet. The city was quiet, with no one around except for a few speeding cars on the boulevard. "Are we going home?" Jamie slurred loudly, his ears still ringing from the loud music inside.

"No need to scream, I can hear you." Juan Pablo playfully pushed him and laughed as he staggered. As Jamie was about to collapse, Juan Pablo quickly pulled him back, surprising him with his strength. The air crackled with anticipation, and their laughter faded as a strange wave of sensation rippled through their bodies – now dangerously close to each other, the heat between them ignited into a wildfire of desire. Their eyes locked, and the world around them faded away until there was nothing but the two of them.

After their crazy night, Jamie realized they were quite different, but both enjoyed playing daring and dangerous games. He caught the back of Juan Pablo's head, tilted his own and sucked on his lips, hard and fiery. A new wave of passion was ignited by the electricity coursing through their veins. They pulled apart, both gasping for air.

"I can't believe I'm doing this," Jamie whispered, his voice husky with emotion.

"Me neither," Juan Pablo said before their tongues met in another erotic dance.

Chapter Twenty

Unusual excitement reeled in the room during breakfast. Juan Pablo's date last night was on the agenda, replacing the usual tedious morning talks about work and errands. It had been a long time since Gabriella had woken up in such an extraordinarily good mood. "Juan Pablo is head over heels. The date with Penelope must have been delightful as he is glowing this morning," she remarked.

"Blah blah!" Isabella murmured, spreading marmalade over her toast. "What could be so pleasant about being with a crocodile?"

"Well, you know what they say, love satiates." Antonio poured himself a juice, throwing a quick glance in Isabella's direction.

"I'd say it makes you look like a fool," Diego said curtly. "He isn't even talking anymore, and I should have asked him to stop before."

"I might as well believe in love at first sight," Gabriella said, grinning as if she had 80 teeth in her mouth.

"What a charming couple they make!" Isabella murmured sarcastically. "What an excitement!"

"Aren't you pleased to see your grandson happy?" Gabriella asked.

"I am more amazed he might like someone like Penelope Hernandez. This boy has quite strange taste!"

Isabella rolled her eyes, denying the slightest possibility this joke could be true at all.

"You better be happy for him. He has chosen a decent lady and not some dirt-poor peasant," Antonio mildly opposed her. "A lot of men have done it recently, and so have some women," he said as a matter of fact.

Lucia involuntarily turned to him, as if he was accusing her of something. The guilt stuck in her throat and she had to sip from her juice.

"That's true!" Gabriella agreed. "So many girls choose the wrong men. Fortunately, we don't have this problem."

Lucia gazed down at the table and ran her hands on her thighs as if wiping off her sweaty hands. Every word spoken at breakfast was turning into dreadful bullets, drilling her brain, and she forced herself to remain impassive under the fire of accusatory looks.

Magnolia had served the full breakfast and threw a quick glance at the table to make sure everything was in order before asking permission to retire. The urge to talk to Mike gripped her tighter. She asked a few other workers for his whereabouts and found him in the storehouse, piling sacks of corn into a wheelbarrow. He turned to her, amazed by the encounter.

"You've changed your plans," Magnolia said curtly. Mike paused for a moment, trying to work out what she meant. "It wasn't difficult to guess after I saw you kissing Mrs Lucia." Mike threw another sack of corn atop the others, seemingly not in the mood of having this sort of conversation with her. "You will not attack Doña Gabriella directly, but you'll use Lucia as a weapon." She raised her tone, hoping to get his attention.

"Don't get involved, Magnolia!"

"I am already involved!" she paused, examining his face, which lacked any trace of emotion. "Mrs Lucia is not to blame for what her father did to your sister."

Mike's blood rushed immediately in his head. He dropped the heavy sack on the ground and kicked it in anger, as the slightest reminder of this could still get under his skin. "Magnolia, please, leave me alone!"

"No, I won't! What I am saying is true. What you're doing to Ms Alvarez is cruel."

"Listen to me, Magnolia." His voice was demanding, his eyes lightning bolts in a dark sky. "I am not following any plan. If it were up to me, everyone would have figured out who we are long time ago."

"But you are courting her. Don't deny it! I saw you."

"Despite the apparent facts, I am not using her as a weapon for revenge. I am scared to death of what's happening, and you know why?" He paused for a moment and cocked his head to one side. "Because I am terrified I can fall in love with a woman who's supposed to be my enemy."

Magnolia found it hard to keep a straight face. The fear of what might come out of such a relationship crawled on her skin as he spoke. *He must be lying*, she said to herself, distracted by pictures of what would follow if someone found out.

"I don't know about her, but there is a feeling arising in me, and it is not hatred, I assure you." He gazed at her one more time, put on his hat and pushed the wheelbarrow towards the exit.

An uncontrollable need to see Lucia spilled into his veins; to hold her in his arms and kiss her soft lips again. He was counting the minutes until she would show up in the servants' room. And when it happened, he entered the room with the warmest smile on his face. Her mesmerizing eyes locked on him. Mike gazed at her for a moment, threw his hat to one side, and with one swift motion, her body was pressed against him; her lips parted at the sweet attack as he couldn't restrain the instant desire to taste them. Lucia gasped as he swiftly swept everything off the table, caught her and laid her head slowly on the wooden surface.

"I need you." He kissed her gently. "I want you, but not here," he whispered against her lips.

She squirmed with desire and anticipation beneath him. As she slowly rose to a sitting position, she ran her fingers through his hair, trying to regulate her intermittent breathing. Lucia brushed her lips against his and lost herself in the moment she had been craving. Her own indecent thoughts intensified her need to kiss him until her mouth could bear no more. A twinge of guilt briefly crossed her mind, but she couldn't bring herself to stop. Oblivious to their surroundings and enchanted by their kisses, they didn't even notice Jamie standing by the door, his lips pressed together in anger. His brother was out of his mind.

Later in the evening, the Williams' house looked like a battlefield. The two brothers acted as if possessed by evil. Chloe screamed at them, horrified. Mike threw another punch at Jamie, causing him to fall onto the table, and when he was ready to throw another one, Jamie kicked him and Mike staggered a few steps back. The muscles in his stomach clenched with pain from Jamie's boots and before he could regain control of himself, Jamie threw another punch, hard, as if he was looking to vent some of his own anger at himself.

"Mike! Jamie! Stop!" Chloe screamed. "What's going on with you?" Desperation and fear gripped her heart, and when Mike finally stopped, he needed a couple of minutes to gather his thoughts.

"He started it. I'm not going to allow him to tell me what to do." He breathed heavily.

"It's for your own good, Mike," Jamie said, wiping the small splotch of blood from beneath his nose. "I warned you not to mess around with Lucia Alvarez. You'll cause trouble for all of us."

"You have no right to warn me about anything."

"Either you stop seeing her, or we are not going back to that damn house!" Jamie screamed and Mike reached to hit him again, but Chloe swiftly moved in between them.

"Chloe, get out of my way! You may get hurt."

"Hit me if you wish, but I am not going to allow you fight like you are enemies," she said curtly. "Mike, you are way stronger than him."

Mike gazed at them hesitantly, grabbed his jacket and stormed outside while Jamie and Chloe hurried to the bathroom to wash off the blood stain.

"He's acting irresponsibly, Chloe, and he doesn't even think about what could happen if her husband catches them," Jamie hissed, touching his upper lip. He splashed more water onto his face, making sure there was no more blood left. "He's acting incredibly foolishly, stalking her in her own home," he added, his frustration obvious in his voice.

"It was foolish of us to tell him to stop," Chloe admitted.

"The worst part is she's responding to his feelings," Jamie continued.

"How do you know?"

"I saw them, Chloe. They were hiding in the servants' room, kissing and making out on the table," he said, a tinge of indignation in his voice.

"Well, this is extreme," she admitted. "But he won't stop."

"You need to talk to him," Jamie urged her, but Chloe only quivered her lips in a semblance of a vague smile.

Chapter Twenty-one

Lucia pulled over in front of the hotel. Her heart pounded in her chest she didn't even notice she had been gripping the steering wheel too tightly. She sighed, trying to bring her nerves under control. She approached Mike from behind but the moment he turned to face her, the hesitation in her mind momentarily dissipated. As she approached him, a fond smile illuminated her face, casting a radiant glow that seemed to dispel the darkness of the night. Lucia's eyes locked onto his, a fleeting expression of desire flickering in her gaze before she turned and made her way to the entrance, as Mike followed silently behind.

The air in the room charged with anticipation as they crossed the threshold. In the softly lit space, Lucia set her purse down gently on the chair, her movements precise and purposeful. Standing before the majestic canopy bed, the coolness of the room enveloped her. With deliberate grace, her fingers found the buttons of her shirt, each one yielding to her touch with a quiet surrender. The fabric slid off her shoulders, revealing her smooth, velvety arms as it pooled softly at her feet, forming a silken contrast against the plush carpet. The ambient glow of the night lamps danced delicately on her exposed skin, casting a luminous sheen over her form. Lucia sank her teeth into her lower lip beneath the heat of Mike's gaze as it traced every contour of her body, causing a delightful rush of anticipation to surge through her, leaving a trail of goosebumps in its wake.

She gasped when his warm arms wrapped around her waist. He could finally appreciate the whole beauty she possessed. Lucia was perfect. "Are you sure?" Mike whispered, and she only nodded in response. His fingers found their way behind her back, deftly undoing the clasps of her bra. Each gentle touch of his fingertips sent an electric current through her, igniting her skin and setting her senses ablaze. His lips found their way to her neck, showering it in thousands of tender kisses that seemed to set her very being on fire.

Guiding her with tender strength, he led her to the bed, the luxurious fabric embracing her form like a lover's embrace. Lucia propped herself up on her elbows, captivated by the sight of him undressing her, his every touch leaving a trail of scintillating sensation. His lips, lush and fervent, traced a tantalizing path from her sternum down to the delicate curve of her navel, eliciting a symphony of heightened breaths that matched the rapid tempo of her heartbeat. With each garment shed, the intensity of the moment seemed to magnify, charging the air with an undeniable fervor. When he delicately removed her thong, his gaze locked onto hers with an intensity that spoke of genuine delight. Lucia let herself sink languorously into the pillows, surrendering to the surging waves of pleasure that cascaded over her with unrestrained force. His hands, like silk, glided over the contours of her thighs, inching upward toward her hips, while his touch caressed her breasts, coaxing forth a symphony of sensations that left her gasping for more.

His lips left a trail of moisture along the soft, vulnerable skin of her inner thigh, a sensation that sent ripples of ecstasy coursing through her entire being. With skillful precision, his fingers lingered on her hardened nipple, coaxing forth a melody of pleasure, while his tongue traced delicate circles around the other. A delicate moan escaped her lips, the sweet sound of surrender mingled with the soft rustle of the sheets as her hands ventured to explore every inch of him.

Mike stood up from the bed, stripped off his clothes as fast as he could and stood immobile for a moment. She was hungrily staring at him, devouring every inch. And when he returned to bed beside her, Mike covered her mouth in a passionate kiss, as his hand trailed down her inner thigh. His long fingers made several circles before entering her. She let out a strangled moan, his manhood throbbing against her hip. "You are so sweet," he moaned in her ear, making her skin prickle with pleasure.

She gasped with joy when he entered her. He started off slowly for his own pleasure, until he reached deeper inside her with every thrust he made. Her breathing rasped and her cries grew louder; she threw her hands around his neck as he sped up bit by bit.

Mike moaned before he gagged her mouth with a kiss. How long had it been since he craved this moment? The bed was moving but he couldn't see past his fluttering eyelids. The radiance of her skin blinded him when she stiffened and came.

"Oh my…" She breathed out, as her hands stopped on his buttocks. Mike closed his eyes as she parted her legs further and curved her waist against him for deeper penetration. He clenched his teeth, close to his own climax. His breathing erratic, his movements reached mayhem speed. He lost himself in the pleasure, until it was too late to pull back, and spilled himself inside her.

He groaned loudly once more before his muscular body crumpled on top of her. Lucia grinned joyously, holding the back of his head. He rolled slowly to her side, dizzy from the blissful moment. He instinctively smiled and gave her a light, gentle kiss on her nose as a thank you for this bliss. He pulled her towards him in a spooning position as the warmth of their bodies pulsed between them.

"Are you okay?" Mike slurred, barely able to keep his eyes open. He left a warm, moist trail of breath on her back as he inhaled the citrus scent of her skin and smiled. She was there in his arms, and he couldn't have asked for more. She had surrendered herself to him.

"More than that," she whispered before they both succumbed to fatigue.

Mike opened his eyes and ran his fingers along the empty side of the bed. "Lucia," he called out a few times, but his own words echoed back to him. His heart sank into a careless gloom as he realized Lucia had left. He went to the window and pulled the curtains aside; the darkness outside made him look towards the watch on the nightstand. Mike picked up his scattered clothes from the floor, rushed to the reception, and headed home, painfully realizing that this night had brought him both joy and sadness. He couldn't be with her like this – having her for a few hours, and then she'd be gone. Yet, she had a husband she needed to return to. *What a pathetic situation*, Mike thought, as the car flew through the empty streets.

⚮

On her way back, Lucia couldn't help but recall every moment of the night. The remorse lurked at the back of her mind as her inner goddess screamed at her for cheating on her husband. But for a few moments, she was forced to ignore her and smiled.

Once at home, she went to the study room and stood there for hours in the ambient light of the desk lamp, bringing her back to the hotel room; a reminder of how she had betrayed her vows and what a bad wife she was. The guilt weighed heavily on her, and she wondered how she could ever face her husband, but the memory of the passion shared with Mike still lingered in her mind, making her both exhilarated and ashamed.

The sound of her husband's voice startled Lucia as she stood at the desk. Antonio switched on the lamp and approached her. "Why aren't you in the bedroom?" His tone was mild, his eyes inquisitive.

"I didn't want to go in there," Lucia said curtly, avoiding eye contact.

Antonio's brow furrowed. "Is something wrong?"

"I can't sleep in the same room as you anymore," she said emphatically, turning to face him.

Antonio's eyes widened in surprise. "What? Is this about me being late?"

"No, it's not that," Lucia replied, chewing on her lower lip. "I just feel like I need to be alone. I'm not sure if you understand."

"No, I don't understand. We've always slept in the same room since we got married,"

"I know, but I can't keep going like this," Lucia said firmly, her gaze locked with his. "I need my space. From now on, I'll be sleeping in another room," Lucia said, turning to leave, but Antonio grabbed her by the arm.

"It's not necessary." He blew up, the unfounded offense taking hold of every fiber of his being. "I will leave the bedroom and sleep in the guest room, or in the stables with the horses," he added and left.

Lucia sat back in her chair, exhaling the air she'd been holding under his menacing glare, and tried to compose herself. Tears welled in her eyes, yet she wasn't ready to cry. At the first hours of dawn, she entered her room, her eyes pointing towards the empty bed, and she sighed with relief.

The morning brought nothing but further quarrels at breakfast. Gabriella was the most affected as Antonio told her about spending the night in the guest room. "Yes, Gabriella, it's true," he said in a defensive tone. "I will be staying there because Lucia refuses to sleep in the same bed as me."

Gabriella jumped from her seat and headed for their bedroom, but Antonio stopped her. He didn't want to look like he was complaining about it. "She's your wife, and she's obligated to live with you," Gabriella whined.

"I will not pressure her because it will make things worse," Antonio said, resting his hands on the back of the chair and turning away from her gaze. "I think it's better this way. We have never been like a family together."

Gabriella emitted a nervous laugh. "No, Antonio, she has to change," she said as she approached to comfort him. "This must be something temporary. I will talk to her and make her realize how absurd this is," she added with a comforting smile.

"Don't insist too much, or she will start treating me worse," he warned, turning his gaze to Gabriella. She nodded before they said goodbye.

Gabriella headed for Lucia's bedroom. "Dominga, please leave me alone with Lucia. I need to talk to her in private," she ordered. The girl did as she was told and closed the door behind her.

Lucia looked in her mother's direction from the upholstered armchair she was curled up in, unsure if she was ready to face what was coming her way. "I know what you're going to tell me, and I'm begging you not to try and change my decision," Lucia said.

"Then at least explain to me what's happening," Gabriella said, cocking her head to one side. "You're undermining the stability of your marriage."

Lucia furrowed her brow in puzzlement. "You're calling this a marriage? It's one big nothing." Her voice was as stern as her gaze.

"Yes, it is a marriage. You've been married for over a year, and you can't ruin something so serious because of a whim," Gabriella said, raising her voice in a desperate attempt to knock some sense into her daughter.

"It's not a whim, Mother," Lucia exploded. "I don't want him near me because I'm tired." Tears pricked at her eyes. "I'm tired of listening to his breathing next to me, of seeing him every morning when I wake up."

"Lucia!" Gabriella exclaimed at her outburst.

"No, Mother, no! I can't anymore! I can't! I can't!" Lucia buried her face in her palms, trying to hide the scorching tears on her cheeks. "I feel this is only doing me harm, Mother, and I should have done it long ago."

"Lucia, you're not okay. Please calm down!" Gabriella's voice trembled with great concern.

"For my own good, and from respect to Antonio, it's better this way," Lucia continued. "If you want to throw me out of this house, well, do it!"

"This is nonsense you're talking." Gabriella approached her. She soothingly ran her hands on Lucia's gentle, wavy hair, trying to calm her down. "You're having a nervous breakdown. I will call a doctor."

"Don't act like I am crazy, Mama!" Lucia screamed. "I fully realize what I am talking about."

"No, I am not saying you're crazy. I am saying you are too nervous." Gabriella's heart sank in sorrow at the unprecedented state her daughter was drowning in. "I will find a way to help you. I promise," she whispered, heading for the door. She glimpsed once more at Lucia's sobbing and closed the door behind her.

She met Diego in the hallway. He threw a quizzical glance at her troubled expression. Gabriella entrusted Diego with her thoughts, quickly explaining the nightmarish morning she had experienced, and all the problems Lucia was going through.

"It's really that bad?" he asked.

"Yes, Diego! I don't know how to handle it." The desperation was evident in her voice.

Diego quickly agreed to speak with her and offered to take her out of the mansion. Perhaps Lucia needed some time away from the mansion.

"What an excellent idea! Are you going to do it for me?" Gabriella smiled gently, and Diego instinctively smiled back in agreement. He phoned Father Thomas to clear his morning and made his way to Lucia's room. He scanned the empty room and went to look for her outside.

Lucia was coming out of the servants' room with Mike, who was holding her hand instinctively. "See you tonight?" Mike asked hopefully.

"Mike, please let go of my hand! Someone might see us," Lucia said, looking around as she tried to pull her hand away.

"Are we going to meet?" he insisted. His hand slid down her cheek and came to rest gently on her chin, causing her heart to pound in her chest. It was risky, too risky even, but this made her alive again.

"I'll give you a sign!" she said slightly above a whisper.

Mike moved his eyes slightly over her head and noticed her brother, Diego, coming towards them. Lucia turned and feverishly tried to pluck her hand from his grip. Diego furrowed his brows in puzzlement as her hand finally slipped free. "I think we need to talk," Diego said curtly, his expression stone-cold, his eyes fixed on his sister. He took a short glance at Mike before he receded into the distance.

Chapter Twenty-two

As soon as they climbed the stairs, Lucia had to steady her steps beneath her brother's penetrating gaze on her back. She had to hurry and find a way to justify her behavior to her brother. She flew into the room and Diego slammed the door behind them.

"What do you want us to talk about?" Lucia answered evasively.

"Not that I particularly want to be involved, but you have to explain everything to me!" he said, his eyes filled with concern. "This morning, you were having a nervous meltdown, you sent your husband to the guest room, and now I find you talking to Mike Williams in a rather intimate setting," Diego stated.

Lucia furrowed her brow sullenly, inwardly cursing the fact no one in this house could keep their mouths shut. "No, we were talking normally," she replied, grateful at least half of what she was saying was true.

"Lucia, he was holding your hand! Why are you allowing him to take such liberties? Should I intervene?" Diego clenched his fist.

"What's wrong with you?" Lucia grumbled. "You're becoming like Mom." Her heart skipped a beat. "You're always looking for problems in everything." Diego emitted a nervous giggle, arched a brow at her, but didn't comment on what she had said. He turned to leave, but Lucia caught him by the arm at the door. "I'm sorry, Diego!" She gazed at him and cocked her head to one side. "I didn't mean to be rude. We're not going to argue over unimportant things, are we?" She plastered an apologetic smile on her face and hugged him tight.

"What's with the sentimentality?" Juan Pablo intervened.

"Nothing!" Lucia stepped back. "Can't I just show my love towards my older brother?" She grinned awkwardly.

"Yes, you can, of course. But don't forget you have another brother," he said, and Lucia hurriedly threw her arms around him too. "Listen, can I use your bathtub? Mine is clogged, and I need to send someone to fix it," Juan Pablo said excitedly. "I have a meeting with Penelope, and I can't keep her waiting," he added with a silly smile.

"Of course. Anytime you want." Lucia said and turned her attention to Diego. "Let's go out!" she suggested, grabbing her purse and leading Diego down the stairs.

"Where are we going?"

"We'll go shopping." She smiled at him as he rolled his eyes in great boredom.

As Lucia and her brother got into the car, she tried to drive past as close to Mike as she could. She rolled down the window. The same hunger as in the hotel room read in her eyes, as she buried her eyes into the side mirror as the car slowly drove away.

"Today you're in a joyful mood." Dominga smiled at him flirtatiously in the kitchen. "You're usually so serious. It's nice to see you like this for a change."

"Yes, he is," Jamie said. "Look at his sly smile." He gazed at Mike, who kept on having his lunch with no comment.

"The masters are happy too, for the engagement of Don Juan Pablo," she said, her mood elevating.

Jamie's stomach clenched at Dominga's words as she told them about the wedding plans in great detail. "Is there any news about it?" Jamie asked hesitantly.

"They already chose the date of the wedding. It's going to be in two months," she said in a gossipy tone before she continued with her duties.

"Two months?" The words echoed in Jamie's mind, and he struggled to hide his sullen demeanor. He didn't understand the game Juan Pablo was playing. He had asked Jamie to go out with him, although they hadn't for a week or so, and had shown interest in him, yet he kept on with this nonsense engagement party. The thought of his plans failing started to replay in his head and that made him even angrier at himself. And what did those supposedly secret looks from the terrace mean?

Jamie's mind was in a stupor. He thought of what could possibly save his plans from going down the drain. What was certain was that he wouldn't let Alvarez's money slip from his hands again. It was his future – he wouldn't be counting the last cents to buy bread or the nice shirt he wanted, or all the other millions of things he had to give up because of their poverty. What's more, Chloe would finally be avenged in a dignified manner.

"Guys?" Dominga called in the distance, interrupting his musings. "Does anyone know anything about plumbing?"

"Why?" Mike asked, finishing his lunch.

"Doña Lucia's bathtub is clogged, and someone needs to fix it," Dominga said.

"I'll come and check it," Mike hurriedly volunteered, raising from his seat, but Jamie caught him almost immediately. "No, you won't! Um… I know about these things," he added, with a trace of embarrassment in his expression.

"I'm going myself!" Mike repeated, his piercing gaze cutting through Jamie as he made another attempt to stop him.

"No, you'll stay here!" He curled his lips into a thin smile. "I don't want any trouble," Jamie hissed close to his ear and followed the girl, indecently looking at her bum every now and then.

Jamie slowly took in the sight of the marvelous room as Dominga left him alone in there. She informed him Lucia was out and he didn't have to hurry. On her way out, she offered him her services in case he needed anything. Jamie gazed at the bed, the furniture, and all the small things, which must cost a fortune. He turned back when Dominga closed the door behind her. *Here is how the wealthy live,* Jamie said to himself, admiring the opulent furnishings. He couldn't help but plaster a smile on his face at the thought that, one day, he might have it all. Or at least part of it, if he played his cards well. Jamie made his way to the bathroom, but as soon as he opened the door, the intense wave of heat and steam hit him in the face. "Of course it will clog," he murmured to himself as he surveyed the thick layer of foam in the bathtub. He took off his vest and kneeled beside the tub, searching for the drain with his hand.

"What the fuck?" Jamie jumped back in surprise when his fingers grabbed a leg under the foam.

"Jamie?" Juan Pablo pulled back the curtain. "What are you doing here?"

"I... I didn't know you were here," Jamie stammered, his cheeks turning crimson. "I came to fix the bathtub. Dominga said it was broken."

"Yes, it is, but it's mine," Juan Pablo pouted.

"Dominga said it was your sister's, so she's the stupid one," Jamie retorted, turning his left side to Juan Pablo while surreptitiously peeking at him. "Why didn't you say something when I came in?"

"I was snoozing," Juan Pablo replied, his irritation evident. "And why didn't you say something?"

"I couldn't see you under this mountain of foam."

"Instead of arguing, you better leave!" Juan Pablo ordered.

"Of course I will. I won't stay and watch you. I'm not some kind of pervert!" Jamie said, offended. As he turned to leave, he slipped on the scattered foam and fell flat on his back. He grunted in pain just as Juan Pablo jumped out of the water, completely naked.

"Oh my God! Are you okay? Are you hurt?" Juan Pablo exclaimed.

"It's because of the fucking foam," Jamie replied, more irritated than hurt at having made a fool of himself. "The whole floor is slippery." As he tried to stand up, Jamie rested on his hand for a moment and instinctively looked at Juan Pablo. "Oh my God!" Jamie gaped at him, longer than he intended.

Juan Pablo caught his stare and quickly grabbed his towel from the curtain rail, wrapping it around his waist. "Don't look at me!" Juan Pablo grunted in embarrassment.

"Then why didn't you stay in the bath?" Jamie snorted, averting his eyes.

Juan Pablo went to Jamie, crouched down, and helped him stand up. "Careful! Like this!"

"I might have broken a bone. It hurts like hell," Jamie groaned as he tried to roll over to his other side, his face an inch away from Juan Pablo's naked chest. "It smells so nice," he mumbled. The bathroom filled with the warm breath of vapor, it transformed into a realm where seconds lingered like hesitant dreams, and reality gently dissolved in the mist. The citrus scent made Jamie dizzy, and he parted his lips to breathe it in. The bathroom's warmth cast a sensual spell that left them lost in the intimacy as Jamie brazenly gazed at the droplets glistened on Juan Pablo's skin, tracing a path from the nape of his necks to the curve of his shoulders.

"Juan Pablo!" Gabriella called from the other room.

"Dios mio!" Juan Pablo nearly choked on the damp air. Jamie turned his head to the other side, hardly hearing Gabriella's footsteps as the embarrassment paralyzed his mind. His heartbeat accelerated in no time, as his eyes momentarily dwelled on Juan Pablo, who stood frozen in his spot, holding his breath.

"Juan Pablo?" Gabriella opened the bathroom door. "Why didn't you respond?"

"I didn't hear you, Mama!" He smiled anxiously, bending over the sink, and pretending to look at himself in the mirror.

"Before you go out with Penelope, I'd like you to help me with the estate accounts." She looked at the wrinkled carpet and the towels on the floor. "Oh, for God's sake, what is this mess?"

"I'll tidy up immediately. It's not right to leave Lucia's bathroom like this," he said, grinning apologetically.

"Hurry up!" she commanded sternly. "It's unbelievable. Why do you always have to turn everything upside down?" Gabriella cast one last scolding look and left.

Juan Pablo nervously exhaled and kneeled beside the bathtub, gently shaking Jamie. "You can come out now."

The water splashed, and Jamie gasped for air, his lungs filling with damp air as he breathed erratically. He swiftly removed the foam from his eyes and ran his hands back through his wet hair. His chest heaved as he struggled to catch his breath, drawing Juan Pablo's curious gaze.

"I am so terribly sorry, but I had to do it! Mother would not have accepted any explanations." Juan Pablo bit his lower lip and furrowed his brows, panic and satisfaction battling on his face.

"Good thing I didn't drown." Jamie coughed, with a pouty face on, trying to come to his senses after being subjected to this ordeal.

Chapter Twenty-three

Rafaela Mendoza and Penelope had arrived at the Alvarez mansion to finalize the details of the engagement party scheduled for the following night. "For God's sake, can you help me out here? I'm all by myself and no matter what I say, nobody seems to like it," Rafaela whined, casting a pleading look at Penelope.

"I can't meddle in your affairs. We must respect our elders," Penelope said shyly.

Juan Pablo's family listened in silence as the old woman voiced her complaints. "First, they refused to host the celebration at home, and now they're saying we can't invite anyone," the woman said, her hand trembling on her cane.

"You can invite your closest friends, but not everyone," Antonio said politely, his smile unwavering. "We want to keep the gathering small and intimate, not an opulent affair," he added.

"Antonio, my family is large, and I don't want to offend anyone," Rafaela replied, looking at him intently.

"We all know you have a battalion of relatives." Isabella fixed her with a stern gaze. "Invite only those who truly care about you. You can count them on one hand." She lifted her chin with a satisfied smile.

Rafaela's mouth gaped open, her eyes squinted, and she turned to her niece, expecting Penelope to defend her, but she stood there meekly, blinking rapidly. "You may burst with envy, but even the most distant of my relatives adore me," she snorted in response. Isabella nodded sarcastically, and the conversation continued with no further comments.

"If you think the guest list is too long, Rafaela can hold the engagement party at her own house," Juan Pablo proposed, looking at his mother, who appeared to have the final say.

"I accept, Rafaela! Invite all your relatives and friends. They will be warmly welcomed in my home," she declared graciously.

With all the final details accordingly planned, Penelope beckoned her fiancé to join her for a stroll around the hacienda. Juan Pablo was surprised at her insistence on walking towards the stables, but he agreed, knowing it would give him a chance to see Jamie. The two were cooing at each other before Penelope finally stopped, transfixed by the sight of Jamie. "I have to admit, your boyfriend looks cooler in work clothes than he does when he's dressed up," she blurted out.

"What nonsense are you talking about?"

She grinned. "Oh, come on, I know you're secretly seeing him while we're going out," she teased mischievously, a little impish glint in her eyes.

"How could you betray me? Were you following me?" His blood rushed to his head. For the first time he felt an uncontrollable surge to slap a woman. Lightning flickered in his eyes, as though he were threatening to turn her to ashes.

"Only last night, but don't worry! I was curious to know who you've been meeting all this time," she reassured him with a wicked grin. "I'm okay with it, seriously."

"So you won't tell anyone?" he replied, his voice softer, his eyes pleading.

"Of course not! I mean, if it were someone of our social status, it would have been better, but your boyfriend most certainly passed the test." She gave him an approving look and bit her lower lip. "Your family would fall into a panic if they ever found out about this," she said, not taking her eyes off Jamie.

"No, my mother will kill me," Juan Pablo said, also glancing in Jamie's direction. "And, to be clear, he's not my boyfriend," Juan Pablo had to clarify, looking around in concern, as Penelope wasn't exactly discreet. For a moment, he regretted telling her about his sexuality or even getting into this giant ball of mess.

"Hey, buddy, come here!" she called out to Jamie.

Juan Pablo nudged her involuntarily, intimidated and exasperated. "What are you doing?" he asked through clenched teeth, his body temperature rising to a hundred degrees.

"Relax! We'll be one big family soon," she said, smiling pleasantly as Jamie approached.

"How can I help you, miss?" Jamie took off his hat and glanced quickly at Juan Pablo, who wished the earth would split open and swallow him.

"When we're alone, you can call me Penelope. It doesn't feel quite right to be called 'miss'," she said, grinning as Jamie looked at Juan Pablo in confusion, chewing on a stick of straw. "What countenance is that?" Penelope arched a brow at Jamie. "Don't worry, I completely approve of your relationship with Juan

Pablo," she added, winking at him and grinning from ear to ear.

"You approve of what now?" Mike roared from a couple of feet behind.

Jamie froze in place and widened his eyes in utmost embarrassment. He lowered his gaze, sensing the impending thunderstorm in Mike's voice. The piercing gaze of Mike's eyes fell like two arrows right into the middle of Jamie's back. For the first time, Jamie didn't even want to be close to his brother. His heart raced in his chest. He wasn't going to get away with just a slightly bleeding nose this time.

Juan Pablo paled and nudged Penelope as she took a few staggering steps aside. He glared at her, grabbed her by the arm, and dashed back towards the house. "What's wrong with you?" she whimpered at the hard squeeze, struggling to keep up with Jamie as he hurried ahead. A few inquisitive eyes followed them as they passed by, and she smiled awkwardly at the workers.

"Shut up and keep moving!" Juan Pablo growled. Mike's distraught look made his heart sink, and for a moment, he wanted to go back and explain what his fiancée had said, but he didn't dare. He had no idea what to say.

Mike and Jamie barely exchanged any words in the car on the way home. When they arrived, Mike slammed the door to the house, almost knocking it off its hinges, and called for Chloe in the living room. His eyes filled with fury, like a predator ready to attack. Jamie's nerves were as tense as guitar strings about to snap.

"What's going on, Mike?" Chloe stood before them, awaiting explanation.

"Speak up!" Mike turned to his brother, who sat guiltily in his chair. "Why are you silent? Are you ashamed?" he added sarcastically.

"I have nothing to be ashamed of! I have done nothing wrong," Jamie snapped, wishing he had sounded more convincing.

"Okay, that's enough! Can someone please explain what's going on!" Chloe roared desperately.

Mike gritted his teeth, trying hard to contain his anger. "Remember when you told me Jamie had a date a few weeks ago? Well, I now know who it was with," he said through clenched teeth. Jamie looked at him contritely, his eyes pleading for him not to continue. "Juan Pablo Alvarez! Lucia's brother. Our brother turned out to be gay." Mike closed his eyes as if trying to erase those words from his memory, as much as he wanted to erase the scene in the hacienda. In a split second, Mike's anger exploded like a looming volcano, and he punched Jamie, sending him flying over the table.

"That's absurd! An absolute lie! This Penelope, or whatever she calls herself, doesn't know what she's talking about. Let me explain!" Jamie rolled to the other side of the table, trying to avoid getting too close to his brother as Chloe stood before him, trying to defend him.

"Explain? What is there to explain? I heard her! She spoke as if I was aware." Mike pounced on him, grabbing his jacket, and shaking him violently before Jamie could escape his brother's grip.

"Mike, please stop!" Chloe begged him, squeezed between them and frightened.

When Mike let go of his brother, he grabbed the vase from the table and smashed it against the wall before reconsidering and redirecting his anger towards Jamie. "Now you're going to tell us everything!" Mike tried to calm himself. "Where have you been seeing each other, what have you been doing, and God help you if you've done anything stupid," he added.

"I'm not going to tell you anything," Jamie snorted, straightening the collar of his worn jacket. "It's not what you think it is! It's part of the plan!" he continued. "And why should I tell you anything when you don't do it either? When was the last time you told us anything about Lucia Alvarez?" His inner self applauded him for standing up to his brother without flinching.

Mike narrowed his eyes and walked over to Jamie. "Listen to me, you silly rascal. Do whatever you want! You can sleep with him for all I care! But if I ever find out you're doing this for money, or even worse, if you jeopardize my relationship with Lucia in any way..." Mike glared at him, the zing in his eyes dangerously going through Jamie's body. "I swear to almighty God, you will never set foot in this house again." He let go of the lapels of Jamie's jacket and marched to his room.

Jamie spent the night in Chloe's room as suggested. With Chloe sleeping over at a friend's place, Jamie had hoped the awkward situation would be gone by morning. Despite the turmoil he had experienced the entire evening, he peacefully fell asleep without any further drama.

Chapter Twenty-four

"Oh my God!" Juan Pablo adjusted his tie at the window, watching the crowd of people arriving. "This isn't a close family gathering, it's a whole wedding," he whimpered.

"You look tense," Diego said nonchalantly.

"I have a good reason. It's not every day you get engaged." Juan Pablo threw a last glance at the mirror to make sure his tie was straight.

"Think carefully about what you're doing! You still have a chance to stop this madness!" Diego looked at Juan Pablo's reflection in the mirror.

"Not the best time to tell me that. The yard is full of people!" Juan Pablo sighed.

"Yes, you're right. It's too late now." Diego turned to his brother, concerned. "Soon, you will be betrothed to Penelope Hernandez, and her husband eventually," he said succinctly, smoothing the sleeves of his brother's suit.

Lucia and Antonio passed through the crowd of guests in the salon, each holding a glass. Most of the invitees were strangers and having to smile through this impending disaster annoyed Lucia to the very core. And the presence of her husband only made her state worse if that was at all possible. "Where's Mom?" she asked, scanning the many heads in front of her.

"Probably in your annoying grandma's room! As always, scandal is inevitable when she's around,"

Antonio said curtly. Lucia glared at him for a moment but didn't comment on his biting remark, choosing instead to continue smiling thinly at the guests.

Gabriella had blocked the door to the room with her body as her mother cried out in her presence. "For God's sake, are you going to lock me in here again like a piece of junk? Get out of my way!" Isabella roared.

"I won't let you go downstairs in those clothes. You look like..." Gabriella paused and pressed her lips together.

"I will dress as I want."

"Unless you change, you're not going downstairs!"

"If you don't back away from the door, I will scream so loud that everyone will know what I think about Juan Pablo's engagement to that crocodile," Isabella threatened flatly. Gabriella sighed deeply. She was desperately trying to convince her mother not to be the center of attention for the evening and not to disparage Rafaela and her family. "The only way I can stay here is with a bottle of tequila and a deck of cards," Isabella murmured. "And since I have neither, I'm going downstairs at once."

Gabriella was dumbfounded by her mother's behavior, rolling her eyes in exasperation. Gabriella suggested she call a maid from the dining room, but her mother raised her eyebrows in disapproval. "No, what am I going to do with her? It'll be as dull as being alone. You'd better call me the two young men – the brothers – Mike and Jamie!"

Gabriella arched her brows quizzically, ready to fulfil her mother's every whim. "Is this your last wish?" Isabella nodded, and Gabriella dashed out of the room before Rafaela and her niece arrived.

She ran to the servants' room where the two brothers were preparing to leave. She urgently asked them to go up to her mother's room and try to keep her company before she got downstairs and ruined everything. Once they were back in the house lounge, Gabriella grabbed a bottle of booze from the waiter's tray and headed up the stairs with the two brothers following her.

Antonio could hardly understand what these peasants were doing at a celebration like this. He clenched his jaw tightly, catching Lucia's brazen gaze at Mike. He gently caressed his wife's cheek as a powerful wave of insecurity threatened to drown him. Startled by her own acts, Lucia turned to him. Her gaze had been fixed in the wrong direction for too long. She quickly mumbled an apology and retreated to the kitchen in dire hope of calming her nerves after the unexpected encounter with Mike.

Once in the room, Gabriella closed the door behind Mike and Jamie. "Here's your drink and the cards," Gabriella hissed. "Do you have any other requests?" Her eyes, like daggers, pierced through the deep V-neck of her mother's dress.

"It's unbelievable!" Isabella exclaimed. "In your eagerness to stop me from mingling with those idiots, you're willing to do anything for me."

Gabriella glared at her once more and asked the boys to keep Isabella occupied. Mike and Jamie looked at the woman, intimidation sparkling in their eyes by her appearance. "Make yourselves comfortable, guys!" Isabella shuffled the cards and plastered a satisfied smile on her face. "One way or another, this witch, my daughter, has brought you here, so let's have some fun."

The hands of the clock struck eight o'clock on the dot when Rafaela and her niece arrived, accompanied by her daughter, Alicia. The young girl was slender and elegant with long, straight burgundy hair and enchanting chestnut eyes. The elegant black dress she wore made her look a couple of inches taller and irresistibly attractive. Penelope immediately went to Juan Pablo, who had already had a bit too much to drink.

"My cousin, Alicia, is also here," she snorted, taking a glass from the walking waiter who kept the guests refreshed. "I can't stand her! She's so puffed up and spoiled, being an only child." Her eyes flickered with envy and she had her first drink in one go.

"You're jealous she'll inherit all the money from your aunt!" Juan Pablo teased, watching the funny face she made from the aftertaste of the cognac.

"No! When we get married, she will leave a large portion of her wealth to me," Penelope said enthusiastically. Juan Pablo rolled his eyes in disbelief but chose not to comment.

The night rolled on imperceptibly as it was well past midnight when Jamie and Mike decided to leave, trying to go unnoticed as they passed through the guests. Doña Isabella was sound asleep in her bed, having drunk too much herself. Outside, the music was playing loudly, and Juan Pablo was dancing with his fiancée, lively and joyful. "What a hypocrite." Jamie gritted his teeth, while Mike gazed helplessly at Lucia, who was standing at one of the tables with her husband. As Lucia rose from her seat, her mesmerizing eyes sank into Mike's. A frantic desire to embrace him coursed through her mind. Her lips parted as if ready to lay them on Mike's. Her stomach churned at the chain of thoughts in her head.

The light from the lamp posts and sconce illuminated her bright, off-shoulder, tight dress. She was perfect.

"What do you think you're doing?" Jamie walked back to Mike. "It's after midnight, and we have a long way to go."

"Get the car and go!"

"You can't stay here!" Jamie grabbed his jacket sleeve. "You're coming with me."

Mike yanked furiously to free himself from Jamie's grip. "I told you to go. What don't you understand?" he snapped, leaving Jamie with no choice but to obey to avoid a scene in front of everyone.

"What an idiot," he murmured to himself. "He's not even hiding." He looked back at his brother who stared at Lucia in front of everyone.

Mike watched the car drive away and headed for the empty barn. The sound of retreating heels on the cement path made him aware of someone following him and he knew well who it was. When he reached the stables, he turned around, fixing his eyes on her V-neck. She smiled at him, provoking an immediate, lustful response. He turned and walked ahead to the barn, and she followed. With every step she took, her heartbeat accelerated like a race car at the start line, the sweetness of the moment guiding her. Mike left the door ajar as a dark shadow appeared before the door.

Mike turned around, towards the creaking sound of the wooden door. The fire ignited for a split second, burning in their loins, as Mike pulled her abruptly into his embrace. He caressed her shoulders, leaning in for a deep, passionate kiss under the scattered light entering through the holes of the wooden walls. Running his fingers down her back, he unzipped her dress, freeing her breasts from their tight confinement. Mike longed for her skin burning under his fingers, and before she could even gasp, his teeth gently gripped her nipple. His tongue made a few full circles around it before he slid his lips up her shoulder and neck. Lucia lifted her leg slightly up his leg, and his hands instinctively slid down her thigh. The heat of every inch of her chiseled body made him groan in her mouth. Lucia's light moan sent a thin stream of air into his ear, getting him ready to possess her right there among the bales of straw and hay. The thought drove him to new mind-blowing heights as he pressed his manhood against her belly, causing her to moan loudly at his hard erection. Lucia pulled her head back, and in one swift motion, she jumped and wrapped her legs around his hips. She wanted to quell this passion, no matter how risky it was. Mike's cool hands roamed over her buttocks, trying to reach her vagina. The new revelation was driving her crazy and as much as she combated her instincts, she could only let out a strangled moan.

"Mike, don't," she whispered hesitantly, but her body betrayed her as his fingers shamelessly wandered around her womanhood. She pressed her breasts tightly against his cool denim jacket, welcoming his touch. She buried her nose in his hair and wrapped her arms tightly around his neck, lost in the intensity of the moment.

Mike responded by delving deeper, and she took a sharp breath as the tip of his finger slid inside her. She moaned lightly in his ear, urging him to go faster. The heat between them intensified, and their eyes locked in a fierce gaze as they were consumed by passion. He pulled her into a fiery kiss, their tongues tangling together in a passionate embrace. They were lost in each other, the world around them fading away until they were the last two people left on the planet. As they finally broke apart, gasping for air, she knew there was no going back. With him, she had found a passion she had never known before.

As if encapsulated in a bubble, they were surrounded by their love and the raw intensity of their connection, completely oblivious to the men who had followed them.

Chapter Twenty-five

Diego paced around his room, trying to process what he had witnessed the previous night. As his mind raced with questions, he knew he couldn't wait any longer for answers. He hurried into Lucia's room, still in his robe, and fixed his gaze intently on her as she was buttoning her white blouse.

"I saw you last night." His voice was cruel and vicious that made her tremble. Confused, she stared back, unsure of what he meant. "In Mike Williams' embrace," he clarified. Lucia's face drained of color as she quickly shut the door behind her brother. "I couldn't believe what I saw," Diego continued, his voice rising. "You were hiding a few steps away from your family and dozens of guests in the garden." Diego's eyes flickered with a mix of rage and disappointment, while Lucia buried her gaze on the floor with embarrassment. "How could you stoop that low?" he snapped loudly, causing her to lift her eyes to meet his. "Have you forgotten you're a married woman?"

"What? Are you surprised to see me with a man like him?" Lucia retorted. "Are you going to judge me now?"

Diego turned away from her, his anger burning like a wildfire, consuming everything in its path. Ever since the day he saw them hold hands, Lucia had given him reasons to doubt her.

"I was convinced you wouldn't understand me," Lucia muttered.

"I probably would understand if it was another man," Diego said, his tone heavy with anger. "Your marriage is clearly not a successful one. You deserve to fall in love. But he's just a simple groom," he added with disgust. Lucia's mouth dropped open as she stared at him in disbelief. "We come from a rich family, we are well-educated, and have dignity. How could you get involved with this guy, Lucia?"

"Mike is a decent man!" Lucia protested.

"If he were, he would have respected you and stayed away from you." Diego waved his finger at her. "How could he have trapped you so much?"

"I was the one who first showed interest in him," Lucia admitted, turning away. She couldn't bring herself to look her brother in the eyes.

"You're lying to protect him."

"It's true! I was the one!" Lucia exploded. She paused and took a deep breath before turning to face Diego. She knew she had to tell him the whole truth, to pull out the thorn that was pricking her heart. "You know why? Because he's the first man I've ever truly liked," she admitted out loud for the very first time. She nervously swallowed and tears welled up in her eyes.

"Did you sleep with him?" Diego asked, unaware of whether he would be able to control his reactions.

"Yes! Several times!" Lucia answered. "And every time I experienced supreme delight," she added, her voice trailing off.

Diego turned his back to her, ran his fingers over his chin, and closed his eyes. The memory of last night flashed into his mind, and the next second, he turned around with his palm wide open. Lucia screamed in pain as her head jerked to one side. "You are shameless!" Diego yelled in Lucia's face. "I swear I will tell everything to Mom and to Antonio," he threatened, his words spilling like venom.

"Very well! Go ahead and tell them if you think it's righteous. I don't care!" Lucia screamed at him before the door opened, and their mother walked in.

"What's going on here?" Gabriella looked at them, puzzled. "What are these cries?"

Lucia went to her brother, stood beside him, and they both stared blankly at her quizzical face. "Diego has something to tell you!" she prompted him.

"What is it, Diego?" Gabriella fixed her gaze on him.

"Nothing. Lucia and I will take a short ride around the hacienda," he said, tightening the sash of his robe. "I'll saddle the horses!" he declared, as he headed towards the door.

It didn't take long for Lucia to get into her riding attire, and soon she was slowly riding her horse alongside her brother, Diego, who appeared much calmer now.

"Why didn't you reveal my secret?" she asked meekly.

"I'm hoping to change your mind and help you see reason."

Lucia took a long pause before speaking again. "You have no idea how I feel, Diego."

Diego's eyes locked onto hers like magnets, holding her in place. He stopped his horse and dismounted. "This is an ignoble passion, an animal attraction! You may have wallowed with this man, but now you must put a stop to it," he declared. "We'll ask Mother to dismiss them, and that will be the end of this embarrassing problem," he added.

"Yes, you're right!" she said. "Mike will leave the mansion, but not my thoughts." She attended to a few tendrils of hair smashing against her face from the wind.

"Lucia, listen to yourself. You're behaving as if you're insane," Diego exclaimed, rolling his eyes. "How could you replace Antonio with a man like this?" He gazed at her face and caught a glimpse of a thin, nervous smile on her lips. "Antonio is a gentleman, with refined tastes and, above all, he's your husband," he added with emphatic tone.

"He can be all of those things, but Mike is special to me," Lucia insisted.

"You can't be serious," Diego said, shaking his head in disbelief. "It sounds ridiculous."

"I'm not a little girl, and I'm not afraid. I won't give up, and I will defend my rights."

"Your rights?" Diego repeated eagerly. "Would you care to explain what your rights are?"

Lucia gazed at him sternly. "Explain? Well, I have the right to be happy, to make mistakes, to live my life!" She raised her voice. "Even if everyone points a guilty finger at me, with you leading the charge. These are my rights!"

Diego let out a heavy sigh and turned away for a moment, pressing his lips together before facing Lucia again. "I can't believe it. First Juan Pablo, and now you. How are these men doing it?" he asked rhetorically in frustration.

Lucia glanced at him, bewildered. "Juan Pablo? What does he have to do with this?"

"What does it matter? In one way or another, he's going to get married to Penelope," Diego replied, sounding resigned. He furrowed his brows at her, both from the merciless sun and the mild anger still rippling through his body. It was pointless to keep insisting. He jumped onto his horse and turned to her. "I'm not going to say anything more, but sooner or later, the truth will come out. And when that moment comes, remember I warned you, and don't count on me for help." He spurred his horse as the fresh summer wind beat against his face.

Lucia's family gathered in the dining room, which was like a pressure cooker. Although her brother had reassured her he would keep quiet, she kept adjusting in her seat. She took another big sip of wine as if trying to wash away the guilt stuck in her throat. The palpable tension between them could be cut off with a knife, yet everyone ate in silence. Antonio threw quick glares at his wife from time to time, inwardly cursing her betrayal. The strained feelings came in waves, each higher and more destructive than the previous. Yet, he managed to compose himself and avoided looking at her too often. The only one who spoke was Juan Pablo, who was in a good mood. "Ah, peace finally reigns!" he exclaimed, sipping his wine.

"Yes, everything is back to normal." Gabriella smiled with satisfaction. "Even my mother hasn't given us a hard time today."

"After last night and all the alcohol, she sleeps like a baby." Dominga poured more wine for Diego and Gabriella.

"You know what they say, after the storm comes the calm," Antonio said with a slight smile, casting an askance glance at his wife.

"I don't believe the calm will last long," Diego said, catching Lucia's stare. "Something tells me the storm is yet to come," he added grimly, taking a sip of his wine. Lucia threw her napkin on the table and headed for the door.

"What's going on?" Gabriella asked. "Today you two are acting weird. Is there a problem?"

"Yes, there is," Diego replied, standing up from the table and leaving his plate full. "But the problem is not mine."

After dinner, Antonio headed towards what was once their bedroom. He sighed heavily before entering, in dire need of keeping his composure. The fact that Diego knew of his sister's cheating made him look like a fool, and he was more than determined to seek his right.

"What do you want?" Lucia jumped out of bed, brushing her wet hair.

"To talk," Antonio said. "Don't you think it's time to put an end to this farce once and for all?" His eyes full of intent, his presumptuous behavior making her muscles clench for a moment. "How long are we going to sleep in separate rooms, Lucia?" He clenched his fist in fury.

"I thought you were used to it."

Antonio arched an eyebrow at her, his cheeks burning with barely contained rage. He swallowed hard. "For the time being, maybe," he said shortly. "I've been waiting for your crisis to subside, but this agony can't continue indefinitely."

"You're right," she agreed, staring at him for a moment. "Antonio, I want a divorce," she stated flatly.

He moved closer to her, pressing his lips into a thin line. He could no longer control his emotions, and he gritted his teeth in frustration. After a moment, he reminded himself to stay calm. "I'm trying to get closer to you, and you're asking me for a divorce," he said, his eyes flashing like lightning against the dark sky.

Lucia's blood froze in her veins as his expression changed. "Antonio, please leave! Just go!" Lucia pointed towards the door.

"I left you alone for too long. Now, I'll take my rightful place as your husband. And if you deny me, I'll have to use force." Lucia screamed in terror as he threw her onto the bed. He quickly took off his suit jacket. "You will accept me as your husband and get to know me as a man," he hissed in a fit of rage. He threw himself on top of her as Lucia vigorously started throwing punches to push him away. His body was too heavy for her, and his lips sent shivers down her spine.

"Leave me alone!" she screamed at him, digging her nails into his neck. Antonio got up from the bed and lightly touched the scratches she had made.

The traces of blood on the tip of his finger woke up his demons. "Is that how you want it?" Antonio gazed at her like a beast ready to pounce. "Is that how you want me to do it?" He slapped her, and she fell hard back onto the bed.

"Antonio!" Gabriella burst into the room with Isabella. Antonio rolled his eyes at their startling entrance and hurriedly got off the bed.

"What did you do to my granddaughter?" Isabella screamed at him, her voice filled with fury. Antonio grabbed his jacket and left without a word, leaving Gabriella trying to process what had just happened. "Did he hurt you, sweetheart?" Isabella sat on the bed, and Lucia rested her head on her chest, crying desolately.

"He didn't do anything to me, but I don't want him anywhere near me. Otherwise, I am capable of the worst," Lucia cried out.

That night, Isabella left to spend the night with her and when the morning came, the first thing Gabriella did was to confront Antonio about his actions. She had known him for a long time and knew he wasn't capable of harming anyone, but she was shocked by his unacceptable behavior.

Diego grasped a few words of their conversation from behind a pillar in the salon, trying to remain unnoticed. The remorse gripped his whole being as he went to his grandma's room, knowing she would tell him everything about the tussle from the previous night between the two of them. As she finished recounting the events, Diego sank in the pool of devastation and regret for having urged Antonio to take control of his marriage. He sat on the sofa in the small hall on the second floor for a long time, waves of guilt crashing down on him. He couldn't bear the ordeal and had to speak with his sister.

He found Lucia taking a bath, and she stood there with indifference in her eyes, or worse, a disdain towards her own brother. Diego lingered before her, leaning against the wooden door, which made Lucia even more irritated. "I can't stop thinking about the situation you're in," he finally said.

Lucia put her hand on her forehead, as if deep in thought. She stared at the wall ahead, avoiding eye contact with her brother. "I assume you know what happened, and I guess you're taking Antonio's side," Lucia replied, her tone bitter.

"You fight like a lioness when he tries to touch you," Diego said, gazing intently at her. The hesitation in his voice echoed in Lucia's ears.

"I cannot stand his attitude," she said with a hint of residual rage in her voice she thought would never dissipate. "His actions last night reminded me of what those men did to me. You know what? To prevent it from ever happening again, I'm capable of the worst."

Diego nervously swallowed and began. "When you were with Mike, do you remember that night?"

Lucia's face brightened and her eyes started glowing. She ran her hands over her shoulders, as if remembering the way he kissed them. "No, I feel the exact opposite with him," she said, a gentle tone in her voice. "He helps me forget this moment. He's gentle, incapable of harming me. Sometimes he seems like a grown kid. I love him and long for him." She opened her eyes, blazing with desire. She'd been lost in thoughts of lust and passion. "I know my words disgust you, so you'd better leave," she said, gazing at him with her knees bent to her chest.

"I don't know what to think, Lucia," Diego said timidly. "I don't want to judge whether what you're doing is right or wrong." His voice trailed off as he stared out the window for a moment. "What I am sure of, though, is that I can't turn against you." A small smile appeared on his lips, breaking his otherwise serious expression. "You're my sister." He paused, his eyes wandering around the room before settling on her. "I have my principles, and I don't condone your behavior, but I'm also not going to stigmatize you." He turned his gaze back to her. His tone was louder and more emphatic. "I just wanted to assure you of that," he said and left.

Chapter Twenty-six

"A divorce. She wants a divorce so she can openly fly into his arms," Antonio raged in the car while driving to a suburban bar in the city to meet an old friend.

He arrived a little early and nervously waited for him. The man, dressed in a black coat and a semi-wide brim hat of the same color, couldn't be missed as he marched through the door. "Armando, man, how long has it been?" He greeted him with a friendly pat on the back.

"Since you ditched me after your marriage," Armando replied with a laugh as they took their seats at the table.

The two friends caught up on old times and almost didn't notice the waiter taking their drinks order. They talked for hours before Antonio brought up the topic of his marriage, quickly filling Armando in on the hell he had been going through for the past year or so. "Not a lucky man!" Armando said with a grim expression.

"Well, it's about to get worse when I tell you what I saw last night," Antonio said, taking a sip of his brandy. "My wife, who I thought would never even look at another man, cheated on me with a simple wastrel who happens to work on the hacienda." Armando leaned back in his chair, taking a full minute to absorb the news. "And you know what I do with my enemies," Antonio said in a low voice.

"Of course!" Armando rested his elbows on the table. "And I know just the right people," he said, a wicked smile forming on his face. "It's good you haven't done anything stupid. I know you well."

"It was hard to keep my composure, but…"

"Well, you take care of your wife. Make her fulfill her marital duties, and as for Mike Williams, leave him to me!" Armando said, putting his hand reassuringly on Antonio's shoulder. "But, for the time being, try not to be a thorn in your wife's side," Armando said, taking a sip of his beer. "She shouldn't see you as an enemy."

"What am I supposed to do?" Antonio raised his voice as hesitation appeared in his gaze. "Give her a divorce and let her go to him?"

"Of course not!" Armando said tersely. "Make her feel guilty. Play the victim," he said, the same wicked smile on his face.

Antonio considered his friend's words. Maybe he was right. After all, his wife held the key to his opulent lifestyle. Without her, he would lose a lot of wealth. For the rest of their meeting, they chatted about more casual topics, lazily drinking their drinks, and even flirted with the women at the neighboring table.

It was well past eight when Antonio finally arrived home. His disheveled appearance sparked the sickest of feelings in Gabriella, who met him at the entrance.

"Is it right to come home at this hour?" Gabriella furrowed her brows in disapproval.

"I have no wife to keep tabs on me," he snapped. "And I insist you don't either!" he added bitingly, almost knocking her over as he barged past her into the house.

Antonio stumbled through the elegant halls of his opulent estate, his mind clouded with a mix of fury and despair. His eyes fell upon Lucia, standing in the grand dining room, her slender figure bathed in the soft glow of the chandelier above. A surge of conflicting emotions gripped him as he approached her, his unsteady steps echoing in the silence. "I don't know if the moment is right, but I want to apologize for my actions." He stood by the door, watching her sip her juice.

"I have no wish to talk to you!" Lucia stated firmly. "You're drunk."

"No, I'm not," he approached her. His breath hit her face and made her stomach churn at the stench.

"Please, just go to your room."

"You keep denying me closeness," he said, grabbing her by the arm as she tried to leave. "Let's talk about our marriage."

"No! Our topic of conversation could be our divorce," she said, gazing at him sternly.

"So that's what you want!" he said, grabbing the glass from the table and throwing it on the floor where it shattered into pieces. He snatched her by the arm; her heart pounded in her chest, and she froze under his stare. "We'll divorce, but it will be my way!"

"Antonio, let go of her!" Gabriella ran into the room with Dominga, completely mortified.

"I won't hurt her! I know I shouldn't do it," Antonio said through clenched teeth.

"Lucia, go to your room!" Gabriella commanded. "Leave us alone."

Lucia quickly did what she was told, fear crawling on her face. She'd never seen her husband like this before. Gabriella ordered Dominga to fetch a tranquilizer.

"She's only talking about divorce, Gabriella," Antonio said desperately. "But I won't give her a divorce. I'll stay in the guest room, but I won't divorce her."

"Antonio, sit down!" Gabriella pulled out a chair from under the table. "You're drunk!"

"Yes, I am. But I drank because of her!" He paused for a moment. The tipsiness made his stomach muscles clench. "I cannot turn my back on her, as she did," he murmured.

Gabriella shook her head in despair. "For God's sake, Antonio, stop talking nonsense. The servants might hear. I won't go through another scandal."

"Gabriella, they already know. Everyone knows that Lucia wants nothing to do with me!" He slammed his hand hard on the table in fury as Dominga entered with a tray of tranquilizers and a bottle of water.

"Dominga, keep an eye on him until I settle things with Marcello," she said and rushed through the door. Dominga nodded. Antonio gazed at her, his eyes blurred and red. He screamed at her to get back to her business, and she did as she was told.

At last, he was alone. He smiled wickedly, staring into emptiness. "Things couldn't have unfolded better than they did," he mumbled. "Now, it's showtime!" he said as he swallowed the entire bottle of pills with a half glass of water.

Twisting and turning, he made his way to the stables. His wrath resurfaced in a split second at the sight of the two brothers. "You're finished with your work here!" he screamed at them. "Your services are no longer required. Don't you hear me?"

Mike crossed his arms over his chest and gazed at him sternly. "You'll have to speak to Doña Gabriella, because she's the one who hired us," Jamie murmured.

"Neither she nor I have hired you! You were sent by the agency!" He grabbed Jamie by the vest. "And I didn't like you from the moment I saw your faces."

With one swift motion, Mike freed his brother from Antonio's grip. "Listen to my brother and act like a gentleman!" Mike snapped. "You can let us go in a more tolerable way. You owe us some respect!"

"Who talks about respect! Who do you think you are, you bottom pauper?"

"A man who won't tolerate your rude attitude," Mike said flatly, while Jamie was on alert to stop him if things got out of hand. "If you want us to stop working, it will happen right this instant, but that doesn't give you the right to insult us." Mike's rage sparkled in his eyes.

"Of all the workers here, you are the most unpleasant one." Antonio pointed his finger at him. "Go away or I will kick you out of here."

"Try us!" Mike dared him. Jamie's heartbeat accelerated; his forehead covered in beads of sweat. He pleaded his brother to stop.

"With dregs like you, I can do whatever I like," Antonio said as he reached to punch him, but Mike quickly blocked his attack, twisting Antonio's arm behind his back as the man struggled to remain upright on his wobbly feet.

"Let him go!" Jamie exclaimed, staring at Antonio's face in pain. "Can't you see he's not okay?"

Mike did what he was told, giving him a light push. Antonio staggered and fell, but he quickly regained his balance on his feet. Antonio caught his throat, his breathing labored, his vision blurred, and he collapsed on the ground unconscious. "Mr Garcia?" Mike bent over Antonio's body.

"What's wrong with him?" Gabriella rushed over and knelt beside him after Dominga had informed her Antonio was quarreling with the workers. "What did you do to him?" Her stare jumped between the brothers and Antonio, vigorously patting his cheek to wake him up. "Help him, for God's sake!" she squealed in horror.

Mike lifted Antonio and brought him into the house, holding him carefully in his arms. He laid him down on the sofa in the salon, and Gabriella immediately ran to call an ambulance. The whole family gathered, drawn by Gabriella's panicked cries.

"What's wrong with him?" Diego asked, bewildered.

"I don't know!" Gabriella muttered, her voice filled with dread. "I gave him a tranquilizer because he was too nervous."

"He must have taken the whole bottle because I found it empty in the kitchen," Magnolia said, holding the empty bottle in her hand.

"What's wrong?" Lucia rushed down the stairs and knelt beside her husband. "What's happened to him?"

"It seems your husband has tried to poison himself, Doña Lucia," Dominga said, her voice shaking.

Lucia's eyes darted between her husband and Mike. The guilt overwhelmed her as she gazed down at her husband's peaceful body. When the ambulance arrived, Lucia jumped in beside Antonio in the back, and they rushed to the hospital.

"Doña Gabriella…" Mike stopped her before she could tell Marcello to get the car ready. "Mr Garcia ordered us to cease work as we are fired. What are we doing?" he asked.

"Nonsense!" Gabriella said emphatically. "Go back to your work!" she ordered Mike and Jamie. "And you, what are you doing, standing here and gossiping!" she said to the rest of the workers who had gathered and ordered them to return to work at once.

On the drive home, Jamie was barely holding his tongue behind his teeth. "Everybody will find out what's going on," Jamie ranted from the passenger seat. "And when her husband dies, there won't be anyone to stop you from throwing yourself into her arms, right? There won't be any obstacle for the love birds."

Mike slammed on the brakes and Jamie almost hit his head on the glove box. The dust from the dirt road filled the car immediately. "Get out!" Mike snorted.

"Why?" Jamie asked.

"Get out!" Mike repeated intently, and Jamie did what he was told. Mike took a few steps in front of the car, trying to calm his nerves. "Do you want to go back and repeat what you said in front of everyone?" Mike said, fist clenched a little above chest level.

"It won't be necessary," Jamie snapped at his brother. "Everything will come out after Garcia is discharged from the hospital. If he's not dead."

Mike punched him and Jamie flew over the hood of the dirty pickup. "If my love of Lucia is such a problem for you, we can get it over with once and for all," Mike said emphatically. "Let's go back! Let's tell them everything. But we'll start with your secret plan, or whatever it is, with Juan Pablo and how you strive to get their money," Mike said, furious. His heartbeat quickened, now matching the speed of his breathing.

"Your relationship wasn't part of the plan."

"I don't give a shit about your plan! I'll finish all of this right now," Mike said as he took off his jacket and threw it aside on the hood of the car, ready to attack.

"Well, if that's how you want it, so be it!" Jamie took off his hat and got into position too. But before they could even start, a car pulled up behind theirs and came to a stop.

Jamie turned back carefully, catching Mike's curious stare, unsure if his brother had tried to trick him. Diego Alvarez put his sunglasses into the pocket of his navy blue suit jacket and stretched his arms to adjust the sleeves to his comfort, checking his watch. "Come closer, Mike Williams," he called out. Mike stepped forward, and Jamie followed right behind him. "I'm guessing you're happy about what happened," Diego said. "Because that was your deed, señor. Should I congratulate you?"

Mike cocked his head to one side, gazing at him appraisingly. "You came all the way here just to tell me that?" he replied, his tone flat.

"I respect my home. I don't talk to wretches, like Lucia and Juan Pablo are doing, under my roof."

"So, you think of us as wretched people?" Mike repeated slowly, taking a few steps closer.

"Yes, I do. I think you're two brothers looking for adventure and wanting to drive my siblings crazy," he shouted. Jamie gazed at the dirty boots he was wearing as a fresh wave of embarrassment washed over him. Diego's intense gaze made him convulsively swallow again. "And Mike, you're the most indecent of all." Diego appraised him with a critical gaze. "Tell me, how could you approach a woman like Lucia? You've ruined her life, you'll ruin her marriage, and you'll humiliate her in the eyes of others."

"If you think that's my goal, you're far from the truth, Mr Alvarez," Mike said through clenched teeth. Diego's baseless accusations and vicious words almost made him scream that it was his father who had inflicted the humiliation upon them and smashed his face on the ground. "I respect Lucia!" he said instead. "Our relationship is based on mutual and sincere feelings."

"Spare me the drama!" Diego smiled thinly. "Tell me what your hidden agenda is and why the hell you came to our house. What gives you the right to act so brazenly in our home?"

"We don't have any hidden agenda," Jamie said. "My brother fell in love with Lucia, and no one is to blame." A few muscles visibly twitched on his face.

"Mr Alvarez, if you're so sure of your righteousness, then go and tell everything to your mother and your family. There's no point in arguing with us," Mike said.

Diego emitted a choked laugh. "You're underestimating me, Mike Williams. You know I wouldn't do it. I wouldn't disappoint them in such a disgraceful way." Diego straightened his posture. "But I demand you leave our home right this instant. For good!" His eyes were smoldering coals.

"Impossible! This won't happen!" Mike's voice was unwavering. "Your threats won't make us leave!"

Diego reached for his sunglasses from his pocket, put them on, and turned to leave. He opened the driver's door and threw a last gaze at them. "I know my value, gentlemen! I don't usually talk to people from your society, but I want to let you know I'm keeping an eye on you!" He got back into the black BMW, skillfully reversed the car, and soon the dust and ash raised from the road hid the car in an impenetrable fog.

Chapter Twenty-seven

Lucia parked her car after returning from the hospital. She was walking towards the entrance of her house when Mike pulled her aside to talk. He had been yearning for her presence those several days since the accident with Antonio and seized every opportunity to speak with her.

"It's dangerous," Lucia cautioned, looking around warily. "We can't be seen talking."

"I need to see you. This situation is tearing me apart," Mike said, his voice laced with pain.

"Mike, please! You must understand that I can't," Lucia pleaded, turning to leave, but Mike halted her.

"I'm begging you," his voice trembled, and the pent-up anguish threatened to bring him to tears.

"I'll come tonight to the same place," Lucia whispered. Mike nodded watching her walk away.

Lucia entered her room as Diego followed and shut the door. Lately, he had grown accustomed to entering her room without knocking or asking permission. "Are you still meeting that man?" The suspicion grabbed his mind the minute he saw them through the window.

"If you had been paying attention, you would have known that I stopped," Lucia retorted.

"I do pay attention, and I just saw you talking to him."

"Please leave me alone."

"Lucia, your husband is in the hospital. He attempted suicide." Diego's voice raised with concern. "He may not have succeeded this time, but he will if he finds out about this." Diego threw one last glance at her before leaving as she had requested.

Lucia lay in bed, her mind besieged by a thousand thoughts, guilt gnawing at her insides. Each time she visited Antonio at the hospital, the sense of responsibility weighed heavily upon her, even though they didn't talk while she was there. And now, her brother's words totally sank her eyes into tears.

That night, when she met Mike at the hotel, she made love to him as if it were their last time together. She craved the feeling of being alive, the need to be a woman. As soon as Mike pressed his lips to hers in a shower of sweet kisses, Lucia's heart bounced back to life after the several rough days she'd been through, like a phoenix rising from the ashes. When they parted, she gazed at his eyes, sorrow, and anguish evident in hers.

"We need to put an end to this madness," Lucia said, her voice wavering with melancholy and sorrow. The guilt wrapped its hands around her throat, as she fastened the belt on her jeans.

Mike looked at her from the bed, halfway through getting dressed himself. "Are you serious?"

"Antonio attempted suicide because of me," Lucia said, placing her face in her hands and sighing heavily.

"You can't be sure! It might be because of something else." Mike went to her, kissing her forehead as the idea of losing her started sinking into his head.

"No, it isn't," she said, slightly raising her voice. "I'm not fulfilling my marital duties, and to top it off, I want a divorce," Lucia added.

"Why don't you admit you're tired of screwing me?" His voice wavered with hesitation.

"Are you really thinking this is a game for me?" Lucia frowned at him. She couldn't believe he had uttered these words out loud. "Mike, I'm crazy about you." She gazed at him with profound, fascinating eyes. "But we can't go on like this. We need to stop," she said, her voice strained with pain, as if the air couldn't reach her lungs.

Mike hugged her tight, and Lucia pressed her cheek against his chiseled chest. The warmth of his body and his musk were a constant reminder of her weakness. His embrace erased every trouble from her mind, and the thought of losing him was driving her to insanity.

"I need you, Lucia. You're in my blood."

"I feel the same way," Lucia said, trying to reassure him. She rubbed her hands on her face, emitting a heavy sigh. She gazed at him again, desperately trying to fight back the welling tears. "I swear, I was going to talk face-to-face with him and my whole family, but this situation is killing me," she said. "I realize he loves me, in his own way, but I can't hurt him like this. The only way for us to be together is for me to get a divorce."

"Then do it!" Mike blurted out.

"It isn't me who should make the decision, but him."

"He'll never give up on you!" Mike snapped. "Nor will I." He jumped on her lips like a predator to its prey. "Lucia, I love you! More than he does! What should I do with my feelings? Should I commit suicide?"

Lucia's fingers on his cheek left traces of the greatest love and deepest pain. The situation had unraveled to the point that she couldn't bear it anymore. "Mike, you need to understand me," she said, as dread filled her pores, "there are things I have to comply with, and as much as I love you, I must not see you anymore." She took her purse and turned to leave.

"Lucia!" Mike called after her, his eyes welling with tears as she opened the door.

"Please, don't look for me anymore! Let's not hurt each other more, because I don't know where this can get us." Lucia looked at him one last time before closing the door.

"Lucia, wait!" He called out her name again, the tears drowning him in a pool of agony and grief. Her words etched in his heart, his world crumbling down. Yet, as the last tear sank into his lips, he whispered, "No, Lucia Alvarez, I'm not ready to lose you."

The following days were like the ninth circle of hell for both of them. Mike watched her from a distance. He couldn't talk to Lucia, and the couple of times he could catch a glimpse of her, she was always with her brothers or someone else. He stared with vacant eyes. The weight of the work seemed overwhelming, and the little jokes his brother was telling made him on the verge of taking out his anger on him. Lucia was so close and yet thousands of miles away from him and this ordeal was pushing him over the edge. It took him a mountain of strength not to rush into her room and kiss her; to possess her like she belonged to him in the same way she did when they were together at the hotel. The agony and nightmare got worse, and intensified to breaking point, when Antonio was discharged from the hospital and returned home as he had to remind himself she'd chosen this clown over him.

Gabriella scurried to help Antonio sit in the comfy armchair, but he fervently refused. "Don't act like I'm an invalid," he said, fixing his gaze on Lucia, who had buried her face in her hands. "Are you not happy to see me home?"

She shifted her gaze toward him, and her expression was sullen when she stood up and left for her room without saying a word.

"Give her time," Gabriella said, trying to excuse her. "Diego, Juan Pablo, come with me to the study. Magnolia, see to it that Antonio has everything he needs." Gabriella smiled at him, as he plastered a thin smile in return.

"You may retire, Magnolia. I will call for you if I need something." He sent her away and carefully headed for the study.

"Father Thomas is furnishing the orphanage, and I promised to send some furniture," Gabriella said, scanning through the papers.

"That's great. We have enough junk in the house," Juan Pablo replied.

Gabriella lifted her head and narrowed her eyes at him. "I'm not going to send him rubbish, but things that will be useful," she said, slightly offended. "Please go to the attic and choose the best ones."

"And why me?" Juan Pablo whined, arching his brow at his mother. "Couldn't Magnolia or Dominga attend to this tedious task?"

"Juan Pablo, please stop being so lazy," Diego said with a great sense of frustration in his voice. "Lately, you've only been preoccupied with your engagement and haven't taken any part in the work on the hacienda."

"Diego is right," Gabriella agreed, turning to Juan Pablo. "Come on, let's get moving!" She scolded him slightly.

Juan Pablo let out a deep sigh of boredom and frustration. "Is there anything else?"

"Yes, at noon Father Thomas will send a truck to pick up the furniture. You'll go with them and deliver the furniture and the money," Gabriella instructed as she handed Juan Pablo the envelope.

He opened it and peeked inside. "This is too much money. Come with me!" Juan Pablo turned to his brother.

"I have to meet with the vet," Diego replied curtly. "Don't think I have nothing to do."

Antonio noticed Juan Pablo standing up from his seat and quickly navigated to his room, instructing the servants not to disturb him. Once alone, he closed the door and fished out his phone from his pocket.

"Antonio, I'm glad to hear from you. Is everything okay? You gave me quite a scare with this move," Armando laughed sarcastically.

"Thankfully, I took the right dose." Antonio plastered a wicked smirk on his face. "Listen, my mother-in-law is sending some junk furniture to Father Thomas today at noon. I think it's the perfect time for something bad to happen to Mike Williams." His eyes flickered with malice when he pulled the curtain aside, gazing at Mike in the front yard.

"Leave that to me," Armando said. "I have found two men, Zylian and Sezar. These must be their nicknames, of course."

"Excellent!" Antonio exclaimed. "The timing is just right to get them in here."

"No worries, my man. I will call them straight away," Armando said before hanging up.

He changed into his pajamas and laid in bed, staring at the chandelier. "Your end is near, you son of a bitch! Your impudence is what is going to kill you!" he muttered, his eyes boring into the ceiling.

Chapter Twenty-eight

The two men raced furiously toward the Alvarez mansion in their truck, concealing their identities in blue overalls and caps. They stopped at the gates, as the guard approached them.

"Good afternoon," the guard greeted them politely and the driver nodded in response. "Did Father Thomas send you, too?"

The men looked at each other before the driver spoke up. "Yes, we're sent by Father Thomas," he said. The guard nodded and let them pass. "What an imbecile!" The men giggled as they drove in.

Once they were at a safe distance, they spied on the crowd of men who were loading expensive furniture onto another truck. "Who of these people is Mike Williams?" Zylian queried his partner.

"He's not around. We'll have to wait. Don Armando said he'd be the only one wearing a black vest."

"How appropriate for the day! When we get there, you know what to do. We need to be quick and clean," Zylian replied, walking his partner through the plan once again as they remained on high alert.

Meanwhile, Dominga called the boys in for lunch. "Thank you, Dominga!" Jamie smiled, inhaling the mouth-watering aroma, and dug in. "What's with the long face, bro?" Jamie peered at his brother. "Trouble in paradise?" Mike glared at him but didn't comment. "What? Lucia is avoiding you and you are helpless. You can't touch her as brazenly as you wish. Am I right?"

"How about eat your soup." Mike threw the rest of his soup on his vest.

Jamie raced from his seat, glaring down at the stain. "Are you crazy?" He blew hard on the hot stain and quickly took off his vest. "Look what you did!" Jamie whined. "And I don't have spare one here." Dominga inhaled in surprise. Her eyes lustfully wandered across Jamie's body.

"This is to teach you not to speak when not necessary," he scolded him. "Don't be such a drama queen." He stared at Jamie's pouty face and gave his in exchange.

"What a sour temper!" Jamie snapped and whipped Mike with his vest in anger. "I've lost my appetite," he hissed and darted off.

"Don't worry, Mike. I'll look for something for you to wear right away," Dominga said, throwing Jamie's dirty tank top in the washing machine. She was a bit flustered by the brothers' little scene and quickly scurried out of the kitchen.

Jamie had returned to the stables when a stranger approached him. "Are you working here?" the man asked in a deep, thick voice.

"Yes, why?"

"We're bringing tubes of concentrates! Someone needs to help us unload them. I'd ask the others, but they're busy loading the other truck with furniture," the man explained, squinting his eyes as his cap couldn't quite protect his eyes from the sun.

"Sure!" Jamie smiled politely and followed the man. When they reached the back of the truck, the man opened the right door. "I don't see anything," Jamie said, straining his eyes at the impenetrable darkness at the bottom of the trailer.

"The tubes are at the end of the trailer," Zylian said, as Jamie jumped on it first to bring them down.

Sezar ambushed him with a few punches, slamming Jamie into the trailer's wall. Zylian also got in and threw several more punches to his stomach and ribs until Jamie lay down, helpless.

Juan Pablo walked around in the distance, making sure everything was running smoothly. "What's this truck?" Juan Pablo asked the guard as the men almost finished loading the first one.

"Father Thomas sent it, probably for more furniture," the guard replied.

"I didn't know there were going to be two," Juan Pablo said, looking quizzical. "My mother mentioned only one."

The guard shrugged his shoulders, and Juan Pablo approached to check. "Who are you, sir?" Juan Pablo gazed at the man who was locking the doors.

"We're bringing tubes of concentrates," Zylian stuttered, completely off guard.

"Um... I thought Father Thomas had sent you?" The man rolled his eyes to the side, as if searching for a credible explanation. He flustered; the sweat on his hands grew until they were completely wet. "Open the door, please!" Juan Pablo ordered.

"Is it really necessary, señor?"

"Open the door!" Juan Pablo repeated in a more demanding voice. "Or should I call the other workers?

There is something fishy! Open!" The man shrugged his shoulders and did as he was told. "What the hell?" Juan Pablo gaped at Jamie, lying on the floor, his hands wrapped in ropes, curled like a baby in a mother's womb. His face scarlet red and his mouth gagged with a band. "What is going on here?" Juan Pablo screamed, mortified. Before he could call for help or do anything else, the man punched him hard and dragged him inside as quickly as he could. He locked the door, hit the pedal to the metal and drove away.

Juan Pablo staggered on the bumpy road, throwing a couple of punches back at Sezar, who was with them in the back. The taste of his own blood in his mouth fueled his rage as he pulled out an injection from his pocket. Within minutes, the needle sank into Juan Pablo's neck and he fell on the floor, unconscious.

Jamie growled and kicked with his legs and feet, but he was powerless. His hands were tightly bound, and the damn band was suffocating him. He rolled his eyes toward Juan Pablo, who was lying peacefully on the floor. Jamie's devastated eyes pointed at Juan Pablo, as if he searched for any signs of life, but the man blocking his sight was preoccupied with tying Juan Pablo up. As he stepped aside, staggering at the unexpected turns of the truck, Jamie cast a glance towards Juan Pablo who was completely immobile. He threw a menacing look at the kidnapper and growled once more.

"Shut up if you don't want your skull blown off!" Sezar slid a gun out of the back of his pants and pointed it at Jamie's forehead. Jamie stilled. Hot and cold waves rippled through his body, and his nostrils flared as he tried to control his erratic breathing. The thought of them being killed shuddered through Jamie, and the idea of dying sent shivers through every bone in his body.

One of workers sent to pick the furniture informed Gabriella that they were ready and waiting for Juan Pablo before setting off. Gabriella feverishly looked around, but he was nowhere to be found.

"He must be in the second truck that came," the guard said.

"What second truck?" Gabriella furrowed her brows, confused. The guard quickly explained as she went inside to phone Father Thomas.

"No, Gabriella, I sent only one as we discussed," Father Thomas said simply. She hung up without saying anything else, her face went blank, and she ordered Magnolia to check the rest of the house.

"Magnolia?" Mike called out. "What's going on? What's all this commotion?"

"We can't find Don Juan Pablo. Have you seen him?" Magnolia asked.

"He was helping with the furniture," Mike replied simply, and Magnolia went off in search of him. "Magnolia, wait! Have you seen Jamie?" Mike called after her.

The woman shook her head, her eyes filled with fear, before she returned to the house.

By early evening, the entire family had gathered in the salon, along with the Mendozas, as they had arranged a dinner at the mansion.

"Mama, please calm down." Diego tried to console her.

"I don't understand – Juan Pablo was carrying a lot of money, but why would they take Jamie too?" Alicia asked, earning a scrutinizing glance from her mother.

"Stop fretting about him and help us soothe Gabriella. Her son is missing." Alicia let out a sigh, rolled her eyes in frustration, and remained silent.

Antonio lazily descended the stairs, his gaze fixated on Mike, who leaned against the pillar in the salon. He froze in shock, his face turning as pale as a sheet at the sight of Mike in his house. "What the hell?" he muttered before Gabriella caught sight of him and immediately threw her arms around his neck, sobbing uncontrollably. As Diego quickly recounted the dreadful afternoon they had, Antonio excused himself and made his way to the study. Antonio slid the doors closed, making sure nobody was following him, and dialed his friend's number. "What kind of incompetent fools have you hired?" Antonio blasted into the handset, his anger boiling over like a tsunami crashing onto the shore.

"What the hell is going on?" Armando's confusion was evident in his voice.

"These two idiots mistook Mike for his brother. He's safe and sound in my house. I thought I was seeing a ghost. And to make matters worse, they've kidnapped my brother-in-law. Do you have any idea what kind of trouble this could cause me?" Antonio raged, his eyes blazing with fury as he impatiently waited for his friend to respond.

"Antonio, I had no idea, I swear. I'll call them right away and have them released," Armando said, embarrassed by the monumental mistake.

"No, leave it as it is for now. It's too risky and the police will be here any minute. We can't be seen to be involved in this," he said tersely into the phone before hanging up.

Mike stood by the pillar, desperation coursing through his veins. He looked over at Gabriella, sobbing and whimpering. His eyes instinctively dwelled on Lucia, who stood meekly by the sofa, trying to sooth his pain from afar. If there was no news about his brother in the next hour, he feared he would lose his mind. He couldn't understand why anyone would kidnap Jamie, and a thousand reasons clashed in his mind, none of them good enough to justify harming him. He asked to call home one more time, hoping Jamie was there and his worries were unfounded. Alas, his hopes drained from his eyes when Chloe said she hadn't seen him, leaving him even more crushed and devastated.

"Mike, what's going on?" She sounded more worried than him.

"I will tell you when I get home," he said curtly and hung up.

Diego peered at him. "Why are you not going home? There is nothing more you could do."

"Diego, please!" Lucia snapped. "His brother is also missing."

"Your brother is right, sweetheart." Antonio turned to her. "There is nothing he can do here. He can wait at home." He glared at Mike, taking Lucia's hand, who was lost in pain and didn't object to the little intimacy.

Magnolia's heart raced with panic. She asked Mike to accompany her to the kitchen and have something to eat since the night was expected to be long. Mike followed her and once alone with her, he couldn't stop racing around the table. His appetite had vanished and seeing Antonio and Lucia holding hands only added salt to his wound.

"Did your brother do it? Is that what you're planning?" Magnolia asked. "To kidnap Juan Pablo so that Doña Gabriella suffers for what she did?"

Mike glared at her for a moment. "How could you believe we have something to do with this?"

"I believe it because I don't know what your plans are," Magnolia said firmly. "I'm wondering why you're still staying in this house."

"If you suspect that we're here to hurt Juan Pablo, then go ahead and tell the whole family!" Mike roared. "I won't tolerate being questioned, especially in moments like this," he added as Magnolia sat at the table, with no further comments.

It was well past ten, and Mike was sitting meekly on the curbstone of the small flower garden next to the parking space in front of the mansion, waiting for any news. The police had come and questioned everyone in the mansion, but the investigation had just begun.

"Mike, why don't you go inside?" Lucia startled him from behind. He turned immediately at the sound of her voice; the voice that echoed in his ears day and night ever since he met her. She took a couple of steps closer. "It looks like we're going through the same hell. We're suffering for our brothers," she said quietly.

Mike's eyes welled with tears, and he reached out to hug her. "No, Mike, don't!" She stopped him.

"I need you, Lucia! Now more than ever," he barely said. In a house of strangers as enemies, she was the light in the black tunnel that helped him survive this ordeal.

"I need you too, believe me! I'm dying to be with you at this moment, but I can't!" She paused for a moment.

"I have high regards for you, Mike. And if you need help, I want you to know I'm ready to do it."

"I know," he said simply. "I believe you." He ran his finger over her cheek to wipe away the trace of tears. "I want you to be brave while we wait."

"Lucia, what are you doing there? Mother is looking for you!" Diego called from a distance, distracting Mike from pulling her into his arms. The pain and sorrow gripped their bodies before she had to leave him alone in the cold dark night.

Chapter Twenty-nine

Jamie and Juan Pablo stood before the men, their hands tied, bands on their eyes, and when the man finally freed Juan Pablo's mouth, he coughed from filling his lungs with air. "What do you want?" he roared, his voice echoing off the vast walls.

"Shut up!" Zylian screamed from behind him. "If you make one more sound, I'll put the gag back. Is that clear?"

He nodded. "No, please, I was going to suffocate," he begged, sensing the man moving away from him.

Jamie's blood rushed to his head. *If only I could see where we are*, Jamie thought, his heart threatening to rip open his chest. He feverishly tried to remain calm. It was too risky to provoke them.

"I want you to answer my questions precisely," the man ordered. Juan Pablo nodded vigorously. "What's your name?" Zylian's husky voice sent a few chills down his spine.

"Juan Pablo Alvarez."

"What were you doing in that mansion?"

"I live there. I am the son of the owner."

The two men exchanged a look before stepping a couple of feet away. "What are we going to do?" Sezar asked.

"For now, nothing," Zylian said. "Get them back in the truck," he commanded, and his partner obeyed, pushing Jamie and Juan Pablo into the vehicle.

Once inside, Sezar untied their blindfolds and removed the gags. "If you start shouting or causing trouble, I won't hesitate to respond," he said menacingly, tying their hands to a wide panel attached to the walls of the trailer. He quickly jumped down and closed the door.

Jamie and Juan Pablo sat facing each other, tied up on opposite sides of the truck. "Could you stop sniveling or whatever you're doing?" Jamie hissed. "You're making me nervous."

Juan Pablo's eyes welled with tears as the overwhelming tension and fear became unbearable. He pulled his knees up to his chest and rested his chin on them. "It's all about the money," he blurted out.

"What money?" Jamie asked.

"The money in my backpack. It's a donation for the orphanage."

"Is it a lot of money?" Jamie asked.

"I don't know, probably," Juan Pablo said, a couple of tears rolling down his cheek. "My mother gave it to me, but I didn't count it. I'll give it to them and beg for them to set us free."

"Don't say a word!" Jamie snapped. "If it was about the money, they would have taken the backpack. Don't be stupid!"

Juan Pablo's irritation crawled on his face. "Don't call me stupid."

"Don't you see they want something else?" Jamie continued. "They want me! They came for me and threw me in the truck before you even came."

"Do you have enemies who might be trying to kill you?" Juan Pablo asked hesitantly.

Jamie turned his gaze to him, his muscles twitching with anger. "Of course not! I'm not someone who deals with dangerous people."

What a jerk! Juan Pablo scolded himself inwardly. *Why did I ask such a silly question?* He looked at Jamie apologetically but didn't say anything. He allowed himself to succumb to his tears, and their rueful situation.

The two men waited outside quietly until the phone rang. "You two are dumb assholes who can't do anything right!" Armando yelled, fuming because of their shortsightedness.

"What are you talking about, Armando?" the man said, frowning in confusion at his partner.

"Do you know what trouble my friend and I could face because of this man, Juan Pablo Alvarez?" Armando blasted. "Plus, you took the wrong man even after I gave you an explicit description of who Mike Williams is."

"No, this can't be! No!" Zylian stuttered.

"Don't do anything," Armando ordered. "The police are launching an investigation. I'll try to come tomorrow with my friend," he said before the connection dropped.

Sezar returned to the truck and informed the others they would be spending the night there.

"Please give us some water," Juan Pablo managed to say. The man took out a bottle of water and poured it into Juan Pablo's mouth. He gulped down as much as he could, somehow grateful for the refreshment. He did the same for Jamie before leaving them miserable in the crappy trailer and the scorching heat.

As morning arrived, Armando and his friend parked their car in a vast, abandoned building, which looked like a garage for large vehicles. Antonio couldn't restrain himself and punched Sezar in the face, causing the man to stagger back. "You stupid bastards!" he roared.

"If you hit him one more time, you're dead!" Zylian pointed his gun at Antonio's horrified face. "I don't allow you to insult us. We are professionals. If someone is to blame, it's him." He gazed at Armando, who blinked rapidly and clenched his jaw tight.

"Antonio, I swear, I gave them clear instructions!" Armando protested, his expression deadpan, and reached to hit one of them but stopped at the sight of the gun in Zylian's hand.

Antonio struggled to calm his breathing and suppress his rage. "What do you plan to do with them? Are you going to kill them?"

The two men exchanged a look. "Yes, we must. It's too risky. They saw our faces." Zylian fixed his gaze on his friend and turned back to the men in suits.

"Whatever you do, I want no part in it! I refuse to burden my conscience with innocent victims," Antonio growled and asked his friend to drive him home.

It took Antonio the entire ride home to compose himself and calm his nerves. When Armando dropped him off, he sped away as fast as he'd come, hoping he'd managed to stay unnoticed. Antonio stared at his house for a moment, considering whether he should have stayed at the hospital. He reluctantly marched ahead, blood rushing to his head at the sight of Mike. "That worthless nobody was supposed to be dead," he muttered. "And yet, he's strolling around my house!"

"Antonio!" Gabriella exclaimed in surprise. "Why didn't you say you were going out? We would have come to pick you up." She fixed him with a blank stare.

"Don't worry, Gabriella. I took a taxi," he replied with a thin smile, and they entered the living room. Antonio looked around at the rest of the family and their usual guests, the Mendoza family, who had gathered, and waved in greeting. "Any news?" he asked hesitantly.

"No," Diego replied.

"We're still waiting for the police to call," Isabella added.

Antonio took his seat on the sofa, next to Lucia. "And Mike? How is he?" Antonio asked.

"Why do you ask?" Lucia turned to him, looking perplexed.

"I'm guessing he's devastated about his brother. And he's our employee," he murmured blithely.

"Like everybody else!" Alicia interjected.

"Well, not everybody! Just his brother! We're more worried about Juan Pablo," Diego said curtly, and Lucia frowned at him.

"Well, I hope they'll return safe and sound." Antonio tried to sound optimistic. "If they're alive!"

Lucia gazed at him, aversion spiking from her eyes, and went to her room.

"Antonio!" Diego reprimanded him, crouching down beside his mother, who began crying even more inconsolably.

Later, Antonio cautiously entered Lucia's room, standing by the door as if afraid to approach her. She threw him a quick glance and disregarded his presence, gazing blankly at the wall with her book open in her lap. "I wanted to apologize for what happened earlier, and for what happened to your family." He paused for a moment, musing. "I know you don't want me to get close to you, but I feel like I have to say this: you and your family can rely on my support," he added after a short pause.

Lucia remained indifferent to what he was saying. She knew his words weren't meant to hurt her, and what was worse, he could be right. She lifted her face up and sighed. "I know," she mumbled. "You have always been empathetic, especially with my mom."

"I have high regard for her." He took a couple of steps towards her bed. "I didn't leave because of her! Otherwise, I wouldn't have waited here to solve our situation."

She mustered her courage to look at him, trying to find meaning in his eyes. "So, now you're in a hurry to divorce?" she asked, arching a brow at him.

"Why should we delay something that cannot be repaired?"

She sighed lightly. "I agree, but I won't discuss it when I'm worried about my brother. I can't think of anything else."

Antonio made a light nod in agreement. "Let's hope it ends in the best possible way. Then, we'll talk about us. It's inevitable," he said, reaching for the door handle. His heart sank in remorse, his rage lulled in the back of his mind.

"Antonio!" Lucia stopped him for a moment. "Thank you! You have the nobility that I lack," she said. He gazed at her for a moment, half-hidden behind the door. When the door closed, Lucia's guilty mind had started to subside as she cried a couple of tears.

Chapter Thirty

The car raced across the vast steppe before screeching to a halt. Zylian and Sezar pulled Jamie out of the car and forced him to kneel. Jamie's hands touched the ground, the dry earth beneath his fingertips. His heart raced with the fear that they might have brought them to a cemetery. "Stay put and don't say a word!" Zylian commanded, removing the gag from Jamie's mouth and letting it hang around his neck like a necklace.

"What are you going to do to us? Please, don't kill us!" Jamie's heart leapt into his mouth as he spoke. "If that's your goal, take off this blindfold. I want to watch!" he screamed, a surge of adrenaline spiking trough his pores.

"I told you not to speak!" Zylian grabbed Jamie by the throat, shook him violently, and let him go. Sezar pushed Juan Pablo down, causing him to almost collapse onto Jamie's lap, before snatching the backpack from his hand and cutting the ropes around his wrists. Jamie instinctively put his arm around Juan Pablo's shoulder to support him, as he was shaking with fear beneath Jamie's fingers.

"You will stay here for at least ten minutes and don't turn around or move!" the man ordered.

Jamie and Juan Pablo both bowed their heads in submission, and Jamie nervously swallowed, waiting meekly for their fate. The wind howled through the endless expanse of the steppe, kicking up dust and debris as it went. The dread was suffocating. The sobs of Juan Pablo made Jamie's heart thud in his chest. The thought of what was coming was unbearable and he rather wished for them to finish it quickly.

After a moment, the man let go of Jamie, stood up, and the car drove away. Jamie quickly removed his blindfold and slowly opened his right eye before the left, adjusting to the bright sunlight. "Juan Pablo, they are gone!"

"Quiet! Don't talk!" Juan Pablo panicked, and Jamie tried to search for the car with his eyes, but it was already gone.

"They've left. Didn't you hear the engine?" Jamie skillfully untied the band from Juan Pablo's eyes. "Be careful with your eyes. The light will blind you!"

"What do you mean gone? So, they've released us?" Juan Pablo finally opened his eyes.

"Yes, they didn't kill us!" Jamie replied. They both looked at each other, rejoicing in the freedom and relief of having survived the most terrifying, dreadful ordeal.

The scorching sun burned them bit by bit, draining their strength. They climbed up a high, rocky hill, and Jamie looked around. The desert stretched endlessly beyond the horizon. Juan Pablo lay down on the rock, completely exhausted from the arduous trek through the narrow canyon. He put his hand over his face to shield his eyes from the blinding sun. His mouth dry, he fished out the bottle of water the kidnappers had left and gulped it gratefully before Jamie took the bottle from Juan Pablo's hands. "Don't drink it all up! We might need it. We don't know how long we'll be here!"

"The sun is dehydrating me!" Juan Pablo barely managed to say, and Jamie handed him the bottle back.

"At least they took pity on us and left us some water," Jamie murmured as he sat on another piece of rock next to Juan Pablo.

Juan Pablo shifted his position and leaned back. "I can't see anything, not even a house or a road leading somewhere." He rested his upper body on his hands, straining his eyes to see into the distance.

"If we at least knew where we were…" Jamie looked around again.

"There's nothing useful here at the moment," Juan Pablo said as he rummaged through his backpack, hoping in vain.

When some money fell out of it, Jamie picked up one of the wads, widening his eyes in surprise. "It's strange they didn't take it!"

"That means their goal wasn't robbery," Juan Pablo said. "But what could they possibly want? Maybe they're sadists who enjoy torturing people."

Jamie arched a brow at him. "Don't talk nonsense." He grimaced. "If that were the case, they wouldn't have left us here." Jamie stood up and looked around again, but there was still no sign of any guidance.

When they were ready to continue, each of them headed in the opposite direction, arguing about which way was better. "Okay, let's not argue. Let's head west," Jamie suggested, holding out an open palm for Juan Pablo to lead the way.

The cold hands of the night fell upon their exhausted bodies. They stopped as hunger and thirst drained their bodies. Juan Pablo rummaged through his backpack again. To his surprise, he found a half block of chocolate they could share, and a box of matches.

"You have matches?" Jamie turned to him, as Juan Pablo nodded.

As the night settled over the desolate landscape, Juan Pablo and Jamie found themselves huddled by the dwindling fire, their silhouettes cast in the warm glow of the embers. Juan Pablo absently traced the contours of the rocks, his gaze drifting toward the endless expanse of stars above. Juan Pablo took off his suit jacket and laid it next to the fire, allowing them to rest their heads on it. "The moon is so beautiful when it's full," Juan Pablo said, a little above a whisper. "And look at all the stars."

"Do you see those three there, lined up straight?" Jamie pointed with his finger. "It's called Ursa Major, which translates to the great bear."

Juan Pablo looked at him for a moment. "I couldn't have held on without you," he admitted, his voice soft and vulnerable.

Jamie looked up from the flames, his smile bridging the gap between fear and uncertainty. "We are in this together." A flicker of warmth danced in his eyes. He stood up and added more twigs to the fire. Juan Pablo reached out a hand, resting it lightly on Jamie's shoulders, his breath catching slightly as their closeness became his lifeline in the darkness.

Their conversation drifted to memories of home, of places and people left behind a long time ago. Jamie spoke of the countryside where he grew up, of the rolling hills and the warmth of a home now lost to ashes and memory.

"What happened then? Why did you leave all that behind?" Juan Pablo turned to him.

Jamie stared into the flames, lost in thought. Memories flooded his mind as if they had happened yesterday – the fire, their house collapsing in flames, The officer announcing the death of his parents.

"Jamie?" Juan Pablo's voice brought him back to the present.

"I'm trying to remember what happened." He sniveled, battling the stinging tears. "Nobody leaves their land and the people they love just like that," he paused. "There's always a reason, and in my case, it was because I was forced to."

Juan Pablo clenched his jaw lightly. He leaned in closely, wiping away Jamie's tear with a finger before planting an involuntary sympathetic kiss on his cheek. "If these memories are torturing you, it's best to let it go," he said softly, meeting Jamie's twinkling eyes for a moment.

"We should try to get some sleep," Jamie said as he rested his head on his hat and turned towards the warmth of the dwindling fire. Juan Pablo stared at the moon for a while, muttering words of a prayer he'd learned during the Sunday services. His heart burned with desire and hope they would escape this ordeal safely. When fatigue overtook him, he rested his head on the backpack and fell asleep as soon as his eyelids closed.

The fire had long since burned out, leaving only smoldering embers. "Jamie? Jamie?" Juan Pablo shook his body lightly as he slowly opened his eyes.

"What happened?" Jamie growled half asleep.

"The fire is out!"

"So?"

"Well, let's get some more wood. This place is full of snakes, scorpions, and other nasty animals."

Jamie sat up, propping himself up with his hand, and let out a sigh. "All that noise for nothing!"

As Jamie disappeared into the darkness, Juan Pablo remained by the dead fire, his thoughts drifting to the unexpected comfort he found in Jamie's presence. Luckily, he returned quickly, his arms laden with branches and twigs. "Here," Jamie murmured, arranging the wood carefully. As the fire roared back to life, they found themselves drawn closer as if the space between them was diminishing.

Jamie lay down and tried to get back to sleep. But soon enough, Juan Pablo shook him awake once more. "Jamie? Jamie?"

"What now?" Jamie snorted and lay on his back, gazing at him.

"I can't sleep now."

"What can I do to help?" Jamie's voice seeped with irony carrying a hint of acrimony.

Juan Pablo took a deliberate moment, his eyes fixated on Jamie's unruly locks that appeared as if they were in a secret rebellion against any form of order. The low light accentuated the depth of his fathomless eyes, resembling the intense darkness of a wintry night. In their depths, the flickering firelight seemed to pirouette, casting a mesmerizing dance within the rich brown irises, giving them an enigmatic allure. A ghost of a smile played upon Juan Pablo's lips, a subtle hint of mischief peeking through the corners of his mouth. "I am sure we can think of something," he murmured, his voice laced with an alluring confidence that seemed to envelop the space around them. Tracing his fingers lightly over the rough fabric of Jamie's vest, he created a tingling sensation that made Jamie's breath catch in his throat. Jamie swallowed, the nervous movement betraying the turmoil within him. His gaze flickered between Juan Pablo's fingers that seemed to have a life of their own and the intensity of his dark, probing gaze.

"Is that so?" Jamie managed, his voice unexpectedly husky, betraying the effect that Juan Pablo's proximity had on him. A faint, almost mischievous chuckle escaped Juan Pablo's lips, the sound carrying an underlying amusement at Jamie's evident unease. With a deliberate tantalizing motion, he lifted the hem of Jamie's tank top with a single finger, slipping his hand beneath the fabric with an effortless grace.

"Does this bother you?" he inquired softly, his eyes fixed unwaveringly on Jamie, as if searching for something beyond the surface. Jamie found himself transfixed, his lips parting involuntarily as he struggled to maintain his composure. His mind desperately attempted to prod him into awareness of what was happening, but his consciousness was as numb as submerged feet in icy water. The pool of saliva in his mouth became an unwelcome reminder of his increasing unease, prompting him to swallow again, the movement almost audible in the charged ambience. "And what if kiss you?"

"I think we've been through this before," Jamie said in a low, husky voice, unsure if he said it out loud. His heartbeat accelerated, matching the speed of his blinking. Juan Pablo leaned in, close enough to feel Jamie's breath, closed his eyes, and their lips touched like feathers falling onto one another.

It was for a short moment as Juan Pablo pulled himself back to a kneeling position, leaving Jamie lying there with his eyes closed. His lips remained parted, allowing a thin stream of cold air to cool down his blood. When he opened his eyes again, he lifted himself up, grabbed Juan Pablo's nape, and gagged his mouth for a longer, hot-blooded kiss.

Jamie lay back, holding Juan Pablo's nape tightly while their tongues met in an erotic dance. Jamie skilfully unbuttoned Juan Pablo's shirt and threw it to one side. Juan Pablo plucked his lips from Jamie's for long enough to slide his vest off over his head. The cold hard ground beneath Jamie's back disappeared, their bodies pressed against each other as the heat of their muscles reaching fever pitch, threatened to burn them entirely. This new wave of unexpected lust made Jamie tremble. It was utterly wrong kissing him, yet he found it arduous to keep his lips restrained.

Juan Pablo gazed at him for a moment as his hand slid across Jamie's forehead. His eyes reading the hunger in Jamie's.

"Why did you stop?" Jamie whispered, as his chest bobbed up and down frantically.

"Are you sure?" Juan Pablo whispered back, and Jamie's nod of approval made Juan Pablo want him even more. His lips trailed down Jamie's chest, leaving moist marks all over his scorching body. Jamie lifted his head up, resting on his elbows, gazing at Juan Pablo, who worked on his belt. Juan Pablo looked at him, as if asking for permission to continue. And when Jamie arched his body to lift his waist, Juan Pablo yanked his jeans down to his ankles and glued his lips to Jamie's abs again.

"Oh wow!" Juan Pablo whispered, his rasped, moist breath making Jamie's skin bristle. Juan Pablo grabbed his own crotch, rubbing it tightly, amazed by his own erection. He pulled down Jamie's boxers slightly, revealing his jutting manhood. Juan Pablo swallowed, and Jamie followed him with stern, lustful eyes as Juan Pablo slid his mouth down before wrapping it with his lips.

"Oh my…" Jamie growled, his manhood wet and pulsating, and rested his head down, unable to prop himself on his elbows. The sweet sensation made Jamie's eyes blur; his mind focused on his wet shaft. His body arched extensively every time Juan Pablo's lips went all the way down along the length.

"Should I stop or keep going?" Juan Pablo looked at him.

In his raspy, frantic breathing, and semi-conscious state, Jamie whispered, "Yes! Keep going!"

Juan Pablo stood up, swiftly removed his pants and boxers, and straddled him again before his moans tore the silence of the desert. The palpable intensity of their connection made Juan Pablo moved with an expert rhythm, driving Jamie to new heights of pleasure. Jamie's fingers gripped the rough fabric of Juan Pablo's shirt, his breaths coming in ragged gasps as he surrendered to the sensations coursing through his body. Juan Pablo's face contorted in ecstasy as he neared his own release, the heat between them igniting sparks of fire. And then, in a burst of pleasure that left them both spent, he collapsed by Jamie's side, limbs entangled and chests heaving. Jamie's eyes sank into the full orb of the moon, his mind preoccupied to discern what had just happened, but a small voice inside him screamed for more. As they lay there, catching their breaths and basking in the afterglow of unexpected passion, Jamie knew he had discovered something new and exciting about himself—a side he found distressing to face, yet he was eager to find out where it would lead him. The air around them seemed to simmer with an invisible energy, the warmth radiating from Jamie's skin blending seamlessly with the crackling heat of the fire. With a slow, deliberate breath, he closed his eyes, allowing the fleeting sensation to envelop him like a comforting shroud. In that moment of respite, the world seemed to pause, as if holding its breath in anticipation.

Chapter Thirty-one

The morning sky was dark and gloomy as heavy rain clouds rolled in over the barren desert landscape. The air was thick with the scent of wet earth. Jamie was woken up by a few drops of rain and instinctively turned to Juan Pablo. Rubbing his arms to warm himself, he inhaled the melancholy that mixed with the humid air, filling his lungs, before shaking his friend awake. "Juan Pablo, we need to go," he urged.

The man slowly stirred his body and lazily slurred, before opening his eyes, "Are we dead?"

"No, but it's morning and it's raining." Jamie frowned at the gray clouds.

"I feel like a steamroller ran over me." Juan Pablo sat up, trying to ignore the pain in his lower back.

"Same here," Jamie muttered. "But we have to keep moving. We need to find someone who can help us."

"Where do you suggest we head towards?"

"Any direction will do. East, west, north, south… Let's go!" Jamie urged and threw a glance at the ravenous, black circle of what once was a campfire.

"Jamie," Juan Pablo whined, struggling to stand up on his sore legs. "Can you give me a hand?"

Jamie reached out his hand and swiftly pulled him back up. "The mattress wasn't very comfortable, was it? I promise next time to find a nicer one. Come on!"

Juan Pablo let out a mock laugh, and they went off. The rain blurred their vision, and their clothes were soaked through. Their shoes stuck in the mud, and they got tired of walking soon.

Jamie squinted his eyes, gazing through the raindrops ahead. The deserted place may have seemed bleak and lifeless, but the rain had brought with it a certain kind of beauty. They didn't comment on the night before and walked in silence as Jamie let the rain wash away the awkwardness in his body and fill the dreadful silence between them. The rain was seeping through his vest, and he found this to be soothing. He stopped and bent down, resting his hands on his knees. After taking a few deep breaths, he straightened back up. His eyes caught a glimpse of a cabin or something, but he wasn't sure if it was a figment of his imagination.

"Juan Pablo, do you see what I see?" Jamie said, his face breaking into a smile. "That's a house!" He turned his head as there was no response. He turned around, squinting his eyes at Juan Pablo lying on the ground. "Juan Pablo!" Jamie rushed over and kneeled at his side, resting Juan Pablo's head in his lap. The rain was mercilessly beating against his skin. "Juan Pablo, come on, open your eyes!" Jamie screamed as he patted his cheek in a desperate attempt to wake him up. There was no response.

Jamie put the backpack on his back, slid one arm beneath Juan Pablo's neck and the other beneath the back of his knees in a bride-like position. The adrenaline gave him a new dose of power as he grabbed Juan Pablo's body, moaned loudly as he tried to stand up on his feet. Juan Pablo growled lightly at the motion, and Jamie gritted his teeth as his arms shook violently for a second under the weight of Juan Pablo's body as he made a couple of small steps forward.

After an eternity of walking, Jamie put Juan Pablo on the ground again and rested on his knees and calves a few meters away from the door of the wooden house. He slowly crawled toward it and stretched his arm to knock on the door with an open palm. The door opened, and Jamie looked at the kid who screamed in horror and darted off inside. A couple of seconds later, Jamie looked up again, and the ghostly figure of a woman stood in front of him. "Help, please!" he barely whispered, resting his head on the wet, cold, cemented threshold.

❧❧

It had been a week since Juan Pablo and Jamie had returned home. Although they had tried hard to erase the ugly moment from their minds, Juan Pablo still found himself going back to those moments with Jamie. The fire... the moon... the wilderness. He closed his eyes, inhaling deeply as if Jamie was standing before him. When he opened his eyes again, he meekly smiled, emitting the long stream of air he'd been holding, as Diego was still bombarding him with questions about the mysterious kidnapping.

Life in the hacienda was returning back to normal as the wedding of Juan Pablo and Penelope drew closer. However, he couldn't focus on that now, not when his mind was full of Jamie. Gabriella had called Jamie into the study and thanked him for saving her son's life, shedding tears at the memory of the dreadful nights without him. Meanwhile, Penelope was over the moon since her fiancé had returned. Mike and Lucia's sense of partial happiness deepened. Their brothers were safe and sound at home, yet they had to keep a distance from each other. Lucia now had to put order into her relationship with her husband, which made her even more distraught than she already was.

Before the weekend arrived, the Mendozas were invited for a friendly lunch. Alicia was spending more and more time with the brothers, particularly with Jamie, despite her mother's disapproval and light protests whenever she caught them together. The two families were gathered in the dining room, and Penelope was complaining about her car acting strange. When Penelope tried to bring up Alicia's interactions with the two brothers to her mother, Alicia quickly deflected by informing her she had asked Mike to fix the car, diffusing the situation.

"Wait, are you saying he's fixing it now?" Antonio asked in great surprise. Alicia nodded, but Antonio scoffed sarcastically. "There's hardly any point. He doesn't know anything about mechanics. He'll only make the engine worse."

Lucia looked at him, annoyed, but didn't comment. Lately, her husband had been acting weird, always jumping to say something negative about Mike whenever he was brought up in conversation.

"It wouldn't hurt to go and check, Antonio," Gabriella interjected. "We shouldn't put too much trust in them," she added with a slight trace of concern on her face.

Antonio reached to stand up and make his way out when Lucia caught his arm. "No, stay here, Antonio," she said politely before leaving. Antonio's face changed, as did Diego's. But he didn't interfere. It had cost him a great amount of pity and remorse the last time he did and nearly broke his relationship with Lucia.

Mike averted his gaze, blinded by her sunny smile. "How's it going? Are you going to be able to fix the car?" she asked in a light, euphonious voice.

"Of course! There's nothing wrong with it. It'll be ready in ten minutes," he replied with a smile. "I know quite a lot about mechanics."

Lucia nodded with great satisfaction. She hadn't known about his passion for cars, and his reassurance made her smile too goofily and for too long at him. "Good!" she said simply before turning to go back.

"Lucia!" Mike ran a few steps to catch up with her.

"Mike, please, don't touch me!" she said insistently. "Someone will see us!"

"Let them! I don't care!" he said blithely. "I can't take it any more. We need to sort out our relationship." The constant avoiding, secret looks, and the never-ending chase were driving him crazy. He needed her, and she needed him.

"Neither the time nor the place is convenient for this, Mike." She looked around to make sure no one was seeing them.

"And they never will be. Because you're avoiding me! You're giving me false hope. You're not helping me, Lucia," Mike blew up in mild anger. "If there's no chance, you'd better tell me. I'll leave your home, and you'll never see me again, even if I'm dying."

Lucia smoothed her hair from the wind and gazed at him with pain. "Mike, please calm down!" she begged. "Please don't complicate things more than they already are."

"I'm not complicating anything. I just want to know what I can rely on," Mike said, as the anguish welled up his eyes with tears. Another strong wave was ready to hit his body, crushing him down. "I'm desperate. I'm going back and forth without knowing where we stand."

"If you must know, I don't feel any better." Lucia looked at him and read the sincerity in his grieving eyes before she emitted a long, heavy sigh. "All right then! You're right! "We can't go on like this any longer." She hid her eyes behind her fingers, rubbing her forehead, lost in thought. "Wait for me in the fields behind the hacienda. But, Mike, please be careful!" she added and looked around once more to assure herself they were alone. When her gaze found his, Lucia smiled timidly at him and turned to leave.

Mike watched her walk away until she disappeared behind the door. He returned to fixing the car, sporting the broadest smile possible, his heart dancing and his thoughts in disarray. It had been weeks since they had met, alone, away from the predators' eyes.

After the Mendoza family had left, Gabriella and her sons prepared to attend the small service in memory of her husband. Lucia excused herself citing a dreadful migraine. Gabriella initially protested feverishly, but eventually gave up after a couple of tries. Lucia stood by the window, and as the car vanished behind the bend in the road, she quickly changed into more comfortable riding clothes.

She swiftly stirred her horse and smiled at the horizon. As soon as she spotted him, Mike reached out his hands and helped her down. In an instant, Lucia flew into his arms and gasped, as her soft, silken lips met his momentarily. "Mike, please," she managed to whisper, "we're still close to my home."

"Come on, get back on!" he replied mildly, gesturing towards the beautiful black stallion with his eyes, and she complied.

Mike didn't say anything more, and Lucia didn't dare to ask. In truth, she didn't care what he was thinking if they were together. With one swift motion, he hopped on behind her, spurred the horse ahead, and she flew in his embrace. The warmth of his solid chest spiked the adrenaline she craved, and that eruption of emotions spilled through her veins. The wind beat against her face, and Mike's face furrowed as her hair brushed against his nose, tickling it gently. The sweet bubblegum scent made him close his eyes for a moment, as if memorizing it. When he opened them again, he steered the horse to their left, and the stallion galloped through the vast golden wheat fields.

Lucia gasped, her chest expanding with awe as she feasted her eyes upon the breathtaking panorama. The undulating expanse of golden fields seemed to stretch endlessly, blending seamlessly with the delicate seam of the distant horizon. A soft breeze swept over the landscape, carrying with it the sweet scent of stalks of wheat and earth.

"Can you see it?" Mike's voice, a gentle murmur, brushed her ear like a caress, sending a shiver down her spine.

"What? I can't see anything!" Her words emerged muffled, barely audible, as if she was afraid to disturb the sanctity of the moment.

"Our future! It's written over there – on the horizon!" His voice resonated with an earnest fervour, pulling her closer, his warmth seeping into her skin. He gently guided her, his hand on her shoulder, urging her to follow the direction of his outstretched finger.

With a tender flutter in her chest, she let her gaze drift to where he pointed. The sky was adorned with scattered cotton clouds, their soft edges painted with the sun's warm embrace. As the colours blended seamlessly – a colourful palette of pinks, oranges, and purples – her smile threatened to split her mouth wide open.

"That's us!" Mike continued. "We are free! Like the wind! Lucia…" He paused for a moment and gazed sternly ahead at the swaying stalks of wheat. "I don't have a lot of money. I can't offer you the life you have now, either. I don't have a university degree because I devoted my life to my family – I worked hard to support them. The most sacred thing happening to me is you." Lucia pulled the bridle sharply, and the horse neighed and stopped. Once they got off, she gazed at him and wiped the few tears on his cheeks. "I don't have many ambitions, nor do I dream of sacks of money. I live day by day, and I only rely on my own hands. For everything. That's me, Lucia, nothing more!" Mike gazed at her, put his hands on her hot, velvet cheeks as she rubbed her skin against his palm. "To this insignificant man, you gave yourself – and not only once. You dared to cheat on your husband. Can you keep being with me and love me the way I am?" Lucia put her hands on his wrists, as he was still caressing her face, and gazed at his fathomless, captivating eyes. "Lucia, why aren't you responding to my question? Are you able to turn your back on the luxuries and comforts you have for a person like me, or do I not deserve such a sacrifice? Don't be afraid to answer me. I'm ready to hear anything."

"Do you really want to know how I feel about you?"

"Yes!" he said emphatically. "I want you to decide! I prefer one last 'no' to me running after you without knowing what to do."

Lucia turned around and let out a heavy sigh. Her eyes welled with tears, but a ghost of a smile appeared on her face. "I think the only man I have truly loved deserves any sacrifice. And that man is you, Mike. You're not promising me wealth or luxury, and somehow, I like that." She faced him again, and the joy brightened his face in an instant. The smile on his face splitting his mouth. "Yes, Mike, you deserve any sacrifice." Lucia threw her hands around his neck, and Mike pulled her into his arms and threatened to suffocate her in a wild, wistful kiss.

"So, you are going to divorce your husband?"

"Yes, I am. Our marriage is a complete farce."

"And you'll come live with me?"

"Yes, I will. I promise."

The intensity of their kiss conveyed more than words ever could. Mike lifted her in his embrace in a bride-like position, their lips kissing passionately as they spun around. "You have no idea how you've made me feel, hearing all this," Mike whispered in her ear.

"I've been waiting for just you to make up my mind!" Lucia said gently before her mouth gagged his in an even more sizzling, hot-blooded kiss. The time stilled, pain and grief fading away, as they spent the rest of the afternoon, lost in conversations and the ocean of their emotions.

It was shortly before dusk when Lucia got home and she looked nothing but elated, full of desires and longing for the man she loved. Gabriella and Diego had been waiting for her in the salon.

"Lucia!" Gabriella called. "I know you're doing whatever you like, but I'd like to know where you were all day."

Lucia looked at her mother, her happiness evaporated in an instant. "No! I'm exhausted, and I don't have the strength to give explanations."

"Don't forget you're not living alone but with your family. We have a right to know where you go," Gabriella reprimanded her sternly. Her cold eyes piercing through her. "You cannot go here and there and forget you're a married woman."

Antonio joined them in the salon in the heat of the small quarrel. "Antonio, are you annoyed when I go out without telling you where I'm going?" Lucia turned to him, without giving him time to adjust to the conversation.

"He has nothing to do with what I've asked," Gabriella said.

"Is that so, Mother? You're rubbing my marriage in my face and I don't have my freedom," Lucia snapped.

"I don't mind at all," Antonio said emphatically. "I don't have the right to impede her freedom, anyway," he added blithely. Lucia looked at him askance, cocking her head to one side at her mother.

"Antonio, please!" Gabriella exclaimed.

"There is no problem as far as I am concerned. It's true we are married, but we'll be divorced soon anyway," Antonio said.

"No, no! You'll need to discuss the divorce before you take any steps," Diego cut in. "You have to analyze things well before jumping to any final decisions."

"We have discussed it, and we have decided already, Diego. And that's that," Lucia said curtly.

Antonio looked at her with a trace of bewilderment at her words. Lucia had made up her mind, and he wasn't going to oppose her. After all, he was the one suggesting they hurry. But one thing he promised himself was if he couldn't be with her, surely neither could Mike Williams.

"Antonio, are you okay?" Lucia took him out of his musing.

"Yes, yes, I am. I am going to pack my luggage at once," he said curtly and turned to head for his bedroom before Gabriella stopped him.

"No, Antonio, no! You are an important member of the family, and we are going to miss you," Gabriella pleaded and went right by his side.

"Maybe you, but Lucia don't care." He gazed at her for a moment.

"Antonio, please!" Lucia said in exasperation. "I am not insisting you leave immediately. I even want us to talk in private."

"What for? We have said everything there is to say," he snapped. Gabriella stood there, looking deadpan at her daughter.

"Antonio, I don't want you to go as if I am the one forcing you to leave," Lucia said, with a light trace of concern in her voice.

"I am taking my decision alone." Antonio's voice was bitter and sharp. "It's not necessarily that someone evicts me. I am leaving this house today." He went upstairs and left no time for Lucia to argue with his decision, nor Gabriella to beg him to stay.

"Did you see what you did, Lucia?" Diego roared. "You must be happy."

Lucia took a step further, but she stopped herself. She rested her hand on the cap of the newel post and sighed before she slowly turned to her brother.

"Are you okay?" Gabriella frowned at her pale face, and before Lucia could respond, she put her hands on her forehead and crumpled onto the floor, unconscious.

Chapter Thirty-two

"A child!" Isabella exclaimed in the dining room. "Lucia is expecting a child, just when she was about to get divorced!" she added, astounded, and somehow raged.

"I don't know whether to congratulate them or keep my mouth shut," Juan Pablo murmured, equally puzzled. Diego stood and listened, speechless. "Let's go to her," Juan Pablo said.

"No, let's not disturb her, at least not at this moment," Gabriella suggested. "Maybe she's with Antonio." She looked lazily at the rest of the family members, hoping this child would save their marriage.

Antonio went behind the house, grabbed a whip, and started venting his rage on the metal-barred fence, completely losing his temper by the ultimate offense Lucia had inflicted upon him. For a moment, the thought of Mike Williams poked his mind, spurring him to go faster.

"Antonio," Lucia called him several times. "If you want to spill your rage, I'm here. Hit me! I deserve it!"

He looked at her for a moment, fragile and divine in her nightgown. Antonio raised his hand and froze. He couldn't do it. Even after what she had done, his heart craved her and wouldn't allow him to slap her. "You made hundreds of excuses every time I tried to make love to you, enraged if I even tried to kiss you," Antonio said in a raspy voice. His eyes turned to daggers, and his words pierced her heart even more. "No! It was all a lie! A lie! You were having a lover, that's the truth. You were avoiding me as your husband to sleep with the other!" He whipped the fence once more.

"I won't make any excuse now!" Lucia said curtly. "I never loved you, and you knew this."

"Why didn't you wait till we got a divorce? Why did you have to strike right now?" He glared at her. "Is it him? Is it Mike Williams? The father of your baby?" His eyes struck her like lightning. Her face paled, and her heart thudded madly, threatening to break every bone in her chest. Her mind frantically tried to fathom his words and how the idea of Mike even existed. "Why are you silent? Respond!" he roared again, startling Lucia.

"I will never tell you!" she screamed at him. "You will find out soon enough anyway!" she added in much milder tone as her mind processed the thought that there was no way out.

"When? When everybody starts laughing at me because you've been cheating on me? What a sight – the husband who never slept with his wife and now she is pregnant. I will not divorce you, Lucia! No!" Antonio leaned against the fence, his breathing erratic, and he almost choked on the air. "I will stay in this hell, so everyone thinks the baby is mine!"

"Antonio, please!" Lucia gaped at him, sobbing.

"You wanted me to punish you! Well, this is it. I will never let you be free so you can run to the father of the baby." He rolled his eyes at her.

"You are saying it because you're mad and angry." Lucia trembled at the threat. "Sooner or later, you'll realize it's best for us to get divorced."

"I am doing it out of respect for your mother! How are you planning on telling her the truth?"

"I've made up my mind, Antonio! I will face my family, and I will tell them the whole truth. That's my problem!" Her voice raised with determination.

"You are unrecognizable, Lucia! I thought I married an angel, but you're evil. You don't even respect your mother!" Antonio said in disbelief.

"What are you doing here? The stables are not the place to discuss such matters," Gabriella interrupted them with Diego.

"We didn't find anywhere better, Gabriella!" Antonio snorted.

Gabriella looked at them both, caught Antonio by his elbow, and they went to have a word in private. Lucia dashed for her room, as Diego followed her. The last thing she wanted was to listen to another tirade, but it was inevitable when he rushed into her room and slammed the door behind him. Lucia glared at him, still deeply hurt, and curled up in the armchair.

"A child changes everything, Lucia!" He walked over to the bed and gazed at her. "You must respect it above anything else, regardless of your intolerance for your husband. You have no right to divorce him in such a moment," Diego added.

"Why don't you leave me in peace?" Lucia snapped at him.

"And why are you not listening to what I am saying?" Diego cut her off.

"Because it's pointless! You are fully aware I am carrying Mike's child!"

"Quiet!" He put his hand over her mouth. "For everyone, including mom, you are expecting Antonio's baby. Understood?"

Lucia gazed at him, perplexed. Her thoughts racing in her mind, she snivelled. "And you think it's that easy to hide the truth?"

"Of course it is!" he said curtly. "Unless Antonio thinks differently!" he added hesitantly. "In that case, I will try to convince him not to speak!"

"He won't say anything because it's convenient for him!"

"Thank God. You are lucky!" Diego sighed.

Lucia stood up and glared at her brother. "Diego, I am ready to take on anything right this instant. I will divorce him, and I will go live with Mike!" she said curtly and turned to leave, determined to take responsibility.

Diego pulled her arm desperately. "No, Lucia, no! You can't act so stupidly."

While they were arguing, her nerves snapped, and she slapped him hard. He closed his eyes, clenched his jaw tight, and let the pain go away. Lucia's regret crawled on her face and she apologised several times, but he said nothing for a long time. He stood by the door, shook his head in pain and disapproval. "If that's what you want, go ahead! If you're willing to hurt Mom in this way, then go to that dirt-poor man and leave us! But sooner or later, you'll have to face reality. You'll have to endure deprivation, and even hunger! Is this the life you want to subject yourself and that little innocent baby to?" he uttered meekly before closing the door behind him.

The news about the pregnancy had quickly spread throughout the entire house and the surrounding mansions. Juan Pablo and Isabella went to congratulate her on the joyous news, before her mother went to speak with her as well.

That evening, Mike and Jamie went out for a drink, and to talk. Mike's brain was still absorbing the shockwave of Lucia's pregnancy and they jumped at the chance to escape the suffocating air in their house. "This baby could be mine!" Mike said, musing over the idea.

"Why do you think that? Wouldn't it be more logical for the baby to be her husband's?" Jamie asked, taking a sip of his beer.

"Because she doesn't love him," Mike replied, gazing at his brother. "She once told me they had never consummated their marriage."

"If that were the case, do you really think he would have accepted this so easily? Come on, Mike, use your head!" Jamie exclaimed. "Do you know what kind of scandal this could cause?"

Mike pondered his brother's words for a while, but he couldn't convince himself. These people were cautious about such things and had to be careful about discussing personal issues in front of the servants. "I told you I saw Antonio Garcia leaving the house!" Mike spoke up again. "He was concerned and tense. Is it normal for a man who's about to become a father to be anxious and oppressed? No, he would have been happy, for God's sake."

Jamie shook his head, giving up on trying to convince his brother, and went to order another drink. When he returned, Mike was grinning foolishly. "What's with your silly smile?" Jamie asked.

"I need to talk to Lucia! I refuse to believe the promise she gave me would go down the drain."

The next morning, over breakfast, the dining room was oppressively silent, and filled with surreptitious, guilty looks exchanged between Lucia, Antonio, and Diego. Lucia couldn't sleep a wink through the night, as her head was burning with questions and doubt. Her baffled thoughts of right and wrong threatened to explode her brain or, worse, cause her another blackout. From all the conversations with Diego, her mother, and even Magnolia, trying to convince her what was best for her and the child, Lucia could only think of one thing – peace. She had to escape this prison of accusations and sorrow she'd locked herself in. Antonio took a last sip of his coffee and excused himself, but Lucia stopped him on his way out. "Antonio, I want to speak with you in private."

"Why in private and not in front of the family? Say whatever you want. I no longer care! I am ready to take everything," Antonio replied.

Lucia didn't even turn to face him as he was standing right behind her. "You have decided not to divorce me. You told me this yesterday."

Her husband returned to his seat. "And I am saying it again. How can I do it when you're pregnant with my child?" He gazed at her intently.

Lucia sighed at his flickering eyes. "I need time to think, to calm myself and take the fairest decision for all. I don't want to hurt anyone."

"Very well, Lucia!" Gabriella agreed.

"I will be leaving for a few days. I wish to be alone," Lucia said in a low, emphatic voice.

"Where?" Diego queried.

"In the small cabin in Santo Domingo!"

"In the mountains?" Juan Pablo exclaimed in bewilderment. "Why don't you choose some place more fun?"

Lucia furrowed her brow at him. "I am going there to be alone, not to party."

"I also agree with the idea," Isabella cut in. "You know, the place is quite remote, but the air is fresh. It will serve you well."

"I am going this afternoon!"

Antonio looked at her doubtfully. He wasn't sure if he wanted to let her go for an entire week. But he didn't protest when Gabriella asked for his opinion. *This way she's away from that bastard*, he thought and curled his lips into a thin smile.

"All right then, I am coming with you," Gabriella said.

"No, Mama! I need to make this decision on my own!"

"I don't think you should go to such a remote place alone." Diego rolled his eyes with concern. "If you don't want Mother coming with you, nor myself, let Juan Pablo accompany you. What would you say?"

"Why me?" Juan Pablo exclaimed in surprise. "I don't like mountains! I will be howling out of boredom."

"Juan Pablo, please!" Isabella added. "Don't be selfish. It's for your sister! You cannot abandon her when she needs you the most."

"Abuelita, I don't want to leave... because of Penelope," he murmured, thinking on his feet. "I will miss her like crazy."

Diego raised a brow at him but didn't comment.

"There won't be any problems with that," Gabriella said. "I will ask someone to drive her there on the weekend."

"Of course! If you want, we can call her!" Diego crossed his arms over his chest, having a little fun on his own.

"No, it's not necessary," Juan Pablo said through clenched teeth. "She will come to the end of the world for me," he added with a thin smile. When he had no more excuses at hand, he reluctantly agreed.

Mike was chewing on a stick of straw, his leg bouncing to the speed of his heartbeat. He couldn't work as his stare was constantly fixed on the house. Lucia had been avoiding him again, and all he knew was he had to talk to her. When the last straw of his patience broke, he made his way steadfastly to the house, ignoring Jamie's desperate attempts to stop him. Magnolia opened the door and went outside instead of letting him in.

"Where are you going, Mike?" she blocked his way.

"I need to speak to Lucia!"

"Doña Lucia is unable to receive anyone," Magnolia responded firmly, emphasizing her title. "You cannot see her without permission."

"You're against me, aren't you?" He cast an unwavering gaze at the woman.

"And do you think I should be on your side?" Magnolia said. "Be cautious! It's best for everyone. You're too impulsive, and you don't know what you're doing."

"Magnolia, you're aware of everything that goes on in this house. You know the child Lucia is expecting could be mine!"

Magnolia averted her eyes, crossed her arms over her chest, and emitted a long, heavy sigh.

"I have rights!" Mike cut in.

"What rights could you have over a married woman?" Magnolia gazed at him with utmost desperation at his stubbornness and audacity. "And who said the baby is yours? Come to your senses, Mike!"

"You don't understand anything!" Mike blew up. "I'm desperate!" The sincerity was evident in his wet eyes. The anger and tension took turns in his heart, which he found extremely difficult to contain with each passing day.

"If she wishes, she will find a way to talk to you! Don't make any moves for now!" Magnolia said and entered the house.

When Lucia was ready to go, she gave a note to Magnolia, asking her to give it to Mike. "It's much better this way," she mumbled to herself. A new wave of tears pricked her eyes, but she managed to compose herself.

Penelope had also taken to the idea of visiting the forest, the rivers, and the peace of Santo Domingo during the weekends. She had accepted the invitation with great pleasure, insisting on spending as much time there as they could. Thus, Lucia was going to take her brother away from the temptation and this foolish boy, Jamie, who was messing with his mind.

"Umm…" Juan Pablo raised an eyebrow at her. "You sound more like an enemy than an ally," he said as they strolled alone in the backyard.

"I'm saying this for your own good. You need a serious reality check!" Penelope stopped and turned to him. "I don't like how much you're consumed with Jamie. You were even kidnapped because of him."

"I'll stop meeting him only in your dreams. I'm ready to go through anything, in case you haven't noticed."

Juan Pablo winked at her with the brightest of all his smiles and left.

Penelope watched him walk away, crossed her arms over her chest, and narrowed her eyes. "When will these workers disappear?" she muttered, as a couple of grooms passed by her and gave her strange looks.

Juan Pablo approached Jamie, called him in a professional manner, and slipped a note into his hands. Jamie looked around and examined the note, which appeared to be a map with directions. Juan Pablo informed him he would be gone for the week. "If you truly meant what you said, you'll come!" Juan Pablo murmured and walked away as Jamie stared after him, his mind a tangled ball of yarn, impossible to unravel.

Chapter Thirty-three

Jamie arrived in the mountain town. The roads were wet and deserted as Jamie drove slowly ahead. Despite being exhausted from the early morning wake-up and long journey, adrenaline kept him wide awake. He parked the car a few houses down the road, turned off the music, and texted Juan Pablo, *I am here*. A few moments later, Juan Pablo appeared from behind the hedge fence of a small mountain house. Jamie let out a heavy sigh, gathered his nerves, and got out of the car as Juan Pablo waved him closer.

"What took you so long? I thought you wouldn't come," Juan Pablo said, anxious not to be seen.

"How could I resist a brazen challenge?" Juan Pablo arched a daring, sexy brow, but didn't comment. He pulled Jamie's arm, urging him to a safer location. "What are you doing?" Jamie snorted.

"I don't want Lucia to see us."

"Is that why you asked me to come, to cause more trouble for both of us?"

"What? Are you afraid?"

"Juan Pablo, why did you ask me to come? What do you want to talk about?" Jamie tried to hide his impatience.

"We can talk about many things, but not here!" Juan Pablo said, glancing towards the house. "Why don't we take a stroll in the forest?" He turned to lead the way, but Jamie hesitated.

"What? Are you scared?" Juan Pablo taunted.

Jamie gazed at Juan Pablo's gray-blue eyes and cursed his weakness inwardly. "Show me the way," he murmured, and they both hurried off on the narrow path, leading to the heart of the mountain forest. Juan Pablo navigated the trees skillfully, as if he wanted to show Jamie something. "Okay, enough!" Jamie said in an irritated, raspy voice. The heat trapped between the trees began to seep into his body. "Where are we going?"

"What? I don't remember you getting tired easily," Juan Pablo said with a broad smile.

Jamie gazed at him and a wave of intimidation rippled through his body. Memories of their brazen encounter in the desert flooded his mind, and the heat in his body rose by a hundredfold. "You're the devil," he murmured.

"In my defense, you are bigger than me," Juan Pablo said, amused, and scooted ahead.

Jamie soon lost sight of him and forced himself to continue alone. "Juan Pablo, wait!" he shouted. "As if the desert wasn't enough, you had to bring me to this jungle! Juan Pablo!"

He took a few steps forward and slipped on something hidden beneath the wild vegetation covering the path. Fortunately, he instinctively grabbed a tree branch, preventing himself from falling face first. After looking around, he turned left and shouted for Juan Pablo once again. He pulled aside a few shrub branches blocking his sight and cursed him for being left alone in this godforsaken place. "You deserved it, Jamie Williams!" he scolded himself. "You let yourself be tricked into something silly. Now you'll get lost here and won't be able to return! Juan Pablo!" He swore once more, to no avail.

The forest began to thin, and the place brightened. The serenity of the place barely made Jamie stop and admire the view for a moment, as his mind was occupied with the rage and anger of his wet shoes. He crossed several other large stones along the bank and shouted for Juan Pablo once again.

"Are you scared of the forest? Is that why you're screaming so loudly?" Juan Pablo teased, standing on a stony plate, the waters of the fall behind him overflowing onto the rocks.

Jamie lifted his gaze from his path and looked at him. "If you heard me, why didn't you respond?" he asked.

"Scared boys entertain me!" Juan Pablo smiled, tucking his hands into the pockets of his jeans, shrugging his shoulders. "And you're like that – sometimes a child, and sometimes a demon," he added in a light, nonchalant tone.

"You know what? I don't like this at all. Let's go back!" Jamie shouted over the sound of the tempestuous waters of the fall pouring into the riverbed.

"No!" Juan Pablo said lazily. "Not yet! I feel hot, and I don't want to go back!" He gazed at Jamie, and his lips curled into a provocative smile. He swiftly removed his t-shirt, sinking his teeth into his bottom lip. In a moment, he freed himself from his jeans too, and threw them aside.

"Hmm... if that's how you want to play it!" Jamie murmured, the corners of his lips curling up mischievously.

Juan Pablo had underestimated how much Jamie liked to be challenged, but he relished the feeling. He enjoyed the adrenaline that surged through him, the tingling excitement of the unknown. With a swift motion, he shed his vest, revealing the sinewy muscles that rippled beneath his skin, and discarded his shoes with a decisive flick, letting them tumble haphazardly to the side. There was something electric about the way Jamie's presence charged the air, an enigmatic allure that kept Juan Pablo spellbound, craving more but unable to define what exactly it was.

Jamie's fingers fumbled with the buckle of his jeans, his breath quickening with anticipation as he gingerly stepped onto the slick stone surface. Despite the numbing cold that seeped into his feet, he inched forward with unwavering determination, his eyes fixed on Juan Pablo. Sensing his approach, Juan Pablo crouched down and scooped up handfuls of icy water, flinging them playfully at Jamie. Jamie gasped sharply as the frigid water crashed over him, the chill seeping into his skin, numbing the heat that coursed through his veins. Summoning his own resolve, he retaliated by kicking a spray of water back at Juan Pablo, who yelped in surprise, throwing his hands up to shield his face, his laughter mingling with the roaring cascade behind them.

In a spontaneous moment of connection, Jamie reached out, his fingers brushing against Juan Pablo's skin as he helped him to his feet. Drawing him closer, Jamie wrapped his arms around Juan Pablo's waist, the embrace firm and possessive. With a surge of longing, Jamie leaned in, parting his lips to meet Juan Pablo's in a fervent, unyielding kiss. Their bodies melded together, the water from the cascading falls drizzling over them in a shimmering curtain, cocooning them in a world of their own creation. As their lips parted, they locked eyes, the intensity of their gaze reflecting the fierce passion that pulsed between them, leaving them both breathless and yearning for more.

"What games are you playing, Juan Pablo?"

"The ones I've always liked."

"Silly?"

"Dangerous!" Juan Pablo murmured and sucked on Jamie's lower lip. Their tongues met again, dancing rhythmically, as Juan Pablo slid his hand down Jamie's manhood, rubbing it vigorously as it elongated beneath his fingers. Jamie took a step back, stripped his pants and underwear, allowing Juan Pablo to fully enjoy the show.

Juan Pablo crouched down, wrapping his hands around Jamie's athletic legs for support, and his lips instinctively parted. His tongue slid between his lips, his teeth sank into his lower lip as he instinctively looked up at Jamie, before he ran his lips against the head of Jamie's manhood, making him shiver. "Fuck!" Jamie moaned.

In a moment, Juan Pablo's wet mouth devoured the entire length of Jamie's shaft. His moans grew louder, more frequent, as he pulled his head back. Jamie put his hand on Juan Pablo's head, closing his eyes at the marvelous sensation this man had brought him. And if he wasn't sure the first time, he was fully convinced now – he craved him in a way he'd never thought he would feel for another man. He pulled back and turned Juan Pablo around against the wall of rocks. Jamie's piercing gaze fixed on Juan Pablo's, as he averted his gaze back to face him, quickly removing his boxers and slightly leaned forward. In a moment, his mouth opened, emitting a loud gasp as Jamie slid deep inside. Their moans lost in the music of the falling waters; their minds lost in the pleasure.

When they dove into the depths of the pool of sweetness, they found it hard to resist the pleasure of their climax. Once they came, exhausted, they kissed and inhaled the invigorating mountain air sharply before jumping into the icy waters of the river, splashing water at each other, then pressing bodies together to keep warm.

When their bodies couldn't take any more of the cold waters, they lay on the riverbank, legs wrapped around each other. Juan Pablo rested his head on Jamie's arm, making circles with his finger on Jamie's chest. Jamie glanced at him for a moment, and turned to one side, facing him. "Juan Pablo, what are we really doing?" he asked, gazing at him with unwavering eyes.

"What do you mean?" Juan Pablo replied.

"I mean, I'm a simple worker at your home who might not even be there tomorrow, and you're getting married in a week."

"Are you jealous?" He couldn't help but smirk.

"This isn't funny."

"All right, all right!" Juan Pablo said, his face straightening as he gazed at him with profound eyes. "I don't know how you feel, but I'm crazy about you." His eyes locked in on Jamie's, barely restraining his hands from touching him. "It's true, I've made such a mess and I don't know how I'm going to get out of it, but I know I don't want to lose you." He kissed the back of Jamie's hand and gazed at him again.

"Then don't get married."

"You think it's that simple?"

Jamie said nothing. His pouty face was hidden behind wet curls of hair as he stood up, picking up his clothes and quickly put them on, still wet here and there.

"What are you doing?" Juan Pablo stood up, trying to work out the change in Jamie's mood.

"I'm going home!" Jamie snorted. "I don't know why I even came."

"No, wait!" Juan Pablo grabbed his wrists as Jamie's eyes momentarily fell on his grip. "I'm sure we can think of something."

"Really? Like what?" Jamie turned to him, casting an inquisitive gaze.

"I don't know," Juan Pablo blurted out, trying to come up with ideas. "Are you okay with seeing each other secretly when I'm married?"

Jamie furrowed his brows in offense and turned to go, before Juan Pablo stood in his way. "Why are you making it such a big deal?"

"Because I love you!" The words slipped off Jamie's tongue in a short scream, as he was caught up in his own tension. "Because I'm in love with you!" Jamie wanted to scream again, but his voice came out as a whisper. The sound of his own words, voiced out loud, made him regret even started this whole thing. *"What a jerk I am,"* he mused scolding himself inwardly before Juan Pablo put his hands on Jamie's cheeks and kissed him deeply, longingly, as if this was the reassurance he'd been waiting for.

"Even if you're lying to me, I don't regret anything that's happened between us." He kissed him again, as they closed their eyes, holding each other's sides, and let the ground beneath them disappear.

By the time Jamie had to leave, Juan Pablo knew he had to think of a way to get out of this marriage, even if it meant standing up to his mother.

"Do you think someone might have seen us?" Jamie asked as he passed by the house.

"I don't think so, but it's getting late, and Lucia must be jumping out of her skin."

"When will I see you again?"

"When I come back." Juan Pablo gave him a small goodbye kiss as Jamie simply smiled and jumped into his car. Juan Pablo stood there, volts of excitement coursing through his body, until the headlights of the car faded into the darkness.

"Lucia!" Juan Pablo exclaimed as he turned to go inside. Her slap tore the silence.

Back in the house, Juan Pablo was in the ninth circle of hell as Lucia paced around the living room, rubbing her forehead. She desperately needed to absorb the scene she had witnessed. "Please, Lucia, let me explain what happened," Juan Pablo begged, desperate.

"Explain? Do you think I need an explanation?" she screamed at him. "I saw you! I saw you with Jamie Williams!"

"I see you're angry, but please listen to me without judging."

"No! I can't! I can't!" She burst into tears. "I can't because..." She buried her face in her hands, still absorbing the event. "I'm in the same situation," she added at last, heavily sighing.

Lucia wasn't even mad at her brother being into men, she was mad at her brother's choice of man. Even though she'd told him about her secret affair, she never mentioned to him who she was seeing. And she blamed herself for that. Her heart sank in remorse, her mind in turmoil. She faced her brother with damp, tear-streaked cheeks. "I am going to pretend I haven't seen anything," Lucia said, wiping her lower eyelids and calming her tone. "Do whatever you want! I have no right to meddle in your life!" She turned to go to her bedroom, but her brother stopped her.

"Lucia, please, let's talk about this," he pleaded.

"No, Juan Pablo, no! There is nothing to talk about. We'll leave. I won't allow this to happen again," she said emphatically. "I came here because I wanted to find an answer for myself, and I found it. You helped me find it! I will do what I have to! Thank you!" she said sarcastically at the door and walked out.

When Jamie got home, he went straight to the shower, humming. As he turned on the hot water, it momentarily brought him back to the waterfall. He could smell him, see him, and touch him. His mind tried to recollect all the women he'd slept with, yet none of them had brought such waves of emotions in him as the dozen dates in secret with Juan Pablo and the couple of intimate ones.

"Can you tell me where you went all day long?" Mike pulled the shower curtain aside, snapping him out of his thoughts.

"What's wrong with you?" Jamie snorted and pulled the curtain back. "Leave me alone! I will tell you later."

"No! You will tell me now!" Mike demanded.

Jamie turned off the water, grabbed his towel, and wrapped himself in it. "For your information, I was with Juan Pablo Alvarez. As the saying goes, I hold him in the palm of my hand, even though neither you nor Chloe believed in me. I got what I wanted. Are we clear?" Jamie plastered a broad, satisfied smile on his face, pulled the curtain back, and headed to his room, humming.

Chapter Thirty-four

Lucia had barely slept the previous night, as the image of her brother and Jamie being naked on the riverbank kept invading her thoughts. She had come to find inner peace, but now her brother had worsened things to new, unbearable heights. When morning arrived, Gabriella and Penelope drove to Santo Domingo to pick up Lucia and Juan Pablo.

As they pulled up to the mansion, Lucia looked at her home and smiled. Antonio was standing next to the entrance, talking business with Magnolia and Mike. Her heart raced at the sight of the two men in her life – her husband, whom she hated, and the man she would die for. The small crowd dispersed when she approached and without saying a word to her husband, she walked into the house, but he stopped her by the staircase.

"What? Have you decided, or do you have nothing to tell me?" he asked impatiently.

"Yes, I have," Lucia replied, her unwavering gaze fixed into his hazel brown eyes. "We'll talk. We'll finally establish some order in our relationship."

Once they entered their bedroom, Lucia threw her bag on the bed and turned to Antonio, determined. "You said you didn't want us to get divorced, regardless of the facts. Well, then, we won't get divorced. I give up on that."

Antonio walked around the room, laughing, leaving her confused by his unexpected reaction. "It seems your lover isn't worth much if you give up on him so easily!" he said, a hint of satisfaction and mockery in his voice.

"It wasn't easy at all, I assure you!" Lucia retorted, with a grim expression. "It took me more than a week to make this decision."

"Wonderful! And now, tell me, what's going to be my role in this?" Antonio asked.

"The one you chose yourself. You'll be my husband and the father of my child." She gazed at him walking around the room.

"As a father of a child that is not mine, I don't know how I will cope with it, but as your husband, I want to know what my rights will be." Antonio cocked his head to one side, his eyes full of intent. "Will I be a real husband or the ornamental object I was all this time?"

Lucia wondered if he meant the question. She forced herself to respond. "You'll be the same as you were so far. Don't look for intimacy. You know I don't love you."

"Yeah, yeah! You are in love with another man," Antonio said with irritation. "You know what? It seems to me that this time you are looking for an easy way to correct a mistake you are regretting." He grabbed her chin and forced her to look at him.

"I am only sharing my decision," she hissed in his face and took a step back from him. "If you are not satisfied, we can always proceed with the divorce." She mollified her anger.

"I am not going to give you this pleasure and clear your way so you can run after him," he said curtly and turned to her. "And I am also not thinking of obeying your terms. I have my own."

"Which are?" She arched an eyebrow.

"First, don't even imagine I will let you ever meet this man! You'll go out only with me! Second, I am not going to stay in the guest room forever. I will ask Gabriella to buy us our own house, and I will look for my marital rights."

Lucia had to bite her lip to stifle a scream as the harrowing image invaded her mind. She didn't know if she could endure a day under his terms. Her eyes welled with tears, and before the anguish spilled out in front of him, Magnolia interrupted them for a moment to announce lunch was served.

Once they went to the dining room, Lucia asked him to announce their decision. "Lucia realized her delicate state. The situation has radically changed, and we don't need to divorce. The topic is no longer on the agenda," Antonio stated, and Lucia guiltily bent her gaze down.

"My dear!" Gabriella gave up her seat and went to her. She gave her daughter a kiss and put her hand in Antonio's, beaming at the news. "Thank you! Thank you both! You've made the best decision," she added, nearly crying at the wonderful news.

After lunch, Lucia headed for the servants' room. She had to bring the news to Mike, trying to ignore the sick feeling in her stomach for doing it. She fervently fought her tears as her mind was still processing the happening. She still wasn't sure if that was what was best for her. Lucia put her hand on her stomach, vigilantly looked around, and entered the room. Mike looked at her and smiled fondly as her presence brightened his world.

How long had it been since she was last here? In the room where everything started. He went to her and tried to kiss her, but she rebuffed him before he could even lean in for a kiss.

"No, Mike, I only want us to talk," she said with a trembling voice. She went further down the room, turned her back to him, and uttered her last decision.

"Lucia, what are you talking about?" Mike said, wishing it was all a nightmare and he would wake up any minute now.

"I am trying to be rational. I know I am hurting you, but I must choose between marital duties and my feelings toward you," she paused. Her voice shaky, she barely stopped herself from falling into his arms.

"And you will leave me?" Mike said hesitantly. "You'll throw me away?"

"Believe me, I am hurt, and I feel miserable," she said, sniffing. "But I am obliged to remain with my husband."

Mike went to her and put his hands on her hot, yet wet, cheeks – her skin, her face, her everything. He couldn't bear the thought of losing her. "Lucia don't do it! I am begging you!" His voice trembled with utmost pain, threatening to tear his heart apart. "What am I going to do with my feelings? My life loses any sense without you."

"It isn't easy for me either." Lucia gazed at his wet eyes, filled with heartfelt grief.

"Well, obviously you don't love me as much as I thought," he uttered in a low voice. "You even promised me we'd be together."

Lucia bit her lip in desperation. "Mike, please. How could this happen when…" She paused and sighed. "Your brother and Juan Pablo are having a relationship."

"What?" Mike exclaimed, frowning. "So this is the real reason?" He gazed back at her, unsure of his own mixed feelings about the news.

"I saw them, Mike. I saw them with my own eyes. I don't know what your brother's intentions with Juan Pablo are, but they seemed serious, and that's why we need to break up completely. I can't deal such a blow on Mom. It's enough that one of her children discredits her."

"Lucia, please!" Mike swallowed, as his mouth went dry. "In the name of what's most sacred to you…"

"Mike, please don't say anything." Lucia sniffled again and wiped her tears. "I must be next to my mom when she finds out about Juan Pablo. The scandal that will follow is going to be terrible." She gazed at him one last time and went to leave.

Mike abruptly pulled her into his embrace and ran his hands through her hair. He kissed her tenderly, fondly, with the deepest affection he possessed, then he stopped. Lucia buried her face in her hands and slowly headed for the door. She wasn't ready to leave him, nor was he, yet she turned to him and said, "I don't want to see you anymore. I am begging you to leave the mansion as soon as possible. I will only suffer if you are around." The cramps in her soul got unbearable and were about to break her into pieces. "You will also be hurt!" she added, and before Mike could say anything, she was gone.

Mike leaned on the table, sweeping everything to one side. The anger consumed him like a bushfire consuming a tree. He didn't even wait for the workday to end. He got into his car and sped home, and when he got there, their home turned into a gladiators' arena when Mike jumped out of the blue at Jamie.

"Mike, please leave him alone!" Chloe begged as the two brothers ran around the table in the living room. "Oh my God, you'll kill him."

"Mike, please stop! Why are you so mad at me?" Jamie said in a breathy voice.

Mike grabbed the fruit from the table, furiously throwing it at Jamie. "You are the devil!" Mike roared. "I lost everything because of you!"

Chloe stood there, panicked, as the fruits from the bowl on the table flew in all directions.

"You don't care about anything but your interests," Mike continued.

"How could I know Lucia would find out and Juan Pablo would confess?" Jamie said apologetically.

"To confess? She saw you with her own eyes." Mike threw a couple of apples, flying an inch above Jamie's head.

"Mike, please calm down!" Chloe screamed at him in tears. "He's your brother!"

"No! This shameless rascal is not my brother! He is a traitor who stole my dreams," Mike said, glaring at Jamie. "He is a selfish man who doesn't love anybody but himself. I love Lucia! I would give my life for her! And him? What does he know about loving another person?"

As the two of them started chasing each other around the table again, Jamie headed for the door, ducking as a couple of oranges flew towards him and broke the window.

"Mike, stop!" Chloe grabbed his shoulder. "Enough! I can't put up with these quarrels anymore." Chloe looked around the room, which looked like it had been hit by a tornado. "We'll have to move out! Every time you fight, you break something." She looked at the chunks of glass scattered on the floor. Mike rested his elbows on his legs, burying his head in his palms. Chloe ran her hands over his back for comfort, but it didn't do much to help.

"I don't care a bit! I don't give a shit when this bastard ruins everything he touches," Mike said in raspy voice. Tears streamed down his face, and his sorrow overwhelmed him. "He is not my brother!"

That night, Mike and Lucia went to bed late, shaken by their emotions. Mike stared blankly at the ceiling for a long time. He wouldn't forget her – her ivory smile, the velvet skin, the enigmatic eyes staring at him. "I am not ready to lose you, Lucia! I cannot lose you."

"I'm sorry, Mike! My hands are tied, and I am so weak and helpless!" Lucia cried in her own bed, colder than it had ever been before. Tears wet her pillow, and anguish stuck in her throat. She ran her fingers on her stomach as if holding onto the strongest connection she had with him.

Chloe gazed out of the window for a long time, thinking about the past four months changing their lives forever. The love lives of her brothers were a mess that never ended. They quarreled almost every evening after work, and Chloe had barely been home in the last month because she couldn't endure it. That night she had finally decided to tell them about Mr Brighton, who had asked her to marry him, but they were so estranged from each other that she found it best to keep quiet. "Why are you still awake?" Jamie startled her by appearing in the doorway.

"I am thinking!" she murmured.

"About what?"

"Everything! How it all started!" She gazed at him for a moment before turning to her brother. "But I am more concerned how this will end." She went to him. "Jamie, please talk to him. I don't want to go back to that house. What he has planned, telling them the entire truth, is absolute madness. They'll kill us!"

Jamie left the glass of juice on the table and looked hopelessly at his sister. "You know him, Chloe, and I don't know if any of us can stop him." He emitted another heavier sigh, his heart thudding madly at the thought of the uncertain tomorrow.

Chapter Thirty-five

As the moon cast its silvery glow through the crack of the nearly pulled-to curtains, Jamie found himself caught in the clutches of a restless night. Tossing and turning in bed, his mind was a whirlwind of worries and anxieties that refused to grant him the solace he desperately sought. "What a stubborn man," he mumbled, casting an inquisitive look over at his brother, making sure he was sound asleep in his bed. Jamie turned to yet another position. His mind, a battlefield of racing thoughts, replayed moments, from the conversation he had with Mike and Chloe earlier that evening, like a relentless movie that might as well turn into reality if Mike carried out his plan.

The illuminating light of his phone blinded him as he peered at the time. He swiftly tossed the blanket to one side, got up and opened the wardrobe, grabbing a bag of clothes he had prepared the night before. The creaking sound made him instinctively turn his gaze to his brother, in dire hope that he could tiptoe out of the room unnoticed. He slid into his jeans and the shirt Chloe had ironed for him, put on his jacket and hat, and closed the door behind him. He headed down the road and stopped several houses from his own. The car stopped, and the two men got out in unusually cheering mood.

"Are we late?" Miguel greeted him with a wave.

"No, right on time." Jamie looked around to make sure no one had seen them. "Are we ready to go?"

"Yes, lead the way!" Carlos, Miguel's brother, said as they all jumped in the car and disappeared into the darkness.

Jamie skillfully navigated them through the streets of the town, and with the first rays of the sun, the Wrangler SUV was flying down the dirt roads between the villages.

"Wow, the journey is long," Miguel said. "You never mentioned we would be driving out of town."

"Yeah, it's a long journey, but we're almost there." Jamie leaned forward against the driver's seat.

"Why do I know this road?" Miguel pondered. "I must have been here before."

"I still can't believe you're getting married. Does she live in a mansion?" Carlos queried with a smirk.

"There are only mansions in this area." Jamie's eyes jumped from one house to another lined along the way. "And about that, it's actually 'him'," he added, clearing his throat with hints of awkwardness. The two brothers gaped at him with bewilderment. "What the hell, man?" Jamie said as the Jeep veered to the right end, but, thankfully, Miguel got it back on track. His heart jumping from his chest to his mouth and back a few times before the car stopped as they neared the man who was nervously waiting. Jamie went to Juan Pablo, who reached to kiss him, but Jamie turned his head to one side, at the awkward stares of his friends and Juan Pablo's lips fell on his cheek.

"Who are those people?" He appraised them closely.

"Our witnesses! The only ones I could find." Jamie rubbed his chin and looked at them doubtfully. Juan

Pablo managed a thin smile in response, and soon the car was flying back to town.

Carlos pulled over right in front of the city hall. Once outside, the air was electrified with anticipation, excitement humming through the bodies. Jamie caught Juan Pablo's hand and rushed inside, but he stopped him midway on the stairs.

"Wait! Are we sure about what we're doing?" Juan Pablo gazed at him, as if waiting for reassurance that they were doing the right thing.

"We've come this far. You can't give up now!" Jamie said, slight annoyance creeping into his voice.

"Juan Pablo, stop right there!" Penelope screamed through the rolled-down window of the green VW Beetle as it came to a stop. She rushed out of the car like a bullet aimed to pierce through them. "What are you thinking? You can do whatever you like?"

"Penelope, what are you doing here?" Juan Pablo stuttered, his gaze darting between her and Jamie.

"Trying to stop you from doing another absurdity."

"The decision is mine alone. You have no right to interfere."

"What do you want? To marry this peasant who isn't even properly dressed?" She appraised him doubtfully and returned her full attention to Juan Pablo. "You're coming with me! He's a good-for-nothing." She clenched her teeth, grabbing him by the wrist and pulling him towards her car.

"Penelope, let him go!" Jamie said with a great dose of annoyance, but Juan Pablo convinced him to stay out of it. His stare dwelled on the girl again. Her eyes were firing bullets in all directions. "Penelope, if you have any respect for me whatsoever, please don't interfere." He made a little pouty face. "We're friends and allies, aren't we?"

"No, we're not! It's over!" she growled. "I'm your fiancé, and you'll marry me."

"But I love Jamie."

"You don't love anyone." She laughed nervously. "You're just a bad boy who does crazy, stupid things, and you're supposed to be smart. I'm the best choice for you." Her tone was as serious as her face.

"Penelope, I've never really thought of marrying you."

"You can't leave me like this. I can't lose my aunt's inheritance!" Penelope's eyes welled with tears at the horrifying thought. "I am calling your family right away," she threatened in a desperate attempt to prevent what was happening.

"Do as you wish!" Juan Pablo snapped at her. "Find another man to gain your aunt's money. Poor or rich, I love this man and that's that!" Juan Pablo said, turning to go back to Jamie, but she pulled him back.

Jamie waved to his friends and they quickly jumped to Juan Pablo's rescue, holding her as she vigorously tried to pluck herself from their strong grip, screaming desperately. Jamie and Juan Pablo looked at each other again, and walked inside, holding hands, pretending not to notice the desperate cries of the girl.

They walked down the aisle between the empty chairs, their eyes fixed on the registrar before them. Their nerves tugged like guitar strings, yet their excitement shone through their smiles.

"Are we ready?" The registrar smiled, and the modest ceremony commenced as Miguel and Carlos joined them.

Once outside, Jamie's heart danced like a butterfly, his smile radiant as the sun. He looked down at the golden ring, stark evidence that he was now a member of a new society, determined to live up to the standards he had dreamed of for so long. His gaze moved onto his husband, a glimpse into their future, and then frowned at the rice Miguel and Carlos were playfully throwing. "That's enough," he protested, squeezing his eyes shut.

"It is tradition," Carlos cheered, teasing him about their honeymoon.

Juan Pablo's attention shifted as he noticed Penelope's car still parked in the same place, her head bent low behind the steering wheel, seemingly trying to remain unnoticed. "This chick isn't giving up," Miguel remarked, his gaze following in the same direction.

"Let's go!" Jamie urged. "I don't want any trouble with her."

"But what if she follows us?" Juan Pablo looked at him, a trace of concern flickered in his eyes.

"Leave her to us and go," Carlos said calmly, bidding them farewell as the newlyweds set off.

The sound of screeching tires echoed as the black Range Rover pulled up. Gabriella slammed the door and hurried towards her son, with Diego and Antonio following. Her anger blazed like an inferno, consuming everything in its path, leaving only ashes and echoes of fury. Seeing Jamie Williams brought back images from the contentious meeting she had just endured with his siblings at her own house. And when Diego informed her of her son's marriage, her fury struck with the precision and speed of a viper, leaving a potent and lingering poison in its wake. The sight of her son standing next to another Williams threatened to push her into a complete nervous breakdown.

"Step away from this man immediately!" Gabriella roared. Her voice pierced like a descending thunderstorm, each word carrying the booming resonance of thunder and the sharp crackle of lightning.

"Why?" Juan Pablo furrowed his brows as Gabriella grabbed his crooked elbow and tugged him toward the car.

"I am your mother, and I am ordering you to do so," she said, but Juan Pablo managed to free himself from her firm grip.

"Don't even look at him and forget about this nonsense wedding."

"He can't forget anything," Jamie interjected. "We are already married, ma'am."

"That's not true!" Gabriella stared at him, her mind feverishly rejecting his words.

"It's true. These are the witnesses. They can confirm it," Jamie explained, gesturing to those around.

Gabriella stood there, her expression blank as she struggled to accept the bitter truth. Her eyes darted between Juan Pablo and his husband, her breath growing shorter.

"It's true, Mama. I am already married," Juan Pablo asserted, summoning his courage. He held Gabriella's gaze, his mouth dry, his words serving as the final blow that shattered her denial. She raised her hand and slapped his cheek with fury, making his head turn to one side.

"Don't you dare, Mrs Alvarez," Jamie hissed from behind. "You don't have the right."

Diego locked eyes with Jamie, his heart racing as wildly as his blood rushed to his head. He fought desperately against the urge to attack Jamie, but his self-control wavered. He reached out to strike, only to be restrained by Antonio at the last possible moment. "Antonio, let go of me! I'll put this scumbag in his place!" Diego roared, his breath ragged. His icy glare bore into Jamie, who managed to steady his nerves under the intense scrutiny.

"Have you lost your mind, Juan Pablo?" Gabriella shouted, her voice cracking with teary frustration. "Please tell me he forced you into this," she implored, her tears welling up.

"Gabriella, please calm down," Antonio intervened, his eyes scanning the gathered onlookers. "Let's go back to the mansion. People are watching."

Gabriella met Antonio's gaze, as if silently conceding. She retreated into the car, slamming the door shut. As the others followed, the screech of tires shattered the otherwise quiet afternoon.

As soon as the cars parked outside the grand hacienda, Magnolia rushed into the reception hall. "Be prepared. They're here!" She paused, trying to catch her breath, before continuing, "Together with Jamie and Mr Juan Pablo."

Mike glanced at his sister, who was trembling with nerves in the white armchair. Chloe swallowed hard as she gazed at Magnolia, and once again pleaded with her brother to leave. She stood up, took a step to the door before Gabriella hurried into the room, coming to an abrupt halt as if she had forgotten that Mike and Chloe were still present. Her intense gaze lingered on Chloe, causing her to lower her head and stand beside her brother, revealing only half of her body, right before the whole family joined them.

"Well, now that we're all here, we can clarify everything," Gabriella said, pacing slowly around the room, as if she were relentlessly fighting the urge to calm herself down. "I blindly trusted Magnolia by putting her in charge of hiring new staff." She stopped in her tracks and turned to her. "And she hired these people knowing full well who they were. She lied to me, saying that they were sent by an agency and deceived us all. Explain!"

Gabriella's booming tone caused Magnolia to visibly shiver. Her eyes were buried in her fidgeting fingers. Gabriella's voice echoed within the sterile walls before Jamie spoke again. "It's better if we explain," he cleared his throat and removed his hat.

"I don't want to hear another word from you," Gabriella said through clenched teeth. Her unwavering gaze pierced through him as he stood there as unyielding as steel, staring back at the woman.

"What's there to explain, gentlemen?" Penelope said. "Let's call the police." She turned to Gabriella, who was visibly shaking with nerves. She turned to Antonio, as if asking his opinion with her stare, and as soon as he gave her a hesitant look, she turned to the brothers and Chloe, who stood petrified before the elegant woman.

"No, I don't want to deal with that," she whimpered. "I won't file any complaints, but I am not going to accept you or this marriage under any circumstances." Her words came as staccato, shifting her gaze to Jamie. "You won't get your way," she hissed as if her hatred intensified each time she looked him in the eyes. "I won't let you into my family."

"I fell in love with Juan Pablo, not with your family," Jamie replied, his tone slightly dry. "And I am married to him, not to you. For me, what matters is that we are lawfully wed," he added, a hint of a contented smile crawling at the corner of his mouth but it was hard to tell.

"Get out of my house right now! Go away! I don't want to see you for the rest of my life!" Gabriella roared as Diego sank his fingers firmly into her fragile shoulders, barely holding her back from lashing out at him.

"No, Mom, how can you just let them go?" Diego threw another menacing look at Jamie and his siblings. "They should pay for what they did."

Gabriella staggered, quickly placing her hand on her forehead, and gripping the armrest of the armchair with the other.

"Jamie, let's go!" Chloe begged as Diego helped his mother to sit down. "Mrs Alvarez needs rest."

"Come on Jamie," Mike said in a low voice. Jamie glanced at Juan Pablo who only nodded in agreement.

As they finally embarked on the journey back home in the worn-out pickup, Chloe's breath began to steady, and a sense of liberation washed over her. She stole a glance at her brothers, their faces etched with a mix of exhaustion and relief. "We made it out of there, didn't we?" Chloe's voice quivered, still tinged with the residual fear that had gripped her.

In the driver's seat, Mike's grip on the wheel tightened, his knuckles turning white. He couldn't shake the haunting image of Lucia's mesmerizing eyes from his mind. They seemed to bore into his soul, leaving an ache he couldn't easily dismiss. With every mile that separated him from her, a pang of regret gnawed at him, threatening to unravel his resolve. He stole a glance at his own reflection in the rearview mirror, searching for answers he couldn't quite articulate. The landscape shifted, the winding road fading behind them. Lucia's face grew distant, a memory held captive by the rear glass. Mike's heart weighed heavy with the finality of their departure, his own silent farewell echoing in the quiet car.

Epilogue

The quietude of the room was stifling as Jamie stood before the mirror, his reflection frowning back at himself and the more he adjusted the collar of his shirt, the deeper his frustration grew. Mike leaned against the doorframe, arms crossed over his chest, his gaze fixed on his brother for a long moment before he pretentiously coughed to get his brother's attention.

"Why have you dressed up like this?" he asked in a casual tone as Jamie flashed a mischievous grin and sauntered over, semi-pleased with his appearance.

"For your information, I'm heading over to the Alvarezs' place," Jamie responded, reaching for his hat. "It's been more than a week now since the wedding, so Doña Gabriella must've had plenty of time to cool down and come to terms with reality," he remarked. His resolute gaze fixed on his brother as Mike's lips curved into a subtle twist of a smile, and he skeptically arched an eyebrow.

"You really don't know what dignity means," Mike retorted. "Do you really think they will accept you?"

Jamie put on his cowboy hat and looked at him once more. "They don't have a choice. Doña Gabriella is very conservative, but she'll have to agree with the facts." He cast one final glance in the mirror, taming the last unruly curl beneath his hat, before he strode out.

The sun, a blazing orb of brilliance, bestowed its warm, golden caress upon the sprawling estate. Jamie's footsteps traced a path through dew-kissed flowers that burst forth in a riot of colors across manicured gardens. With a reverent pause, he stood, hands finding solace within the pockets of his weathered jeans. His gaze was a magnet drawn to the majestic mansion that loomed before him – a monument to both grandeur and enigma. A deep breath surged within him, a fortification for the odyssey awaiting, and he stepped forward, resolutely.

Every inch of the well-known salon beckoned with memories. A fleeting grin danced upon Jamie's lips; a manifestation of a joy so profound it threatened to reshape his very being.

"At last, the miracle happened," he whispered to himself before Gabriella appeared abruptly, stealing away the moment of joy. She led him further, into the hallowed embrace of a small study room.

Once their short conversation concluded, Gabriella's command to the servant to gather the whole family sliced through the air with a cutting urgency. "The situation we face is very delicate and complicated," Gabriella began, her tone a measured cadence. Her voice, a river of tranquility, flowed contrary to the tempestuous clash that had marked their previous encounter. "I tried to reassure Mr Williams how absurd this marriage is, but he relentlessly refuses to give up," she said amidst the hushed anticipation. The remnants of a struggle that had worn her patience was etched into her gaze.

"I will do the same thing if you try to persuade me." Juan Pablo caught Jamie's hand in front of the whole family. Gabriella's gaze fixated on their entwined fingers; she only swallowed hard and continued.

"I know, just as I know there is nothing to be done in this case. Do we have another option but to accept Jamie into our family?" she said, as if pondering for a fleeting moment if this question was more for her to answer than a real question to the rest gathered in the salon.

An awkward silence filled the room instantly. Words were replaced by stares, heavy with sadness and helplessness, before Jamie spoke again, his voice carrying the same determination. "I already told you that I am not interested in whether you'd accept me or not." His gaze was fixed on Gabriella. "What I know is that I am Juan Pablo's husband." His inner God applauded him for his bravery and for a moment, he saw himself as a king in his castle.

"I know," Gabriella said simply, pressing her lips tightly as if trying to bury her sadness within. "You are his husband," she repeated, stealing a glance at the rest of the family. Each bowed their heads, staring blankly at the floor. "And as his husband, you'll be responsible for him," she added, turning her stern gaze toward her son. "And you… you'll depend fully on him because you have nothing more to do with us."

Juan Pablo frowned at his mother, locking his eyes with hers. A perplexed and astonished look crept onto his face. Gabriella's words were a storm that left his emotions in ruins. "Despite everything, you will still be my mother," he replied, his voice carrying the pain within him.

Gabriella rose from the armchair. "Yes, I will be, up to my last day," she continued. "But my obligations toward you finish right here."

Lucia looked at her brother. Her eyes pooled with tears as she just stood and stared in silence, wishing to hug and comfort him. But she remained seated, next to her husband, inwardly cursing the cruelty of the unfolding events.

"Children who marry in secret forfeit their rights." Gabriella spoke without a trace of hesitation. Lucia looked at her mother; her words echoed in her mind like a relentless, painful refrain, and she stole another short, surreptitious glance at her husband. "So you can pack your clothes and leave to live your life the way you have chosen," Gabriella added with a heavy sigh.

"Are you throwing me out?" Juan Pablo almost choked on his words.

"You chose this yourself," Gabriella said, gazing unwavering at the two men standing before her. "Jamie, you can take him now, and I hope you two are very happy." Her voice broke as she spoke, tears threatening to run down her cheek like a relentless river. "It's true that you found a husband, but it's also true that you lost us. Magnolia?"

"Yes, ma'am?"

"Help my son pack his things. He must be in a hurry to leave this house," she added, staring at her son.

Jamie looked at Juan Pablo, the ground beneath his feet disappearing as quickly as his dreams of this home and everything else he had hoped to receive as a new member of the Alvarez family. He squeezed his hat firmly as if to make sure this was not a nightmare.

"Why are you still standing? Why don't you leave? Are you not in a hurry?" Diego stood next to his mother, his posture superior. He put his hands on his hips and buried his fathomless eyes in his brother. Juan Pablo swiftly let go of Jamie, pulling him up from his deep thoughts, and ran upstairs after Magnolia.

"You can wait outside," Gabriella said in a dry, cold tone. "Our meeting is over, and there is nothing else for you to do in my house."

Jamie only nodded. Once outside, he turned back to make sure no one followed him. *You didn't expect that, Jamie Williams*, he said to himself, beating his hat on his leg with fury. The idea of him facing an empty well of options started sinking into his mind, leaving him with a growing sense of desperation. Standing on the cliff's edge of hopelessness, the weight of his failures pressed against him, his heart pounding like the waves crashing below.

A few moments later, his husband joined him outside. "We can go," he said in a low voice.

Jamie looked at him, regret and pain danced in his eyes. He nervously rotated the brim of his hat and could hardly say the words that pressed inside him. "Juan Pablo, I don't have a place to bring you other than my home." His stare filled with shades of pain. "And my house is very modest," he added, burying his eyes into the ground, saving himself the embarrassment of looking his husband in the eyes. "Mike and Chloe live there too."

"That's not important right now."

"I didn't think your mother would allow this," Jamie said. "I always thought she'd do anything to keep you here."

"What do you mean, Jamie?" Juan Pablo raised his voice. "Be more specific," he added as thoughts and doubts battled in his mind.

"You still have a chance to give up on me!" Jamie gazed at him, and his own words almost suffocated him. "I don't want to hurt you by depriving you of all the things you have now. Nor can I make you live in misery."

"Just answer me this." Juan Pablo stared at him with determination. "Do you love me or not?"

"Of course, I do," Jamie uttered leaving no doubts of his sincerity.

"That's what I wanted to hear! Let's go!" He grabbed him by the hand and led him to the car.

The sleek Range Rover pulled off, and the bitter farewell became a distant memory of the past with every mile ahead. The road to the mansion faded away and Juan Pablo smiled fondly at his husband, seeing his future inscribed in his eyes.

Coming soon…

As you turn the final pages of "Whispers of Forbidden Love," my heart is filled with gratitude for the incredible journey we've shared together.

But the story doesn't end here…

In the hushed corridors of passion and the echo of untold secrets, a new chapter unfolds. "De Amor," the sequel to "Whispers of Forbidden Love," takes you deeper into the labyrinth of love and desire. As the embers of the past continue to smolder, new flames are kindled, and the dance of hearts resumes, threatening to consume all in their path.

Amidst the tapestry of emotions, a question lingers: Can love withstand the tests of time and tribulation? Or will it crumble beneath the weight of untold truths? Brace yourself for a riveting journey through the complexities of love, passion, and the undying pursuit of happiness.

On this last page, the story whispers of what's to come, enticing you to step once more into the world of "De Amor." Are you ready for the next act…?